'Donogh[...] t[...]e
cust[...] [...]al
delic[...] ... A thrilling domestic p[...] draws
its power from quotidian detail as well as gothic horror.'

Guardian

'Donoghue's prose is as sturdy and serviceable as a good
pair of brogans, but never nondescript. There are occasional flashes of lyricism – "a cloud loosely bandaged the
waning moon," for instance, a line of perfect description
couched in perfect iambic pentameter – but Donoghue's
main purpose here is story, story, story, and God bless her
for it ... impossible to put down ... it also reminded me
of *The Razor's Edge*, only turned inside out. Maugham's
book is about the power of spirituality to heal. Donoghue
has written with crackling intensity, about its power to
destroy.'
Stephen King, *New York Times*

'Donoghue weaves crunchily convincing period detail
through a pacy narrative with relish and aplomb ... all
of it is vivid and well judged ... she is such an undisputed
master of the small and the slow, of the uneasy fragmenting
of time that happens when human beings are contained
within four walls, that all you want is for her to go on doing what she does so well.'
Observer

'*The Wonder* explores nineteenth-century rural Ireland
with great passion: the profound faith, prayer, superstition, ritual, corruption and collective madness of it all. The
descriptions of Anna's wasting body are agonisingly vivid
and Donoghue is a superb stylist – her prose is stirring and
tender, her period setting alive.'
Sunday Times

THE WONDER

Born in Dublin in 1969, and now living in Canada, Emma Donoghue writes fiction (novels and short stories, contemporary and historical, most recently *Haven* and *The Pull of the Stars*), as well as drama for screen and stage. *Room* was a *New York Times* Best Book of 2010 and a finalist for the Man Booker, Commonwealth and Orange Prizes, selling between two and three million copies in forty languages. Donoghue was nominated for an Academy Award for her 2015 adaptation starring Brie Larson. She co-wrote the screenplay for the film of her 2016 novel *The Wonder*, starring Florence Pugh (Netflix). For more information, visit www.emmadonoghue.com.

THE WONDER

EMMA DONOGHUE

PICADOR

First published 2016 by Little, Brown and Company, New York

First published in the UK 2016 by Picador

First published in paperback 2017 by Picador

This paperback edition first published 2022 by Picador
an imprint of Pan Macmillan
The Smithson, 6 Briset Street, London EC1M 5NR
EU representative: Macmillan Publishers Ireland Ltd, 1st Floor,
The Liffey Trust Centre, 117–126 Sheriff Street Upper,
Dublin 1, D01 YC43
Associated companies throughout the world
www.panmacmillan.com

ISBN 978-1-5290-9300-1

Printed and bound by CPI Group (UK) Ltd, Croydon, CR0 4YY

Visit **www.picador.com** to read more about all our books
and to buy them. You will also find features, author interviews and
news of any author events, and you can sign up for e-newsletters
so that you're always first to hear about our new releases.

For our daughter, Una, an old Irish blessing:

Nár mille an sioc do chuid prátaí,
Go raibh duilleoga do chabáiste slán ó chnuimheanna.

May there be no frost on your potatoes,
nor worms in your cabbage.

CONTENTS

THE WONDER

CHAPTER ONE

Nurse

nurse
> to suckle an infant
> to bring up a child
> to take care of the sick

The journey was no worse than she expected. A train from London to Liverpool; the steam packet overnight to Dublin; a slow Sunday train west to a town called Athlone.

A driver was waiting. "Mrs. Wright?"

Lib had known many Irishmen, soldiers. But that was some years ago, so her ear strained now to make out the driver's words.

He carried her trunk to what he called the jaunting car. An Irish misnomer; nothing jaunty about this bare cart. Lib settled herself on the single bench down the middle, her boots hanging closer to the right-hand wheel than she liked. She put up her steel-frame umbrella against the drizzle. This was better than the stuffy train, at least.

On the other side of the bench, slouching so his back almost touched hers, the driver flicked his whip. "Go on, now!"

The shaggy pony stirred.

The few people on the macadamised road out of Athlone seemed wan, which Lib attributed to the infamous diet of potatoes and little else. Perhaps that was responsible for the driver's missing teeth too.

He made some remark about the dead.

"I beg your pardon?"

"The dead centre, ma'am."

Lib waited, braced against the juddering of the cart.

He pointed down. "We're in the exact middle of the country here."

Flat fields striped with dark foliage. Sheets of reddish-brown peat; wasn't bogland known to harbour disease? The occasional grey remains of a cottage, almost greened over. Nothing that struck Lib as picturesque. Clearly the Irish Midlands were a depression where wet pooled, the little circle in a saucer.

The jaunting car turned off the road onto a narrower gravel way. The pattering on her umbrella's canvas became a continuous thrum. Windowless cabins; Lib imagined a family with its animals in each, huddling in out of the rain.

At intervals a lane led off towards a jumble of roofs that probably constituted a village. But never the right village, evidently. Lib should have asked the driver how long the journey was likely to take. She didn't put the question to him now in case the answer was *Still a long time yet*.

All Matron at the hospital had said was that an experienced nurse was required for two weeks, in a private capacity. The costs of keep and travel to and from Ireland to be furnished, as well as a daily consideration. Lib knew nothing about the O'Donnells except that they had to be a family of means if they were cosmopolitan enough to send all the way to England for a better class of nurse. It occurred to her only now to wonder how they could know that the patient would need her services for no more nor less than a fortnight. Perhaps Lib was a temporary replacement for another nurse.

In any case, she'd be quite well paid for her trouble, and the novelty of the thing held some interest. At the hospital, Lib's training was resented as much as it was appreciated, and only the more basic of her skills were required: feeding, changing dressings, bed-making.

She resisted the impulse to reach under her cloak and pull out her watch; it wouldn't make the time go any faster, and the rain might get into the mechanism.

Another roofless cabin now, turned away from the road, its gabled walls accusing the sky. Weeds had had no success at covering up this ruin yet. Lib glimpsed a mess of black through the door-shaped hole; a recent conflagration, then. (But how did anything manage to catch fire in this waterlogged country?) Nobody had taken the trouble to clear away the charred rafters, let alone frame and thatch a new roof. Was it true that the Irish were impervious to improvement?

A woman in a filthy frilled cap was stationed on the verge, a knot of children in the hedge behind her. The rattle of the cart brought them forward with hands cupped high as if to catch the rain. Lib looked away, awkward.

"The hungry season," muttered the driver.

But this was high summer. How could food be scarce now, of all times?

Her boots were speckled with mud and gravel spat up by the wheel. Several times the jaunting car lurched into a dun puddle deep enough that she had to cling to the bench so as not to be flung out.

More cabins, some with three or four windows. Barns,

sheds. A two-storey farmhouse, then another. Two men turned from loading a wagon, and one said something to the other. Lib looked down at herself: Was there something odd about her travelling costume? Perhaps the locals were so shiftless, they'd break off work to goggle at any stranger.

Up ahead, whitewash glared from a building with a pointed roof and a cross on top, which meant a Roman Catholic chapel. Only when the driver reined in did Lib realize that they'd arrived at the village, although by English standards it was no more than a sorry-looking cluster of buildings.

She checked her watch now: almost nine, and the sun hadn't set yet. The pony dropped its head and chewed a tuft. This appeared to be the sole street.

"You're to put up at the spirit grocery."

"I beg your pardon?"

"Ryan's." The driver nodded left to a building with no sign.

This couldn't be right. Stiff after the journey, Lib let the man hand her down. She shook her umbrella at arm's length, rolled the waxy canvas, and buttoned it tight. She dried her hand on the inside of her cloak before she stepped into the low-beamed shop.

The reek of burning peat hit her. Apart from the fire smouldering under a massive chimney, only a couple of lamps lit the room, where a girl was nudging a canister into its row on a high shelf.

"Good evening," said Lib. "I believe I may have been brought to the wrong place."

"You'll be the Englishwoman," said the girl slightly

6

too loudly, as if Lib were deaf. "Would you care to step into the back for a bit of supper?"

Lib held her temper. If there was no proper inn, and if the O'Donnell family couldn't or wouldn't accommodate the nurse they'd hired, then complaining would be no use.

She went through the door beside the chimney and found herself in a small, windowless room with two tables. One was occupied by a nun whose face was almost invisible behind the starched layers of her headdress. If Lib flinched a little, it was because she hadn't seen the like for years; in England religious sisters didn't go about in such garb for fear of provoking anti-Romish sentiment. "Good evening," she said civilly.

The nun answered with a deep bow. Perhaps members of her order were discouraged from speaking to those not of their creed, or vowed to silence, even?

Lib sat at the other table, facing away from the nun, and waited. Her stomach growled — she hoped not loudly enough to be heard. There was a faint clicking that had to be coming from under the woman's black folds: the famous rosary beads.

When at last the girl brought in the tray, the nun bent her head and whispered; saying grace before the meal. She was in her forties or fifties, Lib guessed, with slightly prominent eyes, and the meaty hands of a peasant.

An odd assortment of dishes: oat bread, cabbage, some kind of fish. "I was rather expecting potatoes," Lib told the girl.

" 'Tis another month you'll be waiting for them."

Ah, now Lib understood why this was Ireland's hungry season — potatoes weren't harvested until the autumn.

Everything tasted of peat, but she set about clearing her plate. Since Scutari, where the nurses' rations had been as short as the men's, Lib had found herself incapable of wasting a bite.

Noise out in the grocery, and then a party of four squeezed into the dining room. "God save all here," said the first man.

Not knowing the appropriate response, Lib nodded.

"And ye too." It was the nun who murmured that, making the sign of the cross by touching her forehead, chest, left and right shoulders. Then she left the room — whether because she'd had all she wanted of her meagre portion or to surrender the second table to the newcomers, Lib couldn't tell.

They were a raucous lot, these farmers and their wives. Had they already been drinking elsewhere all Sunday afternoon? *Spirit grocery;* now she understood the driver's phrase. Not a haunted grocery, but one that served liquor.

From their chatter, which touched on some *extraordinary wonder* they could hardly believe although they'd seen it with their own eyes, Lib decided they must have been to a fair.

" 'Tis the other crowd are behind it, I'd say," said a bearded man. His wife elbowed him, but he persisted. "Waiting on her hand and foot!"

"Mrs. Wright?"

She turned her head.

The stranger in the doorway tapped his waistcoat. "Dr. McBrearty."

That was the name of the O'Donnells' physician, Lib remembered. She stood to shake his hand. Straggly white side-whiskers, very little hair above. A shabby jacket, shoulders flecked with dandruff, and a knob-headed walking stick. Seventy, perhaps?

The farmers and their wives were eyeing them with interest.

"Good of you to travel all this way," the doctor remarked, as if Lib were paying a visit rather than taking up employment. "Was the crossing awful? If you've quite finished?" he went on, without giving her a chance to answer.

She followed him out into the shop. The girl, lifting a lamp, beckoned them up the narrow staircase.

The bedroom was poky. Lib's trunk took up much of the floor. Was she expected to have a tête-à-tête with Dr. McBrearty here? Had the premises no other room free, or was the girl too uncouth to arrange things more politely?

"Very good, Maggie," he told the girl. "How's your father's cough?"

"Better, nearly."

"Now, Mrs. Wright," he said as soon as the girl was gone, and he gestured for her to take the single rush chair.

Lib would have given a great deal for ten minutes alone first to use the chamber pot and the washstand. The Irish were notorious for neglecting the niceties.

The doctor leaned on his cane. "You're of what age, if I may ask?"

So she had to submit to an interview on the spot, although she'd been given to understand that the job was already hers. "Not yet thirty, Doctor."

"A widow, yes? You took up nursing when you found yourself, ah, thrown on your own resources?"

Was McBrearty checking Matron's account of her? She nodded. "Less than a year after I was married."

She'd happened on an article about the thousands of soldiers suffering from gunshot wounds or cholera, and no one to tend them. The *Times* had announced that seven thousand pounds had been raised to send a party of Englishwomen to the Crimea as nurses. *That,* Lib had thought, with dread but also a sense of daring, *I believe I could do that.* She'd lost so much already, she was reckless.

All she told the doctor now was "I was twenty-five."

"A Nightingale!" he marvelled.

Ah, so Matron had told him that much. Lib was always shy of introducing the great lady's name into conversation and loathed the whimsical title that had come to be attached to all those Miss N. had trained, as if they were dolls cast in her heroic mould. "Yes, I had the honour of serving under her at Scutari."

"Noble labour."

It seemed perverse to answer no, arrogant to say yes. It struck Lib now that the name of Nightingale was why the O'Donnell family had taken the trouble to bring a nurse all the way across the Irish Sea. She could tell the old Irishman would like to hear more about her teacher's beauty, sternness, righteous indignation. "I was a lady nurse," she said instead.

"A volunteer?"

She'd meant to clarify, but he'd taken her up wrong, and her face heated. Really, though, why feel the least embarrassment? Miss N. always reminded them that the fact of being paid didn't lessen their altruism. "No, I mean that I was one of the educated nursing sisters rather than the ordinary nurses. My father was a gentleman," she added, a little foolishly. Not a wealthy one, but still.

"Ah, very good. How long have you been at the hospital?"

"Three years come September." Remarkable in itself, as most of the nurses stayed no more than a matter of months; irresponsible scrubbers, Mrs. Gamps in the old mould, whining for their rations of porter. Not that Lib was particularly appreciated there. She'd heard Matron describe veterans of Miss N.'s Crimean campaign as *uppish*. "After Scutari I worked in several families," she added, "and saw my own parents through their final illnesses."

"Have you ever nursed a child, Mrs. Wright?"

Lib was thrown, but only for a moment. "I would expect the principles to be the same. Is my patient a child?"

"Mm, Anna O'Donnell."

"I've not been told her complaint."

He sighed.

Something fatal, then, Lib deduced. But slow enough that it hadn't killed the child yet. Consumption, most likely, in this wet climate.

"She's not exactly ill. Your only duty will be to watch her."

A curious verb. That awful nurse in *Jane Eyre,* charged with keeping the lunatic hidden away in the attic. "I've been brought here to . . . stand guard?"

"No, no, simply to observe."

But observation was only the first piece of the puzzle. Miss N. had taught her nurses to watch carefully in order to understand what the ill required and provide it. Not medicine — that was the doctors' domain — but the things she argued were equally crucial to recovery: light, air, warmth, cleanliness, rest, comfort, nourishment, and conversation. "If I understand you—"

"I doubt you do yet, and the fault's mine." McBrearty leaned on the edge of the washstand as if his strength were failing.

Lib would have liked to offer the old man the chair if she could have done it without insult.

"I don't want to prejudice you in any way," he went on, "but what I may say is that it's a most unusual case. Anna O'Donnell claims — or, rather, her parents claim — that she hasn't taken food since her eleventh birthday."

Lib frowned. "She must be ill, then."

"Not with any known disease. Known to me, that is," said McBrearty, correcting himself. "She simply doesn't eat."

"You mean, no solids?" Lib had heard of that affectation of refined modern misses, to live off boiled arrowroot or beef tea for days on end.

"No sustenance of any kind," the doctor corrected her. "She can't take a thing but clear water."

Can't means won't, as the nursery saying went. Unless . . . "Has the poor child some gastric obstruction?"

"None that I've been able to find."

Lib was at a loss. "Severe nausea?" She'd known pregnant women too sick to stomach food.

The doctor shook his head.

"Is she melancholic?"

"I wouldn't say that. A quiet, pious girl."

Ah, so this was a religious enthusiasm, perhaps, not a medical matter at all. "Roman Catholic?"

The flick of his hand seemed to say *What else?*

She supposed they were virtually all Catholics, this far from Dublin. The doctor might well be one himself. "I'm sure you've impressed on her the dangers of fasting," said Lib.

"I have, of course. So did her parents, at the start. But Anna's immoveable."

Had Lib been dragged across the sea for this, a child's whim? The O'Donnells must have panicked the first day their daughter turned up her nose at her breakfast and shot off a telegram to London demanding not just any nurse, but one of the new, irreproachable kind: *Send a Nightingale!*

"How long has it been since her birthday?" she asked.

McBrearty plucked at his whiskers. "April, this was. Four months ago today!"

Lib would have laughed aloud if it weren't for her training. "Doctor, the child would be dead by now." She waited for some sign that they agreed on the absurdity: a knowing wink, a tap of the nose.

He only nodded. "It's a great mystery."

That wasn't the word Lib would have chosen. "Is she . . . bedridden, at least?"

He shook his head. "Anna walks around like any other girl."

"Emaciated?"

"She's always been a mite of a thing, but no, she seems hardly to have altered since April."

He spoke sincerely, but this was ludicrous. Were they half blind, his rheumy eyes?

"And she's in full possession of all her faculties," added

13

McBrearty. "In fact, the vital force burns so strong in Anna that the O'Donnells have become convinced she can live without food."

"Incredible." The word came out too caustic.

"I'm not surprised you're sceptical, Mrs. Wright. I was too."

Was? "Are you telling me, in all seriousness, that—"

He interrupted, his papery hands shooting up. "The obvious interpretation is that it's a hoax."

"Yes," said Lib in relief.

"But this child . . . she's not like other children."

She waited for more.

"I can *tell* you nothing, Mrs. Wright. I have only questions. For the past four months I've been burning with curiosity, as I'm sure you are now."

No, what Lib burnt with was a desire to end this interview and get the man out of her room. "Doctor, science tells us that to live without food is impossible."

"But haven't most new discoveries in the history of civilization seemed uncanny at first, almost magical?" His voice shook a little with excitement. "From Archimedes to Newton, all the greats have achieved their breakthroughs by examining the evidence of their senses without prejudice. So all I ask is for you to keep an open mind when you meet Anna O'Donnell tomorrow."

Lib lowered her eyes, mortified for McBrearty. How could a physician let himself be snared in a little girl's game and fancy himself among the *greats* as a consequence? "May I ask, is the child under your sole care?" She phrased it politely, but what she meant was, had no better authority been called in?

"She is," said McBrearty reassuringly. "In fact, it was I who took a notion to work up an account of the case and send it to the *Irish Times*."

Lib had never heard of it. "A national paper?"

"Mm, the most lately established one, so I hoped its proprietors might be somewhat less blinded by sectarian prejudice," he added, wistful. "More open to the new and the extraordinary, wherever it may arise. I thought to share the facts with a broader public, don't you know, in the hope that someone could explain them."

"And has anyone done so?"

A stifled sigh. "There've been several fervent letters proclaiming Anna's case to be an out-and-out miracle. Also a few intriguing suggestions that she might be drawing on some as-yet-undiscovered nutritive qualities of, say, magnetism, or scent."

Scent? Lib sucked in her cheeks so as not to smile.

"One bold correspondent proposed that she might be converting sunlight into energy, as vegetation does. Or living on air, even, as certain plants do," he added, his wrinkled face brightening. "Remember that crew of shipwrecked sailors said to have subsisted for several months on tobacco?"

Lib looked down so he wouldn't read the scorn in her eyes.

McBrearty found his thread again. "But the vast majority of the replies have consisted of personal abuse."

"Of the child?"

"The child, the family, and myself. Comments not just in the *Irish Times* but in various British publications that seem to have taken up the case for the sole purpose of satire."

Lib saw it now. She'd travelled a long way to hire herself out as a nursemaid-cum-gaoler, all because of a provincial doctor's injured pride. Why hadn't she pressed Matron for more details before she accepted the job?

"Most correspondents presume that the O'Donnells are cheats, conspiring to feed their daughter secretly and make fools of the world." McBrearty's voice was shrill. "The name of our village has become a byword for credulous backwardness. Several of the important men hereabouts feel that the honour of the county — possibly of the whole Irish nation — is at stake."

Had the doctor's gullibility spread like a fever among these *important men*?

"So a committee's been formed and a decision taken to mount a watch."

Ah, then it wasn't the O'Donnells who'd sent for Lib at all. "With a view to proving that the child subsists by some extraordinary means?" She tried to keep even a hint of the sardonic out of her voice.

"No, no," McBrearty assured her, "simply to bring the truth to light, whatever the truth may be. Two scrupulous attendants will stay by Anna turn and turnabout, night and day, for a fortnight."

So it wasn't Lib's experience of surgical or infectious cases that was called for here, only the rigour of her training. Clearly the committee hoped, by importing one of the scrupulous new breed of nurses, to give some credence to the O'Donnells' mad story. To make this primitive backwater a wonder to the world. Anger throbbed in Lib's jaw.

Fellow feeling, too, for the other woman lured into this morass. "The second nurse, I don't suppose I know her?"

The doctor frowned. "Didn't you make Sister Michael's acquaintance at supper?"

The almost speechless nun; Lib should have guessed. Strange how they took the names of male saints, as if giving up womanhood itself. But why hadn't the nun introduced herself properly? Was that what that deep bow had been supposed to signify — that she and the English-woman were in this mess together? "Was she trained in the Crimea too?"

"No, no, I've just had her sent up from the House of Mercy in Tullamore," said McBrearty.

One of the *walking nuns*. Lib had served alongside others of that order in Scutari. They were reliable workers, at least, she told herself.

"The parents requested that at least one of you be of their own, ah . . ."

So the O'Donnells had asked for a Roman Catholic. "Denomination."

"And nationality," he added, as if to soften it.

"I'm quite aware that there's no love for the English in this country," said Lib, summoning a tight smile.

McBrearty demurred: "You put it too strongly."

What about the faces that had turned towards the jaunting car as Lib was driven down the village street? But those men had spoken about her because she was expected, she realized now. She wasn't just any Englishwoman; she was the one being shipped in to watch over their squire's pet.

"Sister Michael will provide a certain sense of familiarity for the child, that's all," said McBrearty.

The very idea that *familiarity* was a necessary or even helpful qualification for a watcher! But for the other nurse, he'd picked one of Miss N.'s own famous brigade, she thought, to make this watch look sufficiently *scrupulous,* especially in the eyes of the British press.

Lib thought of saying, in a very cool voice, *Doctor, I see that I've been brought here in hopes that my association with a very great lady might cast a veneer of respectability over an outrageous fraud. I'll have no part in it.* If she set off in the morning, she could be back at the hospital in two days.

The prospect filled her with gloom. She imagined herself trying to explain that the Irish job had proved objectionable on moral grounds. How Matron would snort.

So Lib suppressed her feelings, for now, and concentrated on the practicalities. *Simply to observe,* McBrearty had said. "If at any point our charge were to express the slightest wish, even in veiled terms, for something to eat—" she began.

"Then bring it to her." The doctor sounded shocked. "We're not in the business of starving children."

She nodded. "We nurses are to report to you, then, in two weeks?"

He shook his head. "As Anna's physician — and having been dragged into this unpleasantness in the papers — I could be considered an interested party. So it's to the assembled committee that you're to testify on oath."

Lib looked forward to it.

"Yourself and Sister Michael separately," he added, holding up one knobby finger, "without any conferring. We wish to hear to what view each of you comes, quite independently of the other."

"Very good. May I ask, why is this watch not being conducted in the local hospital?" Unless there was none in this all too *dead centre* of the island.

"Oh, the O'Donnells balked at the very idea of their little one being taken off to the county infirmary."

That clinched it for Lib; the squire and his lady wanted to keep their daughter at home so they could carry on slipping food to her. It wouldn't take two weeks of supervision to catch them out.

She chose her words tactfully because the doctor was clearly fond of the young faker. "If, before the fortnight's up, I were to find evidence indicating that Anna has taken nourishment covertly — should I make my report to the committee straightaway?"

His whiskery cheeks crumpled. "I suppose, in that case, it would be a waste of everyone's time and money to carry on any longer."

Lib could be on the ship back to England in a matter of days, then, but with this eccentric episode closed to her satisfaction.

What's more, if newspapers across the kingdom were to give Nurse Elizabeth Wright the credit for exposing the hoax, the whole staff of the hospital would have to sit up and take notice. Who'd call her *uppish* then? Perhaps better things might come of it; a position more suited to Lib's talents, more interesting. A less narrow life.

Her hand shot up to cover a sudden yawn.

"I'd better leave you now," said McBrearty. "It must be almost ten."

Lib pulled the chain at her waist and turned her watch up. "I make it ten eighteen."

"Ah, we're twenty-five minutes behind here. You're still on English time."

Lib slept well, considering.

The sun came up just before six. By then she was in her uniform from the hospital: grey tweed dress, worsted jacket, white cap. (At least it fit. One of the many indignities of Scutari had been the standard-issue costume; short nurses had waded around in theirs, whereas Lib had looked like some pauper grown out of her sleeves.)

She breakfasted alone in the room behind the grocery. The eggs were fresh, yolks sun yellow.

Ryan's girl — Mary? Meg? — wore the same stained apron as the evening before. When she came back to clear away, she said Mr. Thaddeus was waiting. She was out of the room again before Lib could tell her she knew no one by that name.

Lib stepped into the shop. "You wished to speak to me?" she asked the man standing there. She wasn't quite sure whether to add *sir*.

"Good morning, Mrs. Wright, I hope you slept well." This Mr. Thaddeus was more well-spoken than she'd have expected from his faded coat. A pink, not quite youthful snub-nosed face; a shock of black hair sprang out as he lifted his hat. "I'm to bring you over to the O'Donnells' now, if you're ready."

"Quite ready."

But he must have heard the query in her voice, because he added, "The good doctor thought maybe a trusted friend of the family should make the introductions."

Lib was confused. "I had the impression Dr. McBrearty was such a friend."

"That he is," said Mr. Thaddeus, "but I suppose the O'Donnells repose a special confidence in their priest."

A priest? This man was in mufti. "I beg your pardon. Should it be Father Thaddeus?"

A shrug. "Well, that's the new style, but we don't bother our heads much about it in these parts."

It was hard to imagine this amiable fellow as the confessor of the village, the holder of secrets. "You don't wear a clerical collar, or —" Lib gestured at his chest, not knowing the name of the buttoned black robe.

"I've all the gear in my trunk for holy days, of course," said Mr. Thaddeus with a smile.

The girl hurried back in, wiping her hands. "There's your tobacco now," she told him, twisting the ends of a paper package and sliding it over the counter.

"Bless you, Maggie, and a box of matches too. Right, so, Sister?"

He was looking past Lib. She spun around and found the nun hovering; when had she crept in?

Sister Michael nodded at the priest and then at Lib with a twitch of the lips that could have been meant for a smile. Crippled by shyness, Lib supposed.

Why couldn't McBrearty have sent for two Nightingales while he was at it? It occurred to Lib now that perhaps none of the fifty-odd others — lay or religious — had been available at such short notice. Was Lib the only

Crimean nurse who'd failed to find her niche half a decade on? The only one sufficiently at loose ends to take the poisoned bait of this job?

The three of them turned left down the street through a watery sunlight. Ill at ease between the priest and the nun, Lib gripped her leather bag.

Buildings turned different ways, giving one another the cold shoulder. An old woman in a window at a table stacked with baskets — a huckster peddling produce of some sort out of her front room? There was none of the Monday-morning bustle Lib would have expected in England. They passed one man laden with a sack who exchanged blessings with Mr. Thaddeus and Sister Michael.

"Mrs. Wright worked with Miss Nightingale," the priest remarked in the nun's direction.

"So I heard." After a moment Sister Michael said to Lib, "You must have a power of experience with surgical cases."

Lib nodded as modestly as she could. "We also dealt with a great deal of cholera, dysentery, malaria. Frostbite in the winter, of course." In fact the English nurses had spent much of their time stuffing mattresses, stirring gruel, and standing at washtubs, but Lib didn't want the nun to mistake her for an ignorant menial. That was what nobody understood: saving lives often came down to getting a latrine pipe unplugged.

No sign of a market square or green, as any English village would have possessed. The garish white chapel was the only new-looking building. Mr. Thaddeus cut right just before it, taking a muddy lane that led around a grave-yard. The mossy, skewed tombstones seemed to have been planted not in rows but at random. "Is the O'Donnells' house outside the village?" Lib asked, curious as to why the family hadn't been courteous enough to send a driver, let alone put the nurses up themselves.

"A little way," said the nun in her whispery voice.

"Malachy keeps shorthorns," added the priest.

There was more power to this weak sun than Lib would have thought; she was perspiring under her cloak. "How many children have they at home?"

"Just the girl now, since Pat's gone over, God bless him," said Mr. Thaddeus.

Gone where? America seemed most likely to Lib, or Britain, or the Colonies. Ireland, an improvident mother, seemed to ship half her skinny brood abroad. Two children only for the O'Donnells, then; that seemed a paltry total to Lib.

They passed a shabby cabin with a smoking chimney. A path slanted off the lane towards another cottage. Lib's eyes scanned the bogland ahead for any sign of the O'Donnells' estate. Was she allowed to ask the priest for more than plain facts? Each of the nurses had been hired to form her own impressions. But then it struck Lib that this walk might be the only chance she'd get to talk to this *trusted friend of the family*. "Mr. Thaddeus, if I may — can you attest to the honesty of the O'Donnells?"

A moment went by. "Sure I've no reason to doubt it."

Lib had never had a conversation with a Roman Catholic priest before and couldn't read this one's politic tone.

The nun's eyes stayed on the green horizon.

"Malachy's a man of few words," Mr. Thaddeus went on. "A teetotaler."

That surprised Lib.

"Not a drop since he took the Pledge, before the children were born. His wife's a leading light of the parish, very active in the Sodality of Our Lady."

These details meant little to Lib, but she got the drift. "And Anna O'Donnell?"

"A wonderful little girl."

In what sense? Virtuous? Or exceptional? Clearly the chit had them all charmed. Lib looked hard at the priest's curved profile. "Have you ever advised her to refuse nourishment, perhaps as some sort of spiritual exercise?"

His hands spread in protest. "Mrs. Wright. I don't think you're of our faith?"

Picking her words, Lib said, "I was baptized in the Church of England."

The nun seemed to be watching a passing crow. Avoiding contamination by staying out of the conversation?

"Well," said Mr. Thaddeus, "let me assure you that Catholics are required to do without food for only a matter of hours, for instance from midnight to the taking of Holy Communion the following morning. We also abstain from meat on Wednesdays and Fridays and during Lent. Moderate fasting mortifies the cravings of the body, you see," he added as easily as if he were speaking of the weather.

"Meaning the appetite for food?"

"Among others."

Lib moved her eyes to the muddy ground in front of her boots.

"We also express sorrow over the agonies of Our Lord

24

by sharing them even a little," he continued, "so fasting can be a useful penance."

"Meaning that if one punishes oneself, one's sins will be forgiven?" asked Lib.

"Or those of others," said the nun under her breath.

"Just as Sister says," the priest answered, "if we offer up our suffering in a generous spirit to be set to another's account."

Lib pictured a gigantic ledger filled with inky debits and credits.

"But the key is, fasting is never to be carried to an extreme or to the point of harming the health."

Hard to spear this slippery fish. "Then why do you think Anna O'Donnell has gone against the rules of her own church?"

The priest's broad shoulders heaved into a shrug. "Many's the time I've reasoned with her over the past months, pleaded with her to take a bite of something. But she's deaf to all persuasion."

What was it about this spoiled miss that she'd managed to enrol all the grown-ups around her in this charade?

"Here we are," murmured Sister Michael, gesturing towards the end of a faint track.

This couldn't be their destination, surely? The cabin was in need of a fresh coat of whitewash; pitched thatch brooded over three small squares of glass. At the far end, a cow byre stooped under the same roof.

Lib saw all at once the foolishness of her assumptions. If the committee had hired the nurses, then Malachy O'Donnell was not necessarily prosperous. It seemed that all that marked the family out from the other peasants scratching a living around here was their claim that their little girl could live on air.

She stared at the O'Donnells' low roofline. If Dr. McBrearty hadn't been so rash as to write to the *Irish Times,* she saw now, word would never have spread beyond these sodden fields. How many *important* friends of his were investing their hard cash, as well as their names, in this bizarre enterprise? Were they betting that after the fortnight, both nurses would obediently swear to the miracle and make this puny hamlet a marvel of Christendom? Did they think to buy the endorsement, the combined reputability, of a Sister of Mercy and a Nightingale?

The three walked up the path — right past a dung heap, Lib noticed with a quiver of disapproval. The thick walls of the cabin sloped outwards to the ground. A broken pane in the nearest window was stopped up with a rag. There was a half-door, gaping at the top like a horse's stall. Mr. Thaddeus pushed the bottom open with a dull scrape and gestured for Lib to go first.

She stepped into darkness. A woman cried out in a language Lib didn't know.

Her eyes started to adjust. A floor of beaten earth under her boots. Two females in the frilled caps that Irishwomen always seemed to wear were clearing away a drying rack that stood before the fire. After piling the clothes into the younger, slighter woman's arms, the elder ran forward to shake hands with the priest.

He answered her in the same tongue — Gaelic, it had to be — then moved into English. "Rosaleen O'Donnell, I know you met Sister Michael yesterday."

"Sister, good morning to you." The woman squeezed the nun's hands.

"And this is Mrs. Wright, one of the famous nurses from the Crimea."

"My!" Mrs. O'Donnell had broad, bony shoulders, stone-grey eyes, and a smile holed with dark. "Heaven bless you for coming such a distance, ma'am."

Could she really be ignorant enough to think that war still raged in that peninsula and that Lib had just arrived, bloody from the battlefront?

"'Tis in the good room I'd have ye this minute" — Rosaleen O'Donnell nodded towards a door to the right of the fire — "if it wasn't for the visitors."

Now Lib was listening, she could make out the faint sound of singing.

"We're grand here," Mr. Thaddeus assured her.

"Let ye sit down till we have a cup of tea, at least," Mrs. O'Donnell insisted. "The chairs are all within, so I've nothing but creepies for you. Mister's off digging turf for Séamus O'Lalor."

Creepies had to mean the log stools the woman was shoving practically into the flames for her guests. Lib chose one and tried to inch it farther away from the hearth. But the mother looked offended; clearly, right by the fire was the position of honour. So Lib sat, putting down her bag on the cooler side so her ointments wouldn't melt into puddles.

Rosaleen O'Donnell crossed herself as she sat down and so did the priest and the nun. Lib thought of following suit. But no, it would be ridiculous to start aping the locals.

The singing from the so-called good room seemed to swell. The fireplace opened into both parts of the cabin, Lib realized, so sounds leaked through.

While the maid winched the hissing kettle off the fire, Mrs. O'Donnell and the priest chatted about yesterday's drop of rain and how unusually warm the summer was proving on the whole. The nun listened and occasionally murmured assent. Not a word about the daughter.

Lib's uniform was sticking to her sides. For an observant nurse, she reminded herself, time need never be wasted. She noted a plain table, pushed against the windowless back wall. A painted dresser, the lower section barred, like a cage. Some tiny doors set into the walls; recessed cupboards? A curtain of old flour sacks nailed up. All rather primitive, but neat, at least; not quite squalid. The blackened chimney hood was woven of wattle. There was a square hollow on either side of the fire, and what Lib guessed was a salt box nailed high up. A shelf over the fire held a pair of brass candlesticks, a crucifix, and what looked like a small daguerreotype behind glass in a black lacquer case.

"And how's Anna today?" Mr. Thaddeus finally asked when they were all sipping the strong tea, the maid included.

"Well enough in herself, thanks be to God." Mrs. O'Donnell cast another anxious glance towards the good room.

Was the girl in there singing hymns with these visitors?

"Perhaps you could tell the nurses her history," suggested Mr. Thaddeus.

The woman looked blank. "Sure what history has a child?"

Lib met Sister Michael's eyes and took the lead. "Until this year, Mrs. O'Donnell, how would you have described your daughter's health?"

A blink. "Well, she's always been a delicate flower, but not a sniveller or tetchy. If ever she had a scrape or a stye, she'd make it a little offering to heaven."

"What about her appetite?" asked Lib.

"Ah, she's never been greedy or clamoured for treats. Good as gold."

"And her spirits?" asked the nun.

"No cause for complaint," said Mrs. O'Donnell.

These ambiguous answers didn't satisfy Lib. "Does Anna go to school?"

"Oh, Mr. O'Flaherty only doted on her."

"Didn't she win the medal, sure?" The maid pointed at the mantel so suddenly that the tea sloshed in her cup.

"That's right, Kitty," said the mother, nodding like a pecking hen.

Lib looked for a medal and found it, a small bronzed disc in a presentation case beside the photograph.

"But after she caught the whooping cough when it came through the school last year," Mrs. O'Donnell went on, "we thought to keep our little colleen home, considering the dirt up there and the windows that do be always getting broken and letting draughts in."

Colleen; that was what the Irish seemed to call every young female.

"Doesn't she study just as hard at home anyway, with

all her books around her? The nest is enough for the wren, as they say."

Lib didn't know that maxim. She pushed on, because it had occurred to her that Anna's preposterous lie might be rooted in truth. "Since her illness, has she suffered from disturbances of the stomach?" She wondered if violent coughing might have ruptured the child internally.

But Mrs. O'Donnell shook her head with a fixed smile.

"Vomiting, blockages, loose stools?"

"No more than once in a while in the ordinary course of growing."

"So until she turned eleven," Lib asked, "you'd have described your daughter as delicate, nothing more?"

The woman's flaking lips pressed together. "The seventh of April, four months ago yesterday. Overnight, Anna wouldn't take bite nor sup, nothing but God's own water."

Lib felt a surge of dislike. If this were actually true, what kind of mother would report it with such excitement?

But of course it wasn't true, she reminded herself. Either Rosaleen O'Donnell had had a hand in the hoax or the daughter had managed to pull the wool over the mother's eyes, but in any case, cynical or gullible, the woman had no reason to feel afraid for her child.

"Before her birthday, had she choked on a morsel? Eaten anything rancid?"

Mrs. O'Donnell bristled. "There does be nothing rancid in this kitchen."

"Did you plead with her to eat?" asked Lib.

"I might as well have saved my breath."

"And Anna gave no reason for her refusal?"

The woman leaned a little closer, as if imparting a secret. "No need."

"She didn't need to give a reason?" asked Lib.

"She doesn't need it," said Rosaleen O'Donnell, her smile revealing her missing teeth.

"Food, you mean?" asked the nun, barely audible.

"Not a crumb. She's a living marvel."

This had to be a well-rehearsed performance. Except that the gleam in the woman's eyes looked remarkably like conviction to Lib. "And you claim that during the last four months, your daughter's continued in good health?"

Rosaleen O'Donnell straightened her frame, and her sparse eyelashes fluttered. "No false *claims,* no impostures, will be found in this house, Mrs. Wright. 'Tis a humble home, but so was the stable."

Lib was puzzled, thinking of horses, until she realized what the woman meant: Bethlehem.

"We're simple people, himself and myself," said Rosaleen O'Donnell. "We can't explain it, but our little girl is thriving by special providence of the Almighty. Sure aren't all things possible to him?" She appealed to the nun.

Sister Michael nodded. Faintly: "He moves in mysterious ways."

This was why the O'Donnells had asked for a nun, Lib was almost sure of it. And why the doctor had gone along with their request. They were all assuming that a spinster consecrated to Christ would be more likely than most people to believe in miracles. More blinkered by superstition, Lib would call it.

Mr. Thaddeus's eyes were watchful. "But you and Malachy are willing to let these good nurses sit with Anna for the full fortnight, aren't you, Rosaleen, so they can testify before the committee?"

Mrs. O'Donnell flung her skinny arms so wide, her plaid shawl almost fell. "Willing and more than willing, so we'll have our characters vindicated that are as good as any from Cork to Belfast."

Lib almost laughed. To be as concerned for reputation in this meagre cabin as in any mansion . . .

"What have we to hide?" the woman went on. "Haven't we already thrown our doors open to well-wishers from the four corners of the earth?"

Her grandiloquence put Lib's back up.

"Speaking of which," said the priest, "I believe your guests may be leaving."

The singing had ended without Lib noticing. The inner door hung open a crack, shifting in the draught. She walked over and looked through the gap.

The good room was distinguished from the kitchen mostly by its bareness. Apart from a cupboard with a few plates and jugs behind glass and a cluster of rope chairs, there was nothing in it. Half a dozen people were turned towards the corner of the room that Lib couldn't see, their eyes wide, lit as if they were watching some dazzling display. She strained to catch their murmurs.

"Thank you, miss."

"A couple of holy cards for your collection."

"Let me leave you this vial of oil our cousin had blessed by His Holiness in Rome."

"A few flowers is all, cut in my garden this morning."

"A thousand thank-yous, and would you ever kiss the

baby before we go?" That last woman hurried towards the corner with her bundle.

Lib found it tantalizing not to be able to glimpse the *extraordinary wonder* — wasn't that the phrase the farmers had used at the spirit grocery last night? Yes, this must have been what they were raving about: not some two-headed calf but Anna O'Donnell, the *living marvel.* Evidently hordes were let in every day to grovel at the child's feet; the vulgarity of it!

There was that one farmer who'd said something malign about the *other crowd,* how they were *waiting on her hand and foot.* He must have meant the visitors who were so eager to caress the child. What did they think they were doing, setting a little girl up for a saint because they imagined her to have risen above ordinary human needs? It reminded Lib of parades on the Continent, statues in fancy dress promenaded through the reeking alleys.

Though in fact the visitors' voices all sounded Irish to Lib; Mrs. O'Donnell had to be exaggerating about the *four corners of the earth.* The door swung wide now, so Lib stepped back.

The visitors shuffled out. "Missus, for your trouble." A man in a round hat was offering a coin to Rosaleen O'Donnell.

Aha. The root of all evil. Like those well-heeled tourists who paid a peasant to pose with a half-strung fiddle by the door of his mud cabin. The O'Donnells had to be party to this fraud, Lib decided, and for the most predictable of motives: cash.

But the mother flung her hands behind her back. "Sure hospitality's no trouble."

"For the sweet girleen," said the visitor.

Rosaleen O'Donnell kept shaking her head.

"I insist," he said.

"Put it in the box for the poor, sir, if you must leave it." She nodded at an iron safe set on a stool by the door.

Lib rebuked herself for not having spotted that earlier. The visitors all slipped their tips into its slot on their way out. Some of those coins sounded heavy to Lib. Clearly the minx was as much of a paying attraction as any carved cross or standing stone. Lib very much doubted that the O'Donnells would pass a penny on to those even less fortunate than themselves.

Waiting for the crowd to clear, Lib found herself close enough to the mantelpiece to study the daguerreotype. Murky-toned and taken before the son had emigrated. Rosaleen O'Donnell, like some imposing totem. The skinny adolescent boy rather incongruously leaning back in her lap. A small girl sitting upright on the father's. Lib squinted through the glare of the glass. Anna O'Donnell had hair about as dark as Lib's own, down to the shoulders. Nothing to distinguish her from any other child.

"Go on into her room now till I fetch her," Rosaleen O'Donnell was telling Sister Michael.

Lib stiffened. How was the woman planning to prepare her daughter for their scrutiny?

All at once she couldn't bear the smoulder of turf. She muttered something about needing a breath of air and stepped out into the farmyard.

Putting her shoulders back, Lib breathed in and smelled dung. If she did stay, it would be to accept the challenge: to expose this pitiful swindle. The cabin couldn't have more than four rooms; she doubted it would take her more than one night here to catch the girl sneaking food, whether Anna was doing it alone or with help. (Mrs. O'Donnell? Her husband? The slavey, who seemed to be their only servant? Or all of them, of course.) That meant the whole trip would earn Lib just one day's wage. Of course, a less honest nurse wouldn't speak up till the fortnight was gone, to be sure of being paid for all fourteen. Whereas Lib's reward would be seeing it through, making sure sense prevailed over nonsense.

"I'd better be looking in on some others of my flock," said the pink-cheeked priest behind her. "Sister Michael's offered to take the first watch, as you must be feeling the effects of your journey."

"No," said Lib, "I'm quite ready to begin." Itching to meet the girl, in fact.

"As you prefer, Mrs. Wright," said the nun in her whispery voice behind him.

"You'll come back in eight hours, then, Sister?" asked Mr. Thaddeus.

"Twelve," Lib corrected him.

"I believe McBrearty proposed shifts of eight hours, as less tiring," he said.

"Then Sister and I would both be up and down at irregular hours," Lib pointed out. "In my experience of ward nursing, two shifts are more conducive to sleep than three."

"But to fulfil the terms of the watch, you'll be obliged to stay by Anna's side every single minute of the time," said Mr. Thaddeus. "Eight hours sounds long enough."

Just then Lib realized something else: if they worked twelve-hour shifts and she took the first, it would always be Sister Michael on duty during the night, when the girl would have more opportunity to steal food. How could Lib rely on a nun who'd spent most of her life in some provincial convent to be quite as attentive as herself? "Very well, eight hours, then." Calculating in her head. "We might change over at, say, nine in the evening, five in the morning, one in the afternoon, Sister? Those times would seem rather less disruptive to the household."

"Until one o'clock, then?" asked the nun.

"Oh, as we're only beginning now, midmorning, I'm happy to stay with the girl until nine tonight," Lib told her. A long first day would allow her to set up the room and establish the procedures of the watch to her liking.

Sister Michael nodded and glided away down the path back towards the village. How did nuns learn that distinctive walk? Lib wondered. Perhaps it was just an illusion created by the black robes brushing the grass.

"Good luck, Mrs. Wright," said Mr. Thaddeus, tipping his hat.

Luck? As if she were off to the races.

Lib gathered her forces and stepped back inside the house, where Mrs. O'Donnell and the maid were lifting what looked like a massive grey gnome onto a hook. Lib's eyes puzzled it out: an iron crock.

The mother swivelled the pot over the fire and jerked her head towards a half-open door to Lib's left. "I've told Anna all about you."

Told her what, that Mrs. Wright was a spy from across the sea? Coached the brat in the best means of hoodwinking the Englishwoman as she had so many other grown-ups?

The bedroom was an unadorned square. A tiny girl in grey sat on a straight-backed chair between the window and the bed as if listening to some private music. The hair a dark red that hadn't shown in the photograph. At the creak of the door, she looked up, and a smile split her face.

A humbug, Lib reminded herself.

The girl stood and held out her hand.

Lib shook it. Plump fingers cool to the touch. "How are you feeling today, Anna?"

"Very well, missus," said the girl in a small, clear voice.

"Nurse," Lib corrected her, "or Mrs. Wright, or ma'am, if you prefer." She found she couldn't think of anything else to say. She reached into her bag for her miniature memorandum book and measuring tape. She began making notes, to impose something of the systematic on this incongruous situation.

Monday, August 8, 1859, 10:07 a.m.
Length of body: 46 inches.
Arm span: 47 inches.
Girth of skull measured above brows: 22 inches.
Head from crown to chin: 8 inches.

Anna O'Donnell was perfectly obliging. Standing very straight in her plain dress and curiously large boots, she held each position for Lib to measure her, as if learning the steps of a foreign dance. Her face could almost have been described as chubby, which put paid to the fasting story right away. Large hazel eyes bulging a little under puffy eyelids. The whites were porcelain, the pupils dilated, although that could be explained by the faintness of the light coming in. (At least the small pane was open to the summer air. At the hospital, no matter what Lib said, Matron clung to the antiquated notion that windows had to be kept closed against noxious effluvia.)

The girl was very pale, but then Irish skin was generally so, especially on redheads, until the weather coarsened it. Now there was an oddity: a very fine, colourless down on the cheeks. And after all, the girl's lie about not eating didn't preclude her from having some real disorder. Lib wrote it all down.

Miss N. thought some nurses relied on note-taking too much, laming their powers of recall. However, she never went so far as to forbid an *aide-mémoire*. Lib didn't mistrust her own memory, but on this occasion, she'd been hired more as a witness, which called for impeccable case notes.

Something else: Anna's earlobes and lips had a bluish tint to them, and so did the beds of the fingernails. She was chilly to the touch, as if she'd just come in from walking in a snowstorm. "Do you feel cold?" Lib asked.

"Not especially."

Breadth of chest across level of mammae: 10 inches.
Girth of ribs: 24 inches.

The girl's eyes followed her. "What's your name?"

"As I mentioned, it's Mrs. Wright, but you may address me as Nurse."

"Your Christian name, I mean."

Lib ignored that bit of cheek and continued writing.

Girth of hips: 25 inches.
Girth of waist: 21 inches.
Girth of middle of arm: 5 inches.

"What are the numbers for?"

"They're . . . so we can be sure you're in good health," said Lib. An absurd answer, but the question had flustered her. Surely it was a breach of protocol to discuss the nature of her surveillance with its object?

So far, as Lib had expected, the data in her notebook indicated that Anna O'Donnell was a false little baggage. Yes, she was thin in places, shoulder blades like the stubs of missing wings. But not the way a child would be after a month without food, let alone four. Lib knew what starvation looked like; at Scutari, skeletal refugees had been toted in, bones stretching the skin like tent poles under canvas. No, this girl's belly was rounded, if anything. Fashionable belles tight-laced these days in hopes of a sixteen-inch waist, and Anna's was five more than that.

What Lib really would have liked to know was the child's weight, because if it went up even an ounce over the course of the fortnight, that would constitute proof of covert feeding. She took two steps towards the kitchen to fetch a weighing scales before she remembered that she was obliged to keep this child in sight at all times until nine o'clock tonight.

A strange sensation of imprisonment. Lib thought of calling to Mrs. O'Donnell from inside the bedroom, but she didn't want to come off as high-handed, especially so early in her first shift.

"*Beware of spurious imitations,*" murmured Anna.

"I beg your pardon?" Lib said.

One round fingertip traced the words stamped into the ribbed leather cover of the memorandum book.

Lib gave the girl a hard look. *Spurious imitations,* indeed. "The manufacturers are claiming that their velvet paper is unlike any other."

"What's velvet paper?"

"It's been coated to take the mark of a metallic pencil."

The girl stroked the tiny page.

"Anything written on that will be indelible, like ink," said Lib. "Do you know what *indelible* means?"

"A stain that won't come off."

"Correct." Lib took back the memorandum book and tried to think of what other information she needed to extract from the girl. "Are you troubled by any pain, Anna?"

"No."

"Dizziness?"

"Maybe the odd time," Anna admitted.

"Does your pulse pause or skip?"

"Some days it might flutter a bit."

"Are you nervous?"

"Nervous of what?"

Being found out, you swindler. But what Lib said was "Sister Michael and myself, perhaps. Strangers in your home."

Anna shook her head. "You seem kind. I don't think you'd do me any harm."

"Quite right." But Lib felt uncomfortable, as if she'd promised more than she ought. She wasn't here to be kind.

The child had her eyes shut now and was whispering. After a moment Lib realized it had to be a prayer. A show of piety, to make this fast of Anna's more plausible?

The girl finished and looked up, her expression as placid as ever.

"Open your mouth, please," said Lib.

Mostly milk teeth; one or two large adult ones, and several gaps where a replacement had not yet come through. Like the mouth of a much younger child.

Several carious? Breath a little sour.
Clean tongue, rather red and smooth.
Tonsils slightly enlarged.

No cap covered Anna's dark auburn hair, parted in the centre and pulled back in a small bun. Lib undid it now and worked her fingers through the strands, dry and frizzy to the touch. She felt the scalp for anything hidden but found nothing except a scaly patch behind one ear. "You may put it up again."

Anna's fingers fumbled with the hairpins.

Lib went to help — then held back. She wasn't here to tend the girl or be her maid. She was being paid just to stare.

Somewhat clumsy.
Reflexes normal, if a little slow.

Fingernails rather ridged, spotted with white.
Palms and fingers distinctly swollen.

"Step out of your boots for me, please."

"They were my brother's," said Anna as she obeyed.

Feet, ankles, and lower legs very swollen, Lib recorded; no wonder Anna had resorted to the emigrant's discarded boots. Possibly dropsy, water collecting in the tissues? "How long have your legs been so?"

The girl shrugged.

Where the stockings had been tied below Anna's knees, the marks stayed concave. The same with the backs of her heels. Lib had seen this kind of swelling in pregnant women and the occasional old soldier. She pushed her finger into the girl's calf, like a sculptor forming a child out of clay. The pit remained when she removed her finger. "Does that pain you?"

Anna shook her head.

Lib stared at the indented leg. Perhaps it wasn't too serious, but something was wrong with this child.

She carried on lifting one piece of clothing at a time. Even if Anna was a fraud, there was no need to mortify her. The girl shivered, but not as if embarrassed, only as if it were January rather than August. *Few signs of maturity,* Lib jotted down; Anna seemed more like eight or nine than eleven. *Smallpox vaccination on upper arm.* The milk-white skin was dry to the touch, brownish and rough in places. Bruises on the knees, typical in children. But those tiny spots on the girl's shins, blue-red — Lib had never encountered them before. She noticed that same fine down on the girl's forearms, back, belly, legs; like a baby monkey. Was this hairiness common among the Irish, by any chance? Lib recalled cartoons in the popular press depicting them as apish pygmies.

She remembered to check the calf again, the left one. It was as flat as the other now.

Lib glanced through her notes. A few troubling anomalies, yes, but nothing that lent weight to the O'Donnells' grandiose claims of a four-month fast.

Now, where could the child be hiding her food? Lib compressed every seam of Anna's dress and petticoat, feeling for pockets. The clothes had been darned often but well; a decent kind of poverty. She checked each part of the girl's body that could possibly hold the tiniest store, from the armpits down to the crevices (cracked in places) between the swollen toes. Not a crumb.

Anna made no protest. She was whispering to herself again now, lashes resting on cheeks. Lib couldn't make out any of the words except for one that came up over and over and sounded like . . . *Dorothy,* could it be? Roman Catholics were always begging various intermediaries to take up their petty causes with God. Was there a Saint Dorothy?

"What's that you're reciting?" Lib asked when the girl seemed to have finished.

A shake of the head.

"Come now, Anna, aren't we to be friends?"

Lib regretted her choice of word at once, because the round face lit up. "I'd like that."

"Then tell me about this prayer I hear you muttering on and off."

"That one, 'tis . . . not for talking about," said Anna.

43

"Ah. A *secret* prayer."

"Private," she corrected Lib.

Little girls — even honest ones — did love their secrets. Lib remembered her own sister keeping a diary hidden under their mattress. (Not that it stopped Lib reading every anodyne word of it.)

Lib screwed the sections of her stethoscope together. She pressed the flat base to the left side of the child's chest, between the fifth and sixth rib, and put the other end to her own right ear. *Lub-dub, lub-dub;* she listened for the minutest variation in the sounds of the heart. Then for a full minute, by the watch that hung at her waist, she counted. *Pulse distinct,* she wrote, *89 beats per minute.* That was within the expected range. Lib moved the stethoscope to different positions on the child's back. *Lungs healthy, 17 respirations per minute,* she recorded. No crackles or wheezes; despite her odd symptoms, Anna seemed healthier than half her compatriots.

Sitting down on the chair — Miss N. always began by breaking her trainees of the habit of perching on a patient's bed — Lib put the device on the child's belly. She listened for the least gurgle that would betray the presence of food. Tried another spot. Silence. *Digestive cavity hard, tympanitic, drumlike,* she wrote. She percussed the belly lightly. "How does that feel?"

"Full," said Anna.

Lib stared. *Full,* when the belly sounded so empty? Was this defiance? "Uncomfortably full?"

"No."

"You may dress yourself now."

Anna did, slowly and a little awkwardly.

Reports sleeping well at night, seven to nine
  hours.
Intellectual faculties seem unimpaired.

"Do you miss going to school, child?"

A shake of the head.

The O'Donnells' pet apparently wasn't expected to help with the housework, Lib noticed. "Perhaps you prefer to be idle?"

"I read and sew and sing and pray." The child's voice undefensive.

Confrontation was beyond Lib's remit. But she might at least be frank, she decided. Miss N. always recommended it, since nothing preyed on a patient's health like uncertainty. Lib could do this little faker real good by setting an example of candour, holding up a lamp for the girl to follow out of the wilderness into which she'd strayed. Snapping shut her memorandum book, Lib asked, "Do you know why I'm here?"

"To make sure I don't eat."

Of all the skewed ways of putting it . . . "Not at all, Anna. My job is to find out whether it's true that you *aren't* eating. But I would be most relieved if you'd take your meals as other children — other people — do."

A nod.

"Is there anything at all you could fancy? Broth, sago pudding, something sweet?" Lib was only putting a neutral question to the child, she told herself, not pressing food on her in such a way as to influence the outcome of the watch.

"No, thank you."

"Why not, do you suppose?"

A trace of a smile. "I can't say, Mrs. — ma'am," Anna corrected herself.

"Why? Is that *private* too?"

The girl looked back at her mildly. Sharp as a pin, Lib decided. Anna must have realized that giving any explanation would get her into difficulties. If she claimed that her Maker had ordered her not to eat, she'd be comparing herself to a saint. But if she boasted of living by any particular natural means, then she'd be obliged to prove it to the satisfaction of science. *I'm going to crack you like a nut, missy.*

Lib looked around. Until today it must have been child's play for Anna to sneak food from the kitchen next door in the night or for one of the adults to bring it in without the others hearing a thing. "Your maid—"

"Kitty? She's our cousin." Anna took a plaid shawl out of the dresser; its rich reds and browns lent a little colour to her face.

A slavey who was also a poor relation, then; hard for such a subordinate to refuse to take part in a plot. "Where does she sleep?"

"On the settle." Anna nodded towards the kitchen.

Of course; the lower classes often had more family members than they had beds, so they were obliged to improvise. "And your parents?"

"They sleep in the outshot."

Lib didn't know that word.

"The bed built off the cabin, behind the curtain," explained the child.

Lib had noticed the flour-sack drape in the kitchen but assumed it covered a pantry of some kind. How ridiculous for the O'Donnells to leave their good room standing empty and lie down in a makeshift chamber. But Lib supposed they had just enough respectability to aspire to a little more.

The first thing was to make this narrow bedroom proof against subterfuge. Lib touched her hand to the wall, and whitewash flaked off on her fingers. Plaster of some kind, dampish; not wood, brick, or stone, like an English cottage. Well, at least that meant any recess where food might be cached would be easy to discover.

Also, she had to make sure there was nowhere the child could hide from Lib's gaze. That rickety old wooden screen would have to go, for starters; Lib folded its three sections together and carried it to the door.

She looked through without leaving the bedroom. Mrs. O'Donnell was stirring a three-legged pot over the fire, and the maid was mashing something at the long table. Lib set down the screen just inside the kitchen and said, "We won't be needing this. Also, I'd like a basin of hot water and a cloth, please."

"Kitty," said Mrs. O'Donnell to the maid, jerking her head.

Lib's eyes flicked to the child, who was whispering her prayers again.

She moved back to the narrow bed that stood against the wall and began stripping it. The bedstead was wood, and the tick was a straw one, covered in stained canvas. Well, at least it wasn't a feather bed; Miss N. anathemized feathers. A new horsehair mattress would have been more hygienic, but Lib could hardly demand the O'Donnells drum up the money to buy one. (She thought of that strongbox full of coins, nominally destined for the poor.) Besides, she reminded herself, she wasn't here to improve the girl's health, only to study it. She felt the tick all over for any lumps or gaps in the stitching that might reveal hidey-holes.

A strange tinkling in the kitchen. A bell? It sounded once, twice, three times. Calling the family to the table for the noon meal, perhaps. But of course Lib would have to wait to be served in this narrow bedroom.

Anna O'Donnell was on her feet, hovering. "May I go say the Angelus?"

"You need to stay where I can see you," Lib reminded her, testing the flock-stuffed bolster with her fingers.

A voice raised in the kitchen. The mother's?

The child dropped down on her knees, listening hard. *"And she conceived of the Holy Spirit,"* she answered. *"Hail Mary, full of grace, the Lord is with thee . . ."*

Lib thought she recognized that one. This clearly wasn't a *private* prayer; Anna sang out the words so they carried into the next room.

Behind the wall, the women's muffled voices matched the child's. Then a lull. Rosaleen O'Donnell's single voice again. *"Behold the handmaid of the Lord."*

"Be it done to me according to thy word," chanted Anna.

Lib tugged the bedstead well away from the wall so that from now on she'd be able to approach it from three sides. She laid the tick over the footboard to air it out and did the same with the bolster. The ritual was still going on, with its calls, responses, choruses, and occasional chiming of the bell.

"And dwelt amongst us," intoned the girl.

Crouching at each corner of the bed in turn, Lib ran her hand under every bar, felt each knob and angle for scraps. She pawed the floor looking for any patch of beaten earth that might have been gouged up to bury something.

Finally the prayers seemed to be over, and Anna got to her feet. "Do you not say the Angelus, Mrs. Wright?" she asked, a little breathless.

"Is that the name of what you just did?" asked Lib instead of answering.

A nod, as if everyone knew that.

Lib shook the worst of the dust off her skirt and rubbed her hands on her apron. Where was the hot water? Was Kitty just lazy, or was she defying the English nurse?

Anna took something large and white out of her workbag and began hemming it, standing in the corner by the window.

"Sit down, child," Lib told her, waving her to the chair.

"I'm very well here, ma'am."

What a paradox: Anna O'Donnell was a shammer of the deepest dye — but with nice manners. Lib found she couldn't treat her with the harshness she deserved. "Kitty," she called, "could you bring in another chair as well as the hot water?"

No answer from the kitchen.

"Take this one for now," she urged the girl. "I don't want it."

Anna crossed herself, sat down on the chair, and sewed on.

Lib inched the dresser away from the wall to make sure there was nothing hollowed out behind it. Tugging out each drawer — the wood was warped from damp — she went through the girl's small stock of clothes, fingering every seam and hem.

On top of the dresser sat a drooping dandelion in a jar. Miss N. approved of flowers in sickrooms, scorning the old wives' tale about them poisoning the air; she said the brilliancy of colour and variety of form uplifted not only the mind but the body. (In Lib's first week at the hospital, she'd tried to explain that to Matron, who'd called her *la-di-da*.)

It occurred to Lib that the flower might be a source of nourishment hiding in plain sight. What about the liquid — was it really water or some kind of clear broth or syrup? Lib sniffed at the jar, but all her nose registered was the familiar tang of dandelion. She dipped her finger in the liquid, then put it to her lips. As tasteless as it was colourless. But might there be some kind of nutritive element that had those qualities?

Lib could tell without looking that the girl was watching her. Oh, come now, Lib was falling into the trap of the old doctor's delusions. This was just water. She wiped her hand on her apron.

Beside the jar, nothing but a small wooden chest. Not even a mirror, it struck Lib now; did Anna never want to look at herself? She opened the box.

"Those are my treasures," said the girl, jumping up.

"Lovely. May I see?" Lib's hands already busy inside the chest, in case Anna was going to claim that these were *private* too.

"Certainly."

Pious gimcrackery: a set of rosary beads made of — seeds, was it? — with a plain cross on the end, and a painted candlestick in the shape of the Virgin and Child.

"Isn't it beautiful?" Anna reached out for the candlestick. "Mammy and Dadda gave it to me on my confirmation."

"An important day," murmured Lib. The statuette was too sickly-sweet for her taste. She felt it all over to make sure it was really porcelain, not something edible. Only then did she let the girl take it.

Anna held it to her chest. "Confirmation's the *most* important day."

"Why's that?"

" 'Tis the end of being a child."

Darkly comic, Lib found it, this slip of a thing thinking of herself as a grown woman. Next she peered at the writing on a tiny silvery oval, no bigger than the top of her finger.

"That's my Miraculous Medal," said Anna, lifting it out of Lib's hand.

"What miracles has it done?"

That came out too flippant, but the girl didn't take offence. "Ever so many," she assured Lib, rubbing it. "Not *this* one, I mean, but all the Miraculous Medals in Christendom together."

Lib didn't comment. At the bottom of the box, in a glass case, she found a tiny disc. Not metal but white, this one, stamped with a lamb carrying a flag and a coat of arms. It couldn't be the bread from Holy Communion, could it? Surely that would be sacrilege, to keep the Host in a toy box? "What's this, Anna?"

"My Agnus Dei."

Lamb of God; Lib knew that much Latin. She flipped up the lid of the case and grated the disc with her nail.

"Don't break it!"

"I won't." It wasn't bread, she realized, but wax. She laid the box in Anna's cupped hand.

"Each one's been blessed by His Holiness," the child assured her, clicking the lid shut. "Agnus Deis make floods go down and put out fires."

Lib puzzled over the origin of this legend. Considering how fast wax melted, who could imagine it any use against fire?

Nothing left in the chest but a few books. She inspected the titles: all devotional. *A Missal for the Use of the Laity; The Imitation of Christ.* She plucked an ornamented rectangle about the size of a playing card out of the black Book of Psalms.

"Put it back where it lives," said Anna, agitated.

Ah, could there be food hidden in the book? "Just a moment." Lib riffled through the pages. Nothing but more little rectangles.

"Those are my holy cards. Each one has its own place."

The one Lib held was a printed prayer with a fancy-cut border, like lace, and it had another of those tiny medals tied onto it with a ribbon. On the back, in saccharine pastels, a woman cuddled a sheep. *Divine Bergère,* it said at the top. Divine something?

"See, this one matches Psalm One Hundred and Eighteen: *I have gone astray like a sheep that is lost,*" Anna recited, tapping the page without needing to check what it said.

Very "Mary Had a Little Lamb," Lib thought. She saw now that all the books in the chest were studded with these rectangles. "Who gave you these cards?"

"Some were prizes at school or at the mission. Or presents from visitors."

"Where's this mission?"

"It's gone now. My brother left me some of the loveliest ones," said Anna, kissing the sheep card before tucking it into its place and closing the book.

What a curious child. "Do you have a favourite saint?"

Anna shook her head. "They all have different things to teach us. Some of them were born good, but others were very wicked until God cleaned their hearts."

"Oh yes?"

"He can pick anyone to be holy," Anna assured her.

When the door burst open, Lib jumped.

Kitty, with the basin of hot water. "Sorry to keep you. I'm after bringing himself his meal," the young woman said, panting.

Malachy O'Donnell, presumably. Off cutting turf for a neighbour, wasn't he — as a favour? Lib wondered. Or a job of work to supplement the pittance the farm made? It struck her that perhaps only the men got food at midday here.

"What'll I be scrubbing for you?" asked the slavey.

"I'll do that," Lib told her, taking the basin. She couldn't allow any of the family access to this room. Kitty might have food for the child tucked in her apron right now, for all Lib knew.

The maid frowned; confusion or resentment?

"You must be busy," said Lib. "Oh, and could I trouble you for another chair, as well as fresh bedding?"

"A sheet?" asked Kitty.

"A pair of them," Lib corrected her, "and a clean blanket."

"We've none," said the maid, shaking her head.

Such a vacant expression on the broad face; Lib wondered if Kitty was quite all there.

"No clean sheets yet, she means," Anna put in. "Wash day's Monday next, unless 'tis too wet."

"I see," said Lib, suppressing her irritation. "Well, just the chair, then, Kitty."

She added chlorinated soda from a bottle in her bag to the basin of water and wiped every surface; the smell was harsh, but clean. She made the child's bed again, with the same tired sheets and grey blanket. Straightening up, she wondered where else a mouthful of food could possibly be stashed.

This was nothing like the cluttered sickrooms of the upper classes. Apart from the bed, dresser, and chair, there was only a woven mat on the floor, with a pattern of darker lines. Lib lifted it up; nothing underneath. The room would be very cheerless if she took the mat away, as well as chill underfoot. Besides, the most likely place to hide a crust or an apple was in the bed, and surely the committee didn't mean to make the girl sleep on bare boards like a prisoner? No, Lib would just have to inspect the room at frequent and unpredictable intervals to make sure no food had been sneaked in.

Kitty brought in the chair at last, and thumped it down.

"You might take this mat and beat the dust out when you have a moment," said Lib. "Tell me, where would I find a scales to weigh Anna?"

Kitty shook her head.

"In the village, perhaps?"

"We use fists," said Kitty.

Lib frowned.

"Fistfuls of flour, like, and pinches of salt." The slavey mimed them in the air.

"I don't mean household scales," Lib told her. "Something big enough to weigh a person, or an animal. Perhaps on one of the neighbouring farms?"

Kitty shrugged tiredly.

Anna, watching the curling dandelion, gave no sign of hearing any of this, as if it were some other girl's weight that was in question.

Lib sighed. "A jug of cold water, please, then, and a teaspoon."

"Did you want a bit of something?" Kitty asked on her way out.

The phrase confused Lib.

"Or can you wait for your dinner?"

"I can wait."

Lib regretted her words the moment the maid was gone, because she was hungry. But somehow, in front of Anna, she couldn't declare that she was desperate for food. Which was absurd, she reminded herself, since the girl was nothing but a shammer.

Anna was whispering her Dorothy prayer again. Lib did her best to ignore it. She'd put up with far more irksome habits before. There was that boy she'd nursed through scarlet fever who kept hawking up on the floor, and that demented old lady who'd been convinced her medicine was poison and had shoved it away, spilling it all down Lib.

The girl was singing under her breath now, hands folded on her finished needlework. Nothing furtive about this hymn; the Dorothy prayer was the only secret Anna seemed to be keeping. The high notes were a little cracked, but sweet.

> *Hark! the loud celestial hymn,*
> *Angel choirs above are raising,*
> *Cherubim and seraphim,*
> *In unceasing chorus praising.*

When Kitty brought in the jug of water, Lib said, "What's this, may I ask?" Patting the flaking whitewash.

"A wall," said Kitty.

A tiny giggle escaped from the child.

"I mean, of what is it made?" asked Lib.

The slavey's face cleared. "Mud."

"Just mud? Really?"

" 'Tis stone at the base, anyways, for keeping the rats out."

When Kitty was gone, Lib used the tiny bone spoon to taste the water in the jug. No hint of any flavour. "Are you thirsty, child?"

Anna shook her head.

"Hadn't you better take a sip?"

Overstepping her mark; the habits of a nurse died hard. Lib reminded herself that it was nothing to her whether the little fraud drank or not.

But Anna opened her mouth for the spoon and swallowed without difficulty. *"O forgive me, that I may be refreshed,"* she murmured.

Talking not to Lib, of course, but to God.

"Another?"

"No, thank you, Mrs. Wright."

Lib wrote down, *1:13 p.m., 1 tsp. water.* Not that the quantity mattered, she supposed, except that she wanted to be able to give a full account of anything the child ingested on her watch.

Now there really was nothing left to do. Lib took the second chair. It was so close to Anna's that their skirts were almost touching, but there was nowhere else to place it. She considered the long hours ahead with a sense of awkwardness. She'd spent months on end with other private patients, but this was different, because she was eyeing this child like a bird of prey, and Anna knew it.

A soft knock at the door made her leap up.

"Malachy O'Donnell, ma'am." The farmer tapped his faded waistcoat where it buttoned.

"Mr. O'Donnell," said Lib, putting her hand into his leathery one. She would have thanked him for his hospitality except that she was here as a sort of spy on his whole household, so it hardly seemed fitting.

He was short and wiry, as lean as his wife, but with a far narrower frame. Anna took after her father's side. But no spare flesh on any of this family; a troupe of marionettes.

He bent down to kiss his daughter somewhere near the ear. "How are you, pet?"

"Very well, Dadda." Beaming up at him.

Malachy O'Donnell stood there, nodding.

Disappointment weighed on Lib. She'd been expecting something more from the father. The grand showman behind the scenes — or at least a coconspirator, as prickly as his wife. But this yokel . . . "You keep, ah, shorthorns, Mr. O'Donnell?"

"Well. A few now," he said. "I have the lease on a couple of water meadows for the grazing. I sell the, you know, for fertilizer."

Lib realized he meant manure.

"Cattle, now, sometimes . . ." Malachy trailed off. "With their straying and breaking legs and getting stuck when they come out wrong, see — you might say they do be more trouble than they're worth."

What else had Lib seen outside the farmhouse? "You also have poultry, yes?"

"Ah, they'd be Rosaleen's, now. Mrs. O'Donnell's." The man gave one last nod, as if something had been settled, and stroked his daughter's hairline. He headed out, then doubled back. "Meant to say. That fellow from the paper's here."

"I beg your pardon?"

He gestured towards the window. Through the smeary glass Lib saw an enclosed wagon. "To take Anna."

"Take her where?" she snapped. Really, what did the committee men think they were doing, setting up the watch in this cramped and unhygienic cabin and then changing their minds and shipping the child off somewhere else?

"Take her face, just," said her father. "Her likeness."

REILLY & SONS, PHOTOGRAPHISTS, the van said on the side in pompous type. Lib could hear a stranger's voice in the kitchen. Oh, this was too much. She took a few steps before remembering that she wasn't allowed to leave the child's side. She roped her arms around herself instead.

Rosaleen O'Donnell bustled in. "Mr. Reilly's ready to do your daguerreotype, Anna."

"Is this really necessary?" asked Lib.

"'Tis to be engraved and put in the paper."

Printing a portrait of the young chancer, as if she were the queen. Or a two-headed calf, more like. "How far off is his studio?"

"Sure he does it right there in the van." Mrs. O'Donnell jabbed her finger towards the window.

Lib let the child go outside in front of her but tugged her out of the way of an uncovered bucket, pungent with chemicals. Alcohol, she recognized, and . . . was it ether or chloroform? Those fruity stenches brought Lib back to Scutari, where the sedatives always seemed to run out halfway through a run of amputations.

As she handed Anna up the folding steps, Lib wrinkled her nose against a more complicated reek. Something like vinegar and nails.

"Scribbler been and gone, has he?" asked the lank-haired, disheveled man inside.

Lib narrowed her eyes.

"The journalist who's writing the girl up."

"I know nothing of any journalist, Mr. Reilly."

His frock coat was blotched. "Stand by the pretty flowers, now, would you," he said to Anna.

"Mightn't she sit instead, if she'll have to hold position for very long?" asked Lib. On the one occasion when she'd posed for a daguerreotype — in the ranks of Miss N.'s nurses — she'd found it a wearisome business. After the first few minutes one of the flightier young women had shifted and blurred the image, so they'd had to start all over again.

Reilly let out a chuckle and manoeuvred the camera a few inches on the wheeled foot of its tripod. "You're looking at a master of the modern wet process. Three seconds, that's all. The whole thing takes me no more than ten minutes from shutter to plate."

Anna stood where Reilly had put her, beside a spindly table, with her right hand resting next to a vase of silk roses.

He tilted a mirror on a stand so a square of light hit her face, then ducked under the black drape that covered his camera. "Eyes up now, girlie. To me, to me."

Anna's gaze wandered around the room.

"Look to your public."

That meant even less to the child. Her eyes found Lib instead, and she almost smiled, although Lib wasn't smiling.

Reilly emerged and slotted a wooden rectangle into the machine. "Hold that, now. Still as stone." He rolled the brass circle off the lens. "One, two, three . . ." Then he flicked it shut and shook the greasy hair out of his eyes. "Out you go, ladies." He pushed the door open and jumped down from the van, then climbed back in with his reeking bucket of chemicals.

"Why do you keep that outside?" Lib asked, taking Anna by the hand.

Reilly was tugging at cords to let blinds fall over one

window after another and darken the interior of the van. "Risk of explosion."

Lib yanked Anna to the door.

Outside the wagon, the child took a long breath, looking towards the green fields. In sunlight Anna O'Donnell had an almost transparent quality; a blue vein stood out at the temple.

It was a long afternoon back in the bedroom. The girl whispered her prayers and read her books. Lib applied herself to a not-uninteresting article on fungus in *All the Year Round*. At one point Anna accepted another two spoonfuls of water. They sat just a few feet apart, Lib occasionally glancing at the girl over the top of her page. Strange to feel so yoked to another person.

Lib wasn't even free to go out to the privy; she had to make do with the chamber pot. "Do you need this, Anna?"

"No, thank you, ma'am."

Lib left the pot by the door with a cloth over it. She repressed a yawn. "Would you care for a walk?"

Anna brightened. "May we, really?"

"So long as I'm with you." She wanted to test the girl's stamina; did the swelling in Anna's limbs impede her movement? Besides, Lib couldn't bear to stay cooped up in this room any longer.

In the kitchen, side by side, Rosaleen O'Donnell and Kitty were skimming cream off pans with saucer-shaped strainers. The maid looked half the size of the mistress. "Anything you need, pet?" asked Rosaleen.

"No, thank you, Mammy."

Dinner, Lib said silently, *that's what every child needs*. Wasn't feeding what defined a mother from the first day on? A woman's worst pain was to have nothing to give her baby. Or to see the tiny mouth turn away from what she offered.

"We're just stepping out for a walk," Lib told her.

Rosaleen O'Donnell swatted away a fat bluebottle and went back to her work.

There were only two possible explanations for the Irishwoman's serenity, Lib decided: either Rosaleen was so convinced of divine intervention that she had no anxiety for her daughter, or, more likely, she had reason to believe the girl was getting plenty to eat on the sly.

Anna shuffled and clumped along in those boy's boots with an almost undetectable lurch as she shifted her weight from one leg to another. *Perfect thou my goings in thy paths,* she murmured, *that my footsteps be not moved.*

"Do your knees hurt you?" Lib asked as they followed the track past fretful brown hens.

"Not particularly," said Anna, tilting her face up to catch the sun.

"Are these all your father's fields?"

"Well, he rents them," said the girl. "We've none of our own."

Lib hadn't seen any hired men. "Does he do all the work himself?"

"Pat helped, when he was still with us. This one's for oats," said Anna, pointing.

A bedraggled scarecrow in brown trousers leaned sideways. Were these Malachy O'Donnell's old clothes? Lib wondered.

"And over there is hay. The rain usually spoils it, but not this year, it's been so fine," said Anna.

Lib thought she recognized a wide square of low green: the longed-for potatoes.

When they reached the lane, she turned in the direction she hadn't yet been, away from the village. A sun-browned man was mending a stone wall in a desultory way.

"God bless the work," called Anna.

"And you too," he answered.

"That's our neighbour Mr. Corcoran," she whispered to Lib. She bent down and tugged up a brownish stalk topped with starry yellow. Then a tall grass, dull purple at the top.

"You like flowers, Anna?"

"Oh, ever so much. Especially the lilies, of course."

"Why *of course?*"

"Because they're Our Lady's favourite."

Anna spoke about the Holy Family as if they were her relations. "Where would you have seen a lily?" asked Lib.

"In pictures, lots of times. Or water lilies on the lough, though they're not the same." Anna crouched and stroked a minute white flower.

"What's this one?"

"Sundew," Anna told her. "Look."

Lib peered at the round leaves on stalks. They were covered with what looked like sticky fuzz, with the odd black speck.

"It catches insects and sucks them in," said Anna under her breath, as if she feared to disturb the plant.

Could she be right? How interesting, in a gruesome way. It seemed the child had some capacity for science.

When Anna stood up, she wobbled and drew in a deep breath.

Light-headed? Unused to exercise, Lib wondered, or weak from underfeeding? Just because the fast was a hoax of some sort didn't mean that Anna had been getting all the nourishment a growing girl needed; those bony shoulder blades suggested otherwise. "Perhaps we should turn back."

Anna didn't object. Was she tired or just obedient?

When they got to the cabin, Kitty was in the bedroom. Lib was about to challenge her, but the slavey stooped for the chamber pot — perhaps to give herself an excuse for being there. "You'll have a bowl of stirabout now, missus?"

"Very well," said Lib.

When Kitty brought it in, Lib saw that *stirabout* meant porridge. She realized that this was probably her dinner. A quarter past four — country hours.

"Take some salt," said Kitty.

Lib shook her head at the pot with its little spoon.

"Go on," said Kitty, "it keeps the little ones off."

Lib looked askance at the maid. Was she referring to flies?

As soon as Kitty had left the room, Anna spoke up in a whisper. "She means the little people."

Lib didn't understand.

Anna formed dancers out of her plump hands.

"Fairies?" Incredulous.

The child made a face. "They don't like to be called that." But then she smiled again, as if she and Lib both knew there were no tiny beings floundering around in the porridge.

The oatmeal wasn't half bad; it had been boiled in milk rather than water. Lib had trouble swallowing it in front of the child; she felt like some uncouth peasant stuffing herself in the presence of a fine lady. *This is only a small-holder's daughter,* Lib reminded herself, *and a cheat to boot.*

Anna busied herself darning a torn petticoat. She didn't ogle Lib's dinner, nor did she avert her gaze as if struggling with temptation. She just kept on forming her neat little stitches. Even if the girl had eaten something last night, Lib thought, she had to be hungry now, after at least seven hours under the nurse's scrutiny, during which Anna had taken in nothing but three teaspoons of water. How could she bear to sit in a room fragrant with warm porridge?

Lib scraped the bowl clean, partly so that the remains wouldn't be sitting there between the two of them. She was missing baker's bread already.

Rosaleen O'Donnell came in a while later to show off the new photograph. "Mr. Reilly's kindly made us a present of this copy."

The image was astonishingly sharp, though the tints were all wrong; the grey dress had bleached to the white of a nightdress, while the plaid shawl was pitch-black. The girl in the picture was looking sideways, towards the unseen nurse, with a ghost of a smile.

Anna glanced at the photograph as if only for politeness's sake.

"Such a smart case too," said Mrs. O'Donnell, stroking the moulded tin.

This was not an educated woman, Lib thought. Could someone who took such naïve pleasure in a cheap case really be responsible for an elaborate conspiracy? Perhaps — Lib glimpsed Anna out of the corner of her eye — the studious little pet was the only guilty party. After all, until the watch had begun this morning, it would have been easy for the child to snatch all the food she wanted without her family's knowledge.

"It'll go on the mantel beside poor Pat," added Rosaleen O'Donnell, admiring the picture at arm's length.

Was the O'Donnell boy in distressed circumstances now, overseas? Or perhaps his parents had no idea how he was; sometimes emigrants were never heard from again.

When the mother had gone back into the kitchen, Lib stared out at the grass left flattened by Reilly's wagon wheels. Then she turned, and her eye fell on Anna's awful boots. It occurred to Lib that Rosaleen O'Donnell might have said *poor Pat* because he was a natural; simple-minded. That would explain the boy's curious lolling posture in the photograph. But in that case, how could the O'Donnells have brought themselves to ship the unfortunate abroad? Either way, a subject better not raised with his little sister.

For hours on end, Anna sorted her holy cards. Played with them, really; the tender movements, dreamy air, and occasional murmurings reminded Lib of other girls with their dolls.

She read up on the effects of damp in the small volume she always carried in her bag. (*Notes on Nursing*, a gift from its author.) At half past eight she suggested it might be time for Anna to get ready for bed.

The girl crossed herself and changed into her night-dress, eyes down as she did the buttons at the front and wrists. She folded her clothes and laid them on the dresser. She didn't use the pot, so there was still nothing for Lib to measure. A girl of wax instead of flesh.

When Anna undid her bun and combed her hair, masses of dark strands came out on the teeth. That troubled Lib. For a child to be losing her hair like a woman past the prime . . . *She's doing this to herself,* Lib reminded herself. *It's all part of an elaborate trick she's playing on the world.*

Anna made the sign of the cross again as she got into bed. She sat up against the bolster, reading her Psalms.

Lib stayed by the window, watching orange streaks scrape the western sky. Was there any tiny cache of crumbs she could have missed? Tonight was when the girl would seize her chance; tonight, when the nun would be here in place of Lib. Were Sister Michael's ageing eyes sharp enough? Her wits?

Kitty carried in a taper in a stubby brass candlestick.

"Sister Michael will need more than that," said Lib.

"I'll bring another, so."

"Half a dozen candles won't be enough."

The maid's mouth hung a little open.

Lib tried for a conciliatory tone. "I know it's a lot of trouble, but I wonder whether you could get hold of some lamps?"

"Whale oil do be a shocking price these days."

"Then some other kind of oil."

"I'll have to see what I can find tomorrow," said Kitty with a yawn.

She came back in a few minutes with some milk and oatcakes for Lib's supper.

As Lib buttered the oatcakes, her eyes slid to Anna, still lost in her book. Quite a feat, to go all day on an empty stomach and give the impression of not noticing food, let alone caring about it. Such control in one so young; dedication, ambition, even. If these powers could be turned to some good purpose, how far might they take Anna O'Donnell? From having nursed alongside a variety of women, Lib knew that self-mastery counted for more than almost any other talent.

She kept one ear open to the clinks and murmurings around the table on the other side of the half-open door. Even if the mother proved to be blameless as far as the hoax went, she was relishing the fuss, at the very least. And there was the money box by the front door. How did the old proverb go? *Children are the riches of the poor.* Metaphorical riches — but sometimes the literal kind too.

Anna turned the pages, her mouth forming silent words.

A stir in the kitchen. Lib put her head out and saw Sister Michael taking off her black cloak. She gave the nun a courteous nod.

"You'll kneel down with us, won't you, Sister?" asked Mrs. O'Donnell.

The nun murmured something about not liking to keep Mrs. Wright waiting.

"That's quite all right," Lib felt obliged to say.

She turned back to Anna. Who was standing so close behind — spectral in her nightdress — that Lib flinched. That string of brown seeds ready in the child's hand.

Anna slipped past Lib to kneel between her parents on the earth floor. The nun and the maid were down already, each fingering the little cross at the end of her rosary beads. *"I believe in God, the Father Almighty, Creator of Heaven and Earth."* The five voices rattled out the words.

Lib could hardly leave now, because Sister Michael's eyes were shut and her face in its obstructive headdress was bent over her joined hands; nobody was keeping a sharp eye on Anna. So Lib went and sat by the wall, with a clear view of the girl.

The gabbling changed to the Lord's Prayer, which Lib remembered from her own youth. How little she retained of all that. Perhaps faith had never had much of a hold on her; over the years it had fallen away, with other childish things.

"And forgive us our trespasses" — here they all thumped their chests in unison, startling Lib — *"as we forgive those who trespass against us."*

She thought perhaps they'd stand up and say their good nights now. But no, the group plunged into a Hail Mary, and then another, and another. This was ridiculous; was Lib to be stuck here all evening? She blinked to moisten her tired eyes but kept them focused on Anna and on the parents, their solid bodies bracketing their daughter's. It would take only the briefest meeting of hands for a scrap to be passed over. Lib squinted, making sure nothing touched Anna's red lips.

A full quarter of an hour had gone by when she checked the watch hanging at her waist. The child never swayed, never sank down, during all this wearisome clamour. Lib let her eyes flick around the room for a moment, just to relieve them. A fat muslin bag was tied between two chairs, dripping into a basin. What could it be?

The words of the prayer had changed. *"To thee do we cry, poor banished children of Eve . . ."*

At last the whole palaver seemed to be over. The Catholics were standing up, rubbing life back into their legs, and Lib was free to go.

"Good night, Mammy," said Anna.

"I'll be in to say good night in a minute," Rosaleen told her.

Lib picked up her cloak and bag. She'd missed her chance for a private conference with the nun; somehow she couldn't bear to say out loud in front of the child, *Don't take your eyes off her for a second.* "I'll see you in the morning, Anna."

"Good night, Mrs. Wright." Anna led Sister Michael into the bedroom.

Strange creature; she showed no sign of resenting the watch that had been set over her. Behind that calm confidence, surely her mind had to be scurrying like a mouse?

Lib turned left where the O'Donnells' track met the lane, heading back to the village. It wasn't quite dark yet, and red still stained the horizon behind her. The mild air was scented with livestock and the smoke from peat fires. Her limbs ached from sitting for so long. She really needed to talk to Dr. McBrearty about the unsatisfactory conditions at the cabin, but it was too late to go seeking him out tonight.

What had she learned so far? Little or nothing.

A silhouette on the road ahead, a long gun over one shoulder. Lib stiffened. She wasn't used to being out in the countryside at nightfall.

The dog came up first, sniffing at Lib's skirts. Then his owner passed, with barely a nod.

A cock called urgently. Cows filed out of a byre, the farmer behind them. Lib would have thought they'd put their animals outdoors by day and indoors (to keep them safe) by night, rather than the other way around. She understood nothing about this place.

CHAPTER TWO

Watch

watch
> to observe
> to guard someone, as a keeper
> to be awake, as a sentinel
> a division of the night

In her dream the men were calling for tobacco, as always. Underfed, unwashed, hair crawling, ruined limbs seeping through slings into stump pillows, but all their pleas were for something to fill their pipes. The men reached out to Lib as she swept down the ward. Through the cracked windows drifted the Crimean snow, and a door kept banging, banging—

"Mrs. Wright!"

"Here," Lib croaked.

"A quarter past four, you asked to be waked."

This was the room above the spirit grocery, in the dead centre of Ireland. So the voice in the crack of the door was Maggie Ryan's. Lib cleared her throat. "Yes."

Once dressed, she took out *Notes on Nursing* and let it fall open, then put her finger on a random passage. (Like that fortune-telling game Lib and her sister used to play with the Bible on dull Sundays.) Women, she read, were often more *exact and careful* than the stronger sex, which enabled them to avoid *mistakes of inadvertence*.

But for all the care Lib had taken yesterday, she hadn't managed to uncover the mechanism of the fraud yet, had she? Sister Michael had been there all night; would she have solved the puzzle? Lib doubted it somehow. The nun had probably sat there with eyes half closed, clacking her beads.

Well, Lib refused to be gulled by a child of eleven. Today she'd have to be even more *exact and careful,* proving herself worthy of the inscription on this book. She reread it now, Miss N.'s beautiful script: *To Mrs. Wright, who has the true nurse-calling.*

How the lady had frightened Lib, and not only at first meeting. Every word Miss N. pronounced rang as if from a mighty pulpit. *No excuses,* she'd told her raw recruits. *Work hard and refuse God nothing. Do your duty while the world whirls. Don't complain, don't despair. Better to drown in the surf than stand idly on the shore.*

In a private interview, she'd made a peculiar remark. *You have one great advantage over most of your fellow nurses, Mrs. Wright: You're bereft. Free of ties.*

Lib had looked down at her hands. Untied. Empty.

So tell me, are you ready for this good fight? Can you throw your whole self into the breach?

Yes, she'd said, *I can.*

Dark, still. Only a three-quarter moon to light Lib along the village's single street, then a right turn down the lane, past the tilting, greenish headstones. Just as well she hadn't a superstitious bone in her body. Without moonlight she'd never have picked the correct faint path leading off to the O'Donnells' farm, because all these cabins looked like much of a muchness. A quarter to five when she tapped at the door.

No answer.

Lib didn't like to bang harder in case of disturbing the family. Brightness leaked from the door of the byre, off to her right. Ah, the women had to be milking. A trail of melody; was one of them singing to the cows? Not a hymn this time but the kind of plaintive ballad that Lib had never liked.

But Heaven's own light shone in her eyes,
She was too good for me,
And an angel claimed her for his own,
And took her from Lough Ree.

Lib pushed the front door of the cabin and the upper half gave way.

Firelight blazed in the empty kitchen. Something stirring in the corner — a rat? Her year in the foul wards of Scutari had hardened Lib to vermin. She fumbled for the latch to open the lower half of the door. She crossed and bent to look through the barred base of the dresser.

The beady eye of a chicken met hers. A dozen or so birds, in behind the first, started up their soft complaint. Shut in to save them from the foxes, Lib supposed.

She spotted a new-laid egg. Something occurred to her: Perhaps Anna O'Donnell sucked them in the night and ate the shells, leaving no trace?

Stepping back, Lib almost tripped on something white. A saucer, rim poking out from beneath the dresser. How could the slavey have been so careless? When Lib picked it up, liquid sloshed in her hand, soaking her cuff. She hissed and carried the saucer over to the table.

Only then did it register. She put her tongue to her wet

hand: the tang of milk. So the grand fraud was that simple? No need for the child to hunt for eggs, even, when there was a dish of milk left out for her to lap at like a dog in the dark.

Lib felt more disappointment than triumph. Exposing this hardly required a trained nurse. It seemed this job was done already, and she'd be in the jaunting car on her way back to the railway station by the time the sun came up.

The door scraped open, and Lib jerked around as if it were she who had something to hide. "Mrs. O'Donnell."

The Irishwoman mistook accusation for greeting. "Good morning to you, Mrs. Wright, and I hope you got a wink of sleep?"

Kitty behind her, narrow shoulders dragged down by two buckets.

Lib held up the saucer — chipped in two places, she noticed now. "Someone in this household has been secreting milk under the dresser."

Rosaleen O'Donnell's chapped lips parted in the beginnings of a silent laugh.

"I can only presume that your daughter's been sneaking out to drink it."

"You *presume* too much, then. Sure in what farmhouse in the land does there not be a saucer of milk left out at night?"

"For the little ones," said Kitty, half smiling as if marvelling at the Englishwoman's ignorance. "Otherwise wouldn't they take offence and cause a ruction?"

"You expect me to believe that this milk is for the fairies?"

Rosaleen O'Donnell folded her big-boned arms. "Believe

what you like or believe nothing, ma'am. Putting out the drop of milk does no harm, at least."

Lib's mind raced. Both maid and mistress just might be credulous enough for this to be the reason why the milk was under the dresser, but that didn't mean Anna O'Donnell hadn't been sipping from the fairies' dish every night for four months.

Kitty bent to open the dresser. "Get out with ye, now. Isn't the grass full of slugs?" She hustled the chickens towards the door with her skirts.

The bedroom door opened and the nun looked out. Her usual whisper: "Is anything the matter?"

"Not at all," said Lib, unwilling to explain her suspicions. "How was the night?"

"Peaceful, thank God."

Presumably meaning that Sister Michael hadn't caught the child eating yet. But how hard had she tried, given her trust in God's *mysterious ways*? Was the nun going to be any help to Lib at all, or only a hindrance?

Mrs. O'Donnell swung the iron crock off the fire now. Broom in hand, Kitty flicked the hens' greenish dirt out of the dresser.

The nun had disappeared into the bedroom again, leaving the door ajar.

Lib was just untying her cloak when Malachy O'Donnell stepped in from the farmyard with an armful of turf. "Mrs. Wright."

"Mr. O'Donnell."

He dumped the sods by the fire, then turned to go out again.

She remembered to ask: "Might there be a platform scales hereabouts on which I could weigh Anna?"

"Ah, I'm afraid there would not."

"Then how do you weigh your livestock?"

He scratched his purplish nose. "By eye, I suppose."

A child-size voice in the room within.

"Is it herself up already?" asked the father, face lighting.

Mrs. O'Donnell cut past him and went in to their daughter just as Sister Michael stepped out with her satchel.

Lib moved to follow the mother, but the father held up his hand. "You had, ah, another question."

"Did I?" She should have been by the child's side already to prevent a moment's gap between one nurse's shift and the next. But she found it impossible to walk away in the middle of a conversation.

"About the walls, Kitty said you were after asking."

"The walls, yes."

"There do be some, some dung in there, with the mud. And heather and hair for grip," said Malachy O'Donnell.

"Hair, really?" Lib's eyes slid towards the bedroom. Could this apparently ingenuous fellow be a decoy? Might his wife have scooped something out of the cooking pot in her hands before she rushed in to greet her daughter?

"And blood, and a drop of buttermilk," he added.

Lib stared at him. Blood and buttermilk — as if poured out on some primitive altar.

When she finally got into the bedroom, she found Rosaleen O'Donnell sitting on the little bed, and Anna on her knees beside her mother. There'd been enough time for the child to have gulped down a couple of griddle cakes.

Lib cursed herself for the politeness that had kept her chit-chatting with the farmer. And cursed the nun, too, for slipping away so fast; considering that Lib had sat through the entire Rosary yesterday evening, couldn't Sister Michael have stayed a minute longer this morning? Although they weren't supposed to share their views of the girl, surely the nun should have given Lib — the more experienced nurse — a report on any pertinent facts of the night shift.

Anna's voice sounded low but clear, not as if she'd just bolted food. *"My love is mine, and I am his, in me he dwells, in him I live."*

That sounded like poetry, but knowing this child it was Scripture.

The mother wasn't praying, just nodding along, like an admirer in the balcony.

"Mrs. O'Donnell," said Lib.

Rosaleen O'Donnell put her finger to her dry lips.

"You mustn't be here," said Lib.

Rosaleen O'Donnell's head tilted to one side. "Sure can't I say good morning to Anna?"

Face closed like a bud, the child gave no sign of hearing anything.

"Not like this." Lib spelled it out: "Not without one of the nurses present. You mustn't rush into her room ahead of us or have access to her furnishings."

The Irishwoman reared up. "Isn't any mother eager for a little prayer with her own sweet child?"

"You may certainly greet her night and morning. This is for your own good, yours and Mr. O'Donnell's," Lib added, to soften it. "You wish to prove you're innocent of any sleight of hand, don't you?"

For answer, Rosaleen O'Donnell sniffed. "Breakfast will be at nine," she threw over her shoulder as she left.

That was still almost four hours away. Lib felt quite hollow. Farms had their routines, she supposed. But she should have asked the Ryan girl for something at the spirit grocery this morning, a crust in her hand, even.

At school Lib and her sister had always been hungry. (It was the time the two of them had got along best, she remembered; the fellow feeling of prisoners, she supposed now.) A sparing diet was considered beneficial for girls in particular because it kept the digestion in trim and built character. Lib didn't believe she lacked self-control, but she found hunger pointlessly distracting; it made one think of nothing but food. So in adult life she never skipped a meal if she could help it.

Anna made the sign of the cross and got up off her knees now. "Good morning, Mrs. Wright."

Lib considered the girl with grudging respect. "Good morning, Anna." Even if the girl had somehow snatched a sip or a bite of something during the nun's shift or just now with her mother, it couldn't have been much; only a mouthful, at most, since yesterday morning. "How was your night?" Lib got out her memorandum book.

"I have slept and have taken my rest," quoted Anna, crossing herself again before pulling off her nightcap, *"and I have risen up, because the Lord hath protected me."*

"Excellent," said Lib, because she didn't know what else to say. Noticing that the inside of the cap was streaked with shed hair.

The girl unbuttoned her nightdress, slipped it down, and tied the sleeves around her middle. A strange disproportion between her fleshless shoulders and thick wrists and hands, between her narrow chest and bloated belly. She sluiced herself with water from the basin. *"Make thy face to shine upon thy servant,"* she said under her breath, then dried herself with the cloth, shivering.

From under the bed Lib pulled out the chamber pot, which was clean. "Did you use this at all, child?"

Anna nodded. "Sister gave it to Kitty to empty."

What was in it? Lib should have asked but found she couldn't.

Anna pulled her nightdress back up over her shoulders. She wet the small cloth, then reached down under the linen to wash one leg modestly as she balanced on the other, holding the dresser to steady herself. The shimmy, drawers, dress, and stockings she put on were all yesterday's.

Lib usually insisted on a daily change, but she felt she couldn't in a family as poor as this one. She draped the sheets and blanket over the footboard to air before she began her examination of the girl.

Tuesday, August 9, 5:23 a.m.
Water taken: 1 tsp.
Pulse: 95 beats per minute.
Lungs: 16 respirations per minute.
Temperature: cool.

Although temperature was guesswork, really, depending on whether the nurse's fingers happened to be warmer or colder than the patient's armpit.

"Put out your tongue, please." By training Lib always noted the condition of the tongue, though she'd have been hard-pressed to tell what it said about the subject's health. Anna's was red, with an odd flatness at the back instead of the usual tiny bumps.

When Lib put her stethoscope to Anna's navel, she heard a faint gurgling, though that could be attributed to the mixing of air and water; it didn't prove the presence of food. *Sounds in digestive cavity,* she wrote, *of uncertain origin.*

Today she'd have to ask Dr. McBrearty about those swollen lower legs and hands. Lib supposed it could be argued that any symptoms arising from a limited diet were all to the good, because sooner or later, surely they'd provoke the girl to give up this grotesque charade. She made the bed again, tightening the sheets.

Nurse and charge settled into a sort of rhythm on this second day. They read — Lib caught up on Madame Defarge's nefarious doings in *All the Year Round* — and chatted a little. The girl was charming, in her unworldly way. Lib found it hard to keep in mind that Anna was a trickster, a great liar in a country famous for them.

Several times an hour the child whispered what Lib thought of as the Dorothy prayer. Was it meant to strengthen her resolve every time emptiness cramped her belly?

Later in the morning Lib took Anna out for another constitutional — only around the farmyard, because the skies were threatening. When Lib remarked on Anna's halting gait, the child said that was just how she walked. She sang hymns as she went, like a stoical soldier.

"Do you like riddles?" Lib asked her when there came a break in the music.

"I don't know any."

"Dear me." Lib remembered the riddles of childhood more vividly than all the things she'd had to memorize in the schoolroom. "What about this: 'There's not a kingdom on the earth, but what I've travelled o'er and o'er, and whether it be day or night I neither am nor can be seen. What am I?'"

Anna looked mystified, so Lib repeated it.

"'I neither am nor can be seen,'" echoed the girl. "Does that mean that I amn't — I don't exist — or I amn't seen?"

"The latter," said Lib.

"Someone invisible," said Anna, "who travels all across the earth—"

"Or some*thing*," Lib put in.

The child's frown lifted. "The wind?"

"Very good. You're a quick study."

"Another. Please."

"Hmm, let's see. 'The land was white,'" Lib began, "'the seed was black. It'll take a good scholar to riddle me that.'"

"Paper, with ink on it!"

"Clever puss."

"It was because of *scholar*."

"You should go back to school," Lib told her.

Anna looked away, towards a cow munching grass. "I'm all right at home."

"You're an intelligent girl." The compliment came out more like an accusation.

Low clouds were gathering now, so Lib hurried the two of them back into the stuffy cabin. But then the rain held off, and she wished they'd stayed out longer.

Kitty finally brought in Lib's breakfast: two eggs and a cup of milk. This time greed made Lib eat so fast, tiny fragments of shell crunched in her teeth. The eggs were gritty and reeked of peat; roasted in the ashes, no doubt.

How could the child bear not just the hunger, but the boredom? The rest of humankind used meals to divide the day, Lib realized — as reward, as entertainment, the chiming of an inner clock. For Anna, during this watch, each day had to pass like one endless moment.

The child accepted a spoonful of water as if it were some rich wine.

"What's so special about water?"

Anna looked confused.

Lib held up her own cup. "What's the difference between water and this milk?"

Anna hesitated, as if this were another riddle. "There's nothing in the water."

"There's nothing in the milk but water and the goodness of the grass the cow ate."

Anna shook her head, almost smiling.

Lib dropped the subject because Kitty was coming in to take the tray.

She watched the child, who was embroidering a flower on the corner of a handkerchief. Head bent over her stitches, just the tip of her tongue sticking out, in the way of little girls trying their hardest.

A knock at the front door, shortly after ten. Lib heard a muffled conversation. Then Rosaleen O'Donnell tapped on the door of the bedroom and looked past the nurse. "More guests for you, pet. Half a dozen of them, some of them come all the way from America."

The big Irishwoman's sprightliness sickened Lib; she was like some chaperone at a debutante's first ball. "I should have thought it obvious that such visits must be suspended, Mrs. O'Donnell."

"Why so?" The mother jerked her head over her shoulder towards the good room. "These seem like decent people."

"The watch requires conditions of regularity and calm. Without any way of checking what visitors might have on them—"

The woman interrupted. "What kind of what?"

"Well, food," said Lib.

"Sure there's food in this house already without anyone shipping it all the way across the Atlantic." Rosaleen O'Donnell let out a laugh. "Besides, Anna doesn't want it. Haven't you seen proof of that by now?"

"My job is to make sure not only that no one passes the child anything, but that nothing is hidden where she can find it later."

"Why ever would they do that when they've come all this way to see the amazing little girl who *doesn't* eat?"

"Nonetheless."

Mrs. O'Donnell's lips set hard. "Our guests are in the house already, so they are, and 'tis too late to turn them away without grave offence."

At this point it occurred to Lib to slam the bedroom door and set her back against it.

The woman's pebble eyes held hers.

Lib decided to give in until she could speak to Dr. McBrearty. *Lose a battle, win the war.* She led Anna into the good room and took up a position right behind the child's chair.

The visitors were a gentleman from the western port of Limerick with his wife and in-laws as well as a mother and daughter of their acquaintance who were visiting from the United States. The older American lady volunteered the information that she and her daughter were Spiritualists. "We believe the dead speak to us."

Anna nodded, matter-of-fact.

"Your case, my dear, strikes us as the most glorious proof of the power of Mind." The lady leaned over to squeeze the child's fingers.

"No touching, please," said Lib, and the visitor jerked back.

Rosaleen O'Donnell put her head in the door to offer them a cup of tea.

Lib was convinced the woman was provoking her. *No food,* she mouthed.

One of the gentlemen was interrogating Anna about the date of her last meal.

"April the seventh," she told him.

"That was your eleventh birthday?"

"Yes, sir."

"And how do you believe you've survived this long?"

Lib expected Anna to shrug or say she didn't know. Instead she murmured something that sounded like *mamma.*

"Speak up, little girl," said the older Irishwoman.

"I live on manna from heaven," said Anna. As simply as she might have said, *I live on my father's farm.*

Lib shut her eyes briefly so as not to roll them in disbelief.

"Manna from heaven," the younger Spiritualist repeated to the elder. "Fancy that."

The visitors were pulling out presents now. From Boston, a toy called a thaumatrope; did Anna have anything like it?

"I haven't any toys," she told them.

They liked that; the charming gravity of her tone. The Limerick gentleman showed her how to twist the disc's two strings, then twirl it, so the pictures on the two sides blurred into one.

"The bird's in the cage now," marvelled Anna.

"Aha," he cried, "mere illusion."

The disc slowed and stopped, so the empty cage was left on the back, and the bird on the front flew free.

After Kitty brought the tea in, the wife produced something even more curious: a walnut that popped open in Anna's hand to let out a crumpled ball that relaxed into a pair of exquisitely thin yellow gloves. "Chicken skin," said the lady, fondling them. "All the rage when I was a child. Never made anywhere in the world but Limerick. I've kept this pair half a century without tearing them."

Anna drew the gloves on, finger by fat finger; they were too long, but not by much.

"Bless you, my child, bless you."

Once the tea was drunk, Lib made a pointed remark about Anna needing to rest.

"Would you say a little prayer with us first?" asked the lady who'd given her the gloves.

Anna looked to Lib, who felt she had to nod.

"Infant Jesus, meek and mild," the girl began.

Look on me, a little child.
Pity mine and pity me,
Suffer me to come to thee.

"Beautiful!"

The elderly lady wanted to leave some homeopathic tonic pills.

Anna shook her head.

"Ah, keep them, do."

"She can't take them, Mother," the woman's daughter reminded her in a hiss.

"I don't believe absorption under the tongue would count as eating, exactly."

"No, thank you," said Anna.

As they left, Lib listened to the coins clink into the money box.

Rosaleen O'Donnell was hooking a pot out of the dull heart of the fire and knocking ashen sods off its lid. Hands padded with rags, she lifted the lid and took out a round loaf with a cross marked on top.

Everything was religion here, thought Lib. Also, she was beginning to see why all her meals tasted of peat. If she did stay the full fortnight, she'd have consumed a good handful of boggy soil; the thought soured her mouth. "Those will be the last visitors admitted," she told the mother in her firmest voice.

Anna was leaning on the half-door, watching the party climb into their carriage.

Rosaleen O'Donnell straightened up, shaking out her skirts. "Hospitality's a sacred law with the Irish, Mrs. Wright. If anyone knocks, we must open up and feed and shelter them, even if the kitchen floor do be thick with sleeping people already." The sweep of her arm encompassed a horde of invisible guests.

Hospitality, my foot. "This is hardly a matter of taking in paupers," Lib told her.

"Rich, poor, we're all alike in the eyes of God."

It was the pious tone that pushed Lib over the edge. "These people are gawkers. So keen to see your daughter apparently subsist without food, they're willing to pay for the privilege!"

Anna was twirling her thaumatrope now; it caught the light.

Mrs. O'Donnell chewed her lip. "If the sight moves them to almsgiving, what's wrong with that?"

The child went up to her mother just then and handed over her gifts. To distract the two women from their quarrel? Lib wondered.

"Ah sure these are yours, pet," said Rosaleen.

Anna shook her head. "The gold cross that lady left the other day, didn't Mr. Thaddeus say it'd raise a good sum for the needy?"

"But these are only toys," said her mother. "Well, the gloves in the shell, maybe, I suppose those could be sold . . ." She turned the walnut over in her palm. "Keep the spinny thing, though. Sure what harm. Unless Mrs. Wright sees any?"

Lib held her tongue.

She marched into the bedroom behind the girl and

examined all the surfaces again, just as she had yesterday — the floor, the treasure box, the dresser, the bedding.

"Are you cross?" asked Anna, twirling her thaumatrope between her fingers.

"About your toy? No, no." What a child Anna was still, for all the dark complications of her situation.

"About the visitors, then?"

"Well. They don't have your welfare at heart."

The bell chimed in the kitchen and Anna dropped to the floor. (No wonder the child's shins were bruised.) The minutes ticked by while the prayers of the Angelus filled the air. Like being locked up in a monastery, Lib thought.

"Through the same Christ Our Lord, amen." Anna got up and gripped the back of the chair.

"Dizzy?" asked Lib.

Anna shook her head and readjusted her shawl.

"How often must you all do this?"

"At noon only," said the child. " 'Twould be better to say it at six in the morning and in the evening as well, but Mammy and Dadda and Kitty are too busy."

Yesterday Lib had made the mistake of telling the maid she could wait for her dinner. This time she went to the door and called out that she'd like something to eat.

Kitty brought in some fresh cream cheese; that must have been the white stuff dripping in the bag slung between the chairs last night. The bread, still warm, was too dense with bran for Lib's liking. Waiting for the new potatoes of autumn, the family had to be getting down near the dust at the bottom of the meal bin.

Although she was used to eating in front of Anna by now, she still felt like a sow, nose in the trough.

Once Lib had finished, she tried the first chapter of a novel called *Adam Bede*. She was startled when the nun tapped on the door at one o'clock; she'd almost forgotten that her shift would end.

"Look, Sister," said Anna, making her thaumatrope spin.

"What a thing!"

Lib could see she and the other nurse weren't going to get a moment alone this time either. She stepped closer, till her face was at the side of the nun's headdress, and whispered: "I've noted nothing untoward so far. You?"

A hesitation. "We're not to confer."

"Yes, but—"

"Dr. McBrearty was very firm that there should be no sharing of views."

"I'm not looking for your views, Sister," snapped Lib. "Only basic facts. Can you assure me that you're keeping a careful note of anything excreted, for instance? Any solids, I mean."

Very low: "There's been nothing of that kind."

Lib nodded. "I've explained to Mrs. O'Donnell that there's to be no contact without supervision," she went on. "One embrace at rising, say, and another when going to bed. Also, none of the family are to enter Anna's room while she's not there."

The nun was like some undertaker's hired mute.

Lib picked her way along the dirty lane, which was potholed with ovals of blue sky; last night's rain. She was coming to the conclusion that without a fellow nurse working to Lib's own high standards — Miss N.'s standards — the whole watch was flawed. For lack of due vigilance over a crafty child, all this trouble and expense might go to waste.

And yet Lib had seen no real evidence of craftiness in the girl yet. Except for the one vast lie, of course: the claim of living without food.

Manna from heaven, that's what she'd forgotten to ask Sister Michael about. Lib might not have much faith in the nun's judgment, but surely the woman would know her Bible?

It was almost hot this afternoon; Lib took off her cloak and carried it over her arm. She tugged at her collar and wished her uniform were less thick and scratchy.

In the room above the spirit grocery, she changed into a plain green costume. She couldn't bear to stay in, not for a moment; she'd spent half the day shut up already.

Downstairs, two men were carrying an unmistakeable shape out of a passage. Lib recoiled.

"Beg your pardon, Mrs. Wright," said Maggie Ryan, "they'll have him out of your way in two ticks."

Lib watched the men steer the unvarnished coffin around the counter.

"My father's the undertaker too," the girl explained, "on account of having the couple of gigs for hire."

So the carriage outside the window stood in for a hearse as needed. Ryan's combination of trades struck Lib as unsavoury. "A quiet place, this."

Maggie nodded as the door swung shut behind the coffin. "There used to be twice as many of us before the bad time."

Us, meaning the people in this village or in the county? Or the whole of Ireland, perhaps? The *bad time*, Lib assumed, was that terrible failure of the potato ten or fifteen years back. She tried to call up the details. All she could generally remember of old news was a flicker of headlines in grim type. When she was young, she'd never really studied the paper, only glanced at it. Folded the *Times* and laid it beside Wright's plate, every morning, the year she'd been his wife.

She thought of the beggars. "On the drive here I saw many women alone with their children," she mentioned to Maggie Ryan.

"Ah, lots of the men are gone for the season, just, harvesting over your way," said Maggie.

Lib took her to mean England.

"But the most part of the young folk do have their hearts set on America, and then there's no coming home." She jerked her chin, as if to say good riddance to those *young folk* who weren't anchored to this spot.

Judging from her face, Lib thought Maggie herself couldn't have been more than twenty. "You wouldn't consider it?"

"Sure there's no hearth like your own, as they say." Her tone more resigned than fond.

Lib asked her for directions to Dr. McBrearty's.

His house was a substantial one at the end of a lane, some way out on the Athlone road. A maid as decrepit as her master showed Lib into the study. McBrearty whipped off his octagonal glasses as he stood up.

Vanity? she wondered. Did he fancy he looked younger without them?

"Good afternoon, Mrs. Wright. How are you?"

Irked, Lib thought of saying. *Frustrated. Thwarted on all sides.*

"Anything of an urgent nature to report?" he asked as they sat.

"Urgent? Not exactly."

"No hint of fraud, then?"

"No positive evidence," Lib corrected him. "But I thought you might have visited your patient to see for yourself."

His sunken cheeks flushed. "Oh, I assure you, little Anna's on my mind at all hours. In fact, I'm so very concerned for the watch that I've thought it best to absent myself so it can't be insinuated afterwards that I exerted any influence over your findings."

Lib let out a small sigh. McBrearty still seemed to be assuming that the watch would prove the little girl a modern-day miracle. "I'm concerned that Anna's temperature seems low, especially in her extremities."

"Interesting." McBrearty rubbed his chin.

"Her skin's not good," Lib went on, "nor her nails, nor her hair." This sounded like petty stuff from a magazine of beauty. "And there's a downy fuzz growing all over her. But what worries me most is the swelling in her legs — her face and hands, too, but the lower legs are the worst. She's resorted to wearing her brother's old boots."

"Mm, yes, Anna's been dropsical for some time. However, she doesn't complain of pain."

"Well. She doesn't complain at all."

The doctor nodded as if that reassured him. "Digitalis is a proven remedy for fluid retention, but of course she won't take anything by mouth. One might resort to a dry diet—"

"Limit her liquids even further?" Lib's voice shot

upwards. "She has only a few spoonfuls of water a day as it is."

Dr. McBrearty plucked at his side-whiskers. "I could reduce her legs mechanically, I suppose."

Bleeding, did he mean? Leeching? Lib wished she hadn't said a word to this antediluvian.

"But that has its own risks. No, no, on the whole, safer to watch and wait."

Lib was still uneasy. Then again, if Anna was imperiling her own health, whose fault was it but her own? Or the fault of whoever was putting her up to this, Lib supposed.

"She doesn't look like a child who hasn't eaten in four months, does she?" the doctor asked.

"Far from it."

"My sense of it exactly! A wonderful anomaly."

The old man had misunderstood her. He was wilfully blind to the obvious conclusion: the child was getting fed somehow. "Doctor, if Anna were really taking no nourishment at all, don't you think she'd be prostrated by now? Of course you must have seen many famished patients during the potato blight, far more than I," Lib added, as a sop to his expertise.

McBrearty shook his head. "As it happens I was still in Gloucestershire then. I inherited this estate only five years ago and couldn't rent it out, so I thought I'd return and practice here." He rose to his feet as if to say their interview was over.

"Also," she went on in a rush, "I can't say I have the utmost confidence in my fellow nurse. It will be no easy task to maintain complete alertness during night shifts in particular."

"But Sister Michael should be an old hand at that," said McBrearty. "She nursed at the Charitable Infirmary in Dublin for twelve years."

Oh. Why had nobody thought to tell Lib this?

"And at the House of Mercy, they rise for Night Office at midnight, I believe, and again for Lauds at dawn."

"I see," said Lib, mortified. "Well. The real problem is that the conditions at the cabin are most unscientific. I have no way to weigh the child, and there are no lamps to provide adequate light. Anna's room can easily be accessed from the kitchen, so anyone might go in when I take her out walking. Without your authority, Mrs. O'Donnell won't even let me shut the door to oglers, which makes it impossible to watch the child rigourously enough. Could I have it in your hand that there are to be no visitors admitted?"

"Quite, yes." McBrearty wiped his pen on a cloth and took up a fresh page. He fumbled in his breast pocket.

"The mother may resist turning away the mob, of course, on account of the loss of money."

The old man blinked his rheumy eyes and kept digging in his pocket. "Oh, but the donations all go into the poor box that Mr. Thaddeus gave the O'Donnells. You don't understand these people if you think they'd keep a farthing."

Lib's mouth set. "Are you by any chance looking for your spectacles?" She pointed to where they lay among his papers.

"Ah, very good." He jammed the side arms over his

ears and began to write. "How do you find Anna otherwise, may I ask?"

Otherwise? "In spirits, you mean?"

"In, well, in character, I suppose."

Lib was at a loss. *A nice girl. But a cheat of the deepest dye.* Anna had to be. Didn't she? "Generally calm," she said instead. "What Miss Nightingale used to describe as an accumulative temperament, the kind that gathers in impressions gradually."

McBrearty brightened up at the name, so much so that Lib wished she hadn't used it. He signed the note, folded it, and held it out.

"Could you have it sent over to the O'Donnells', please, to put a stop to these visits this very afternoon?"

"Oh, certainly." He tugged off his glasses again, folded them in half with tremulous fingers. "Fascinating letter in the latest *Telegraph*, by the by." McBrearty stirred the papers on his desk without finding what he was looking for. "It mentions a number of previous cases of 'fasting girls' who've lived without food — have been said to do so, at least," he corrected himself, "in Britain and abroad over the centuries."

Really? Lib had never heard of the phenomenon.

"The writer suggests that they might possibly have been, ah — well, not to put too fine a point on it — reabsorbing, subsisting on their own menses."

What a revolting theory. Besides, this child was only eleven. "In my view, Anna is a long way from being pubescent."

"Mm, true." McBrearty looked dashed. Then the corners of his mouth turned up. "To think I might have stayed in England and never had the luck to encounter such a case!"

After leaving the doctor's house, Lib strode away, trying to loosen her stiff legs and shake off the atmosphere of that fusty study.

A lane led towards a clump of woodland. She noticed leaves lobed like oak but on straighter branches than English oaks. The hedges were spiky with furze, and she breathed in the bouquet of the tiny yellow blooms. There were drooping pink flowers that no doubt Anna O'Donnell could have named. Lib tried to identify some of the birds twittering in the bushes, but the low boom of the bittern was the only one she knew for sure — the foghorn of some unseen ship.

One tree stood out at the back of a field; something odd about its dangling branches. Lib picked her way along the outside furrow — although her boots were so muddy already, she wasn't sure why she was bothering to be careful. The tree was farther away than it seemed, a good stretch beyond where the cultivated strips ran out, past an outcropping of grey limestone cracked by sun and rain. Nearing, Lib saw that it was a hawthorn, new twigs coming in red against the glossy leaves. But what was that dangling in strips from the pinkish branches? Moss?

No, not moss. Wool?

Lib almost stumbled into a tiny pool in a cleft rock. Two azure dragonflies clung together a few inches above the water. Could it be a spring? Something like bladderwort fringed the edge of the pool. She was suddenly terribly thirsty, but when she crouched down, the dragonflies disappeared, and the water looked as black as the peaty soil. She cupped some in her palm. It had a whiff like creosote, so she swallowed her thirst and let it spill again.

Not wool hanging from the hawthorn branches above her; something man-made, in strips. How peculiar. Ribbons, scarves? They'd been knotted onto the tree for so long, they were grey and vegetal.

Back at Ryan's, in the tiny dining room, she found a redhaired man finishing a chop and filling in a memorandum book much like hers with a rapid hand. He jumped to his feet. "You're not from hereabouts, ma'am."

How could he tell? Her plain green dress, her bearing?

The man was about her height, a few years younger, with that unmistakeably Irish milky skin under garish curls, and an accent, but an educated one. "William Byrne, of the *Irish Times*."

Ah, the *scribbler* the photographist had mentioned. Lib accepted his handshake. "Mrs. Wright."

"Touring the sights of the Midlands?"

He didn't guess why she was here, then; he took her for a lady tourist. "Are there any?" That came out too sardonic.

Byrne chuckled. "Well, now, it depends how much your soul is stirred by the enigmatic atmosphere of stone circles, ring forts, or round barrows."

"I'm not familiar with the second or the third."

He made a face. "Variations on the stone circle, I suppose."

"So all the sights hereabouts are rocky and circular?"

"Apart from the latest one," said William Byrne, "a magical girl who lives on air."

Lib stiffened.

"Not what I'd call hard news, but my editor in Dublin thought it'd do for August. However, I lamed my mare in a pothole outside Mullingar, had to tend her two nights till she was mended, and now that I'm here, I've been turned away from the girl's humble cot!"

A quiver of embarrassment; he must have arrived just after the note she'd made McBrearty send the O'Donnells. But, really, more publicity for this case would fan the flames of delusion, and the watch could only be hindered by the prying of a newspaper reporter.

Lib would have liked to excuse herself and go upstairs before Byrne could say anything else about Anna O'Donnell, but she needed her dinner. "Could you not have left your horse and hired another?"

"I suspected they'd have shot Polly instead of feeding her hot mash as I did."

She smiled at the image of the journalist curled up in the horse stall.

"My cold welcome at the prodigy's cabin is the real catastrophe," complained Byrne. "I've shot off a caustic paragraph to the paper by telegraph, but now I have to conjure up a full report to send by tonight's mail coach."

Was he always so free-spoken with strangers? Lib couldn't think of anything to say except "Why *caustic*?"

"Well, it speaks ill of the family's honesty, doesn't it, if they won't even let me in the door for fear I'll see through their wunderkind at first glance?"

That wasn't fair to the O'Donnells, but Lib could hardly tell him that he was talking to the very person who'd insisted on banning visitors. Her eyes fell and slid to his notes.

How illimitable is the gullibility of mankind, especially, it must be said, when combined with provincial ignorance. But Mundus vult decipi, ergo decipiatur; *that is to say, "If the world will be gulled, let it be gulled." Thus quoth Petronius, in the days of Our Lord, an aphorism just as pertinent to our own time.*

Maggie Ryan came in with more ale for Byrne.

"The chops were delicious," he told her.

"Ah, now," said Maggie with a touch of scorn, "hunger's the best sauce."

"I believe I'll have a chop," said Lib.

"They're all ate, ma'am. There's mutton."

Lib agreed to mutton, not having a choice. Then she put her head down over *Adam Bede* immediately so William Byrne wouldn't feel invited to linger.

When she reached the cabin at nine that night she recognized the moaning chorus of the Rosary: *Holy Mary, Mother of God, pray for us now and at the hour of our death, amen.*

She let herself in and waited on one of the three-legged stools the Irish called creepies. Like babies, the Catholics, babbling as they squeezed their beads. Sister Michael's head was up, at least, eyes on the little girl, but was she concentrating on her or on the prayers?

Anna was in her nightdress already. Lib watched her

lips shaping the words over and over: *Now and at the hour of our death, amen.* She trained her gaze in turn on the mother, the father, the poor cousin, wondering which of them was plotting to evade her scrutiny tonight.

"Sister, you'll stay for a cup of tea with us?" asked Rosaleen O'Donnell afterwards.

"I won't, Mrs. O'Donnell, but thank you kindly."

Anna's mother was flaunting her preference for the nun, Lib decided. Of course they'd like Sister Michael, familiar and inoffensive.

Rosaleen O'Donnell was using a little rake to tidy the embers into a circle. She set down three fresh sods like spokes in a wheel and sat back on her heels, crossing herself. Once the fresh turf flared up, she scooped ash from a bin and shook it over the flames, damping them down.

Lib had a dizzying sense that time could fall into itself like the embers. That in these dim huts nothing had changed since the age of the Druids and nothing ever would. What was that line in the hymn they'd sung at Lib's school? *The night is dark, and I am far from home.*

While the nun was doing up her cloak in the bedroom, Lib asked her about the day.

Three spoonfuls of water taken, according to Sister Michael, and a short walk. No symptoms any better or worse.

"And if you'd seen the girl engage in any surreptitious behaviour," asked Lib in a whisper, "I hope you'd consider this a relevant *fact* and mention it to me?"

The nun nodded guardedly.

It was maddening; what could they be missing? Still,

the girl couldn't hold out much longer. Lib would catch her out tonight, she was almost sure of it.

She chanced saying one more thing. "Here's a fact. Manna from heaven," she murmured in Sister Michael's ear, "that's what I heard Anna tell a visitor this morning, that she's living on manna from heaven."

The nun gave another tiny nod. Merely acknowledging what Lib had said, or affirming that such a thing was quite possible?

"I thought you might know the scriptural reference."

Sister Michael furrowed her forehead. "The Book of Exodus, I believe."

"Thank you." Lib tried to think of some more conversational note to end on. "It's always intrigued me," she said, letting her voice rise, "why you Sisters of Mercy are called walking nuns."

"We walk out into the world, you see, Mrs. Wright. We take the usual vows of any order — poverty, chastity, obedience — but also a fourth, service."

Lib had never heard the nun say so much before. "What kind of service?"

Anna broke in: "To the sick, the poor, and the ignorant."

"Well remembered, child," said the nun. "We vow to be of use."

As Sister Michael left the room, Rosaleen O'Donnell came in but didn't say a word. Was she refusing to speak to the Englishwoman now, after this morning's spat about the visitors? She turned her back on Lib, bending to wrap the tiny girl in her arms. Lib listened to the whispered endearments and watched Anna's thick hands, dangling at her sides, empty.

Then the woman straightened up and said, "Let you sleep well tonight, pet, and may only the sweetest of dreams come to your bed. *Angel of God, my guardian dear, to whom God's love commits me here.*" Dipping again, her forehead almost touching the child's. "*Ever this night be at my side, to light and guard, to rule and guide.*"

"*Amen.*" The girl joined in on the last word. "Good night, Mammy."

"Good night, pet."

"Good night, Mrs. O'Donnell," Lib put in, conspicuously civil.

After a few minutes, the slavey came in with an unshaded lamp and set it down. She struck a match and lit the wick till it flared, then crossed herself. "There you go, ma'am."

"That's a great help, Kitty," said Lib. The lamp was an old-fashioned thing with a burner like a forked stick inside a conical glass chimney, but its light was snowy white. She sniffed. "Not whale oil?"

" 'Tis burning fluid."

"What's that?"

"I couldn't tell you."

This mysterious burning fluid smelled something like turpentine; alcohol in the mix, perhaps.

We must be scavengers in a time of calamity; that line of Miss N.'s came back to Lib now. At Scutari the nurses had had to root through storerooms for chloride of lime, tincture of opium, blankets, socks, firewood, flour, lice combs . . . What they couldn't find — or couldn't persuade the purveyor to release — they had to improvise. Torn-up sheets became slings, sacks were stuffed to make tiny mattresses; desperation was the mother of the makeshift.

"Here's the can, and the lamp scissors," said Kitty. "After six hours you snuff it and trim off the charred bit and top it up and light the yoke again. And watch out for draughts, the fellow said, or they can shoot soot through the room like a black rain!"

The child was on her knees by the bed, pressing her hands flat together in prayer.

"Good night, pet," Kitty told her with a wide yawn, and she trudged back to the kitchen.

Lib opened to a new page and took up her metallic pencil.

Tuesday, August 9, 9:27 p.m.
Pulse: 93 beats per minute.
Lungs: 14 respirations per minute.
Tongue: no change.

Her first night shift. She'd never minded working these hours; there was something steadying about the quiet. She made a last pass over the sheets with the flat of her hand. Searching for hidden crumbs had already become routine.

Lib's eyes fell on the whitewashed wall, and she thought of the dung, hair, blood, and buttermilk mixed into it. How could such a surface ever be clean? She imagined Anna sucking it for a trace of nourishment, like those wayward babies who ate fistfuls of earth. But no, that would stain her mouth, surely. Besides, Anna was never alone anymore, not since the watch had begun. Candles, the girl's own clothes, pages out of her books, fragments of her own skin — she had no chance to nibble on any of these things unobserved.

Anna finished her prayers by whispering the Dorothy one. Then she made the sign of the cross and climbed under the sheet and the grey blanket. Her head nestled into the thin bolster.

"Have you no other pillow?" asked Lib.

A tiny smile. "I didn't have one at all till the whooping cough."

It was a paradox: Lib meant to expose the girl's stratagems to the world, but she wanted her to get a good night's sleep in the meantime. Old nursing habits died hard.

"Kitty," she called at the door. The O'Donnells had disappeared already, but the maid was setting up an old tick on the base of the settle. "Could I have a second pillow for Anna?"

"Sure take mine," said the maid, holding out a lumpen shape in a cotton slip.

"No, no—"

"Go on, I'll hardly notice, I'm that ready to drop."

"What's the matter, Kitty?" Rosaleen O'Donnell's voice from the alcove; the outshot, that was what they called it.

"She's wanting another pillow for the child."

The mother pushed aside the flour-sack curtain. "Is Anna not well?"

"I simply wondered if there might be a spare pillow," said Lib, awkward.

"Have the both of them," said Rosaleen O'Donnell, carrying her pillow across the floor and piling it on the maid's. "Lovey, are you all right?" she demanded, poking her head into the bedroom.

"I'm grand," said Anna.

"One will do," said Lib, taking Kitty's pillow.

Mrs. O'Donnell sniffed. "The smell of that lamp's not making you sick, is it? Or stinging your eyes?"

"No, Mammy."

The woman was parading her concern, that was it, making it seem as if the hardhearted nurse was doing the child damage by insisting on a brutally bright light.

Finally the door was shut, and nurse and child were alone. "You must be tired," Lib said to Anna.

A long moment. "I don't know."

"It may be hard to drop off, as you're not used to the lamp. Would you like to read? Or have me read you something?"

No answer.

Lib went closer to the girl, who turned out to be asleep already. Snowy cheeks as round as peaches.

Living on *manna from heaven*. What hogwash. What exactly was manna, some sort of bread?

The Book of Exodus, that was in the Old Testament. But the only volume of Scripture Lib could find in Anna's treasure box was the Psalms. She riffled through it, careful not to disturb the little cards. No mention of manna that she could see. One passage caught her eye. *The children that are strangers have lied to me, strange children have faded away, and have halted from their paths*. What on earth did that mean? Anna was a *strange child*, certainly. She'd *halted* from the ordinary *path* of girlhood when she'd decided to lie to the whole world.

It came to Lib then that the question to ask was not *how* a child might commit such a fraud, but *why?* Children told fibs, yes, but surely only one with a perverse nature would invent this particular story. Anna showed not the slightest interest in making her fortune. The young craved attention, perhaps even fame — but at the price of an empty belly, an aching body, the constant fretting about how to carry on the hoax?

Unless the O'Donnells had come up with the monstrous scheme, of course, and bullied Anna into it so they could profit from the visitors beating a path to their door. But she didn't seem like a child under compulsion. She had a quiet firmness about her, an air of self-command unusual in one so young.

Adults could be barefaced liars too, of course, and about no subject so much as their own bodies. In Lib's experience, those who wouldn't cheat a shopkeeper by a farthing would lie about how much brandy they drank or whose room they'd entered and what they'd done there. Girls bursting out of their stays denied their condition till the pangs gripped them. Husbands swore blind that their wives' smashed faces were none of their doing. Everybody was a repository of secrets.

The holy cards were distracting her, with their fancy details — edges like filigree lace, some of them — and exotic names. Saint Aloysius Gonzaga, Saint Catherine of Siena, Saint Philip Neri, Saint Margaret of Scotland, Saint Elizabeth of Hungary; like a set of dolls in national dress. *He can pick anyone,* Anna had said, any sinner or unbeliever. A whole series about the final sufferings of Christ, *Our Lord Stripped of his Garments.* Who could think it a good idea to put such grim images in the hands of a child, and a sensitive one at that?

One card showed a little girl in a boat with a dove over her head: *Le Divin Pilote*. Did the title mean that Christ was piloting her boat invisibly? Or perhaps the pilot was the dove. Wasn't the Holy Ghost often shown as a bird? Or was the figure Lib had taken for a girl actually Jesus, with childish proportions and long hair?

Next, a woman in purple — the Virgin Mary, Lib guessed — bringing a flock of sheep to drink at a pool with a marble rim. What a curious mixture of elegance and rusticity. In the next card, the same woman was bandaging a round-bellied sheep. That dressing would never stay on, in Lib's view. *Mes brebis ne périssent jamais et personne ne les ravira de ma main.* She struggled to make sense of the French. Her somethings never perished and no person could ravish them from her hand?

Anna stirred, her head rolling off the two pillows to lie crooked against her shoulder. Lib quickly closed the cards up in their book.

But Anna slept on. Angelic, as all children looked in that rapt state. The creamy lines of her face proved nothing, Lib reminded herself; sleep could make even adults look innocent. *Whited sepulchres.*

Which reminded her of something: the Madonna and Child. She reached past the books in the little chest and took out the candlestick. What might Anna have entrusted to this pastel-painted figurine? Lib shook it; no sound. It was a hollow tube, open at the bottom. She peered up into the shadowy head of the Virgin, looking for a tiny store of some richly sustaining food. When she put the candlestick to her nose, she smelled nothing. Her prob-ing finger felt . . . something she could barely brush with her short nail. A miniature packet?

The scissors in her bag. Lib slid the blades down the rough inside of the statuette, digging. A hook was what she needed, really, but how to find one in the middle of the night? She gouged harder—

And hissed as the whole thing cracked in two. China child broke away from china mother in her hands.

The packet — insubstantial, after all that — peeled away from its hiding place. When Lib undid the paper, all she found was a lock of hair; dark, but not red like Anna's. The yellowing paper had been torn, apparently at random, out of something called the *Freeman's Journal* towards the end of the preceding year.

She'd broken one of the child's treasures for nothing, like some clumsy novice on her first shift. Lib set the pieces back in the box with the hair packet between them.

Anna slept on. There was nowhere else for Lib to look, nothing else to do except stare at the girl like some wor-shipper venerating an icon. Even if the child was somehow stealing the odd bite, how could it be enough to dull the pangs of hunger? Why weren't they racking her till she woke?

Lib angled the hard-backed rope chair so it faced the bed directly. Sat and squared her shoulders. She looked at her watch: 10:49. No need to press the button to learn the hour, but she did anyway, just for the sensation — the dull thud against her thumb, ten times, rapid and strong at first, then getting slower and fainter.

Lib rubbed her eyes and fixed them on the girl. *Could*

you not watch one hour with me? She remembered that line from the Gospels. But she wasn't watching *with* Anna. Nor watching *over* her, to keep her safe from harm. Just watching her.

Anna seemed restless at times. She rolled herself up in the blanket like a fern furling. Was she cold? There wasn't another blanket; something else Lib should have asked for while Kitty was still up. She draped a plaid shawl over the child. Anna muttered as if saying prayers, but that didn't prove she was awake. Lib didn't make a sound, just in case. (Miss N. never let her nurses wake a patient, because the jarring effect could do great mischief.)

The lamp needed trimming twice and refilling once; it was a cumbersome, stinking thing. For a while after midnight, it sounded as if the O'Donnells were talking by the fire next door in the kitchen. Refining their plots? Or just chatting in the desultory way people often did between their first sleep and their second? Lib couldn't make out Kitty's voice; perhaps the maid was exhausted enough to sleep through it all.

At five in the morning, when the nun tapped on the bedroom door, Anna was taking the long, regular breaths that meant the deepest slumber.

"Sister Michael." Lib leapt up, stiff-legged.

The nun nodded pleasantly.

Anna stirred and rolled over. Lib held her breath, waiting to be sure the child was still asleep. "I couldn't find a Bible," she whispered. "What was this manna, exactly?"

A small hesitation; clearly the nun was deciding whether or not this was the kind of conversation their instructions allowed. "If I remember right, it fell every day to feed the children of Israel when they were fleeing across the desert from their persecutors." As she spoke, Sister Michael took a black volume out of her bag and leafed through the shimmering onionskin. She peered at one page, then the one before, then the one before that. She put one broad fingertip to the paper.

Lib read over her shoulder.

In the morning, a dew lay round about the camp. And when it had covered the face of the earth, it appeared in the wilderness small, and as it were beaten with a pestle, like unto the hoar frost on the ground. And when the children of Israel saw it, they said one to another: Manhu! which signifieth: What is this! for they knew not what it was. And Moses said to them: This is the bread, which the Lord hath given you to eat.

"A grain, then?" asked Lib. "Solid, even though it's described as a dew?"

The nun's finger shifted down the page and came to rest at another line: *And it was like coriander seed, white, and the taste thereof like to flour with honey.*

It was the simplicity of it that struck Lib, the silliness: a child's dream of picking up sweet stuff from the ground. Like finding a gingerbread house in the woods. "Is that all there is?"

"And the children of Israel ate manna forty years," the nun read. Then she slid the book shut.

So Anna O'Donnell believed herself to be living off some kind of celestial seed flour. *Manhu,* meaning "What is this?" Lib was strongly tempted to lean in close to the other woman and say, *Admit it, Sister Michael, for once can't you suspend your prejudices and acknowledge that this is all balderdash?*

But that would be exactly the kind of conferral that McBrearty had forbidden. (For fear the Englishwoman might prove too skilled at brushing away the old cobwebs of superstition with the broom of logic?) Besides, perhaps it was better not to ask. It was bad enough, to Lib's mind, that the two of them were working under the supervision of an aged quack. If she were to be confirmed in her suspicion that her fellow nurse believed a child could live off bread from the Beyond, how could she carry on working with the woman?

In the doorway stood Rosaleen O'Donnell.

"Your daughter's not awake yet," said Lib.

The face disappeared.

"This lamp's to be kept burning all night from now on," she told the nun.

"Very good."

Finally, a small humiliation: Lib opened the little chest and pointed to the broken candlestick. "I'm afraid this was knocked over. Could you pass on my apologies to Anna?"

Sister Michael pursed her lips as she fitted Mother and Child back together.

Lib picked up her cloak and bag.

She shivered on the walk to the village. Something was kinked in her spine. She was hungry, she supposed; she hadn't had a bite since supper at the inn yesterday before her night shift. Her mind was foggy. She was tired. This was Wednesday morning, and she hadn't slept since Monday. What was worse, she was being outwitted by a little girl.

By ten Lib was up again. Hard to keep her eyes shut with all the clattering in the grocery below.

Mr. Ryan, her red-faced host, was directing a pair of boys as they hauled barrels into his cellar. He coughed over his shoulder with a sound like cardboard tearing and said it was too late for any breakfast because didn't his daughter Maggie have the sheets to boil, so Mrs. Wright would just have to wait till noon.

Lib had been going to ask if her boots could be cleaned, but instead she requested rags, polish, and brush so she could do it herself. If they'd thought the Englishwoman too high-and-mighty to get her hands dirty, they couldn't have been more wrong.

When her boots were gleaming again, she sat reading *Adam Bede* in her room, but Mr. Eliot's moralizing was getting tedious, and her stomach kept growling. The Angelus bells rang out across the street. Lib checked her watch, which said two minutes past noon already.

When she went down to the dining room there was no one else there; the journalist must have gone back to Dublin. She chewed her ham in silence.

"Good day, Mrs. Wright," said Anna when Lib came in that afternoon. The room smelled close. The child was as alert as ever, knitting a pair of stockings in creamy wool.

Lib raised her eyebrows interrogatively at Sister Michael.

"Nothing new," murmured the nun. "Two spoons of

water taken." She closed the door behind her on her way out.

Anna didn't say a word about the broken candlestick. "Maybe you might tell me your Christian name today?" she asked.

"I'll tell you a riddle instead," offered Lib.

"Do."

" 'No legs have I, yet I dance,' " she recited.

I'm like a leaf, yet I grow on no tree.
I'm like a fish, but water kills me.
I'm your friend, but don't come too close!

" 'Don't come too close,' " murmured Anna. "Why, what would happen if I did?"

Lib waited.

"No water. No touching. Only let it dance..." Then her smile burst out. "A flame!"

"Very good," said Lib.

This afternoon felt long. Not in the silent, stretching way of the night shift; this was tedium broken by jarring interruptions. Twice there came knocks at the front of the house, and Lib steeled herself. A loud conversation on the doorstep, and then Rosaleen O'Donnell would bustle into Anna's room to announce that — as per Dr. McBrearty's orders — she'd had to turn away visitors. Half a dozen important personages from France the first time, and then a group from the Cape; imagine! These good folk had heard of Anna as they passed through Cork or Belfast and come all this way by train and carriage because they couldn't think of leaving the country without making her acquaintance. They'd insisted Mrs. O'Donnell pass on this bouquet, these edifying books, their fervent regret at being denied even a glimpse of the marvellous little girl.

The third time, Lib was ready with a notice that she suggested the mother paste on the front door.

PLEASE REFRAIN FROM KNOCKING.
THE O'DONNELL FAMILY ARE NOT TO
BE DISTURBED. THEY ARE GRATEFUL
TO BE KEPT IN YOUR THOUGHTS.

Rosaleen took it with a barely audible sniff.

Anna seemed to pay no attention to any of this as she formed her stitches. She went about her day like any girl, Lib thought — reading, doing needlework, arranging the visitors' flowers in a tall jug — except that she didn't eat.

Didn't *seem* to eat, Lib corrected herself, annoyed that she'd lapsed into accepting the sham even for a moment. But one thing was true: The girl wasn't getting so much as a crumb on Lib's watch. Even if by any chance the nun had dozed off on Monday night and Anna had snatched a few mouthfuls then, this was Wednesday afternoon, Anna's third full day without a meal.

Lib's pulse began to thump because it struck her that if the strict surveillance was preventing Anna from getting food by her previous methods, the girl might be starting to suffer in earnest. Could the watch be having the perverse effect of turning the O'Donnells' lie to truth?

From the kitchen, on and off, came the swish and bump of the slavey working an old-fashioned plunge churn. She sang in a low drone.

"Is that a hymn?" Lib asked the child.

Anna shook her head. "Kitty has to charm the butter for it to come." She half sang the rhyme.

Come, butter, come,
Come, butter, come,
Peter stands at the gate,
Waiting for a buttered cake.

What went through the child's mind when she thought of butter or cake? Lib wondered.

She stared at a blue vein on the back of Anna's hand and thought of the weird theory McBrearty had mentioned about the reabsorption of blood. "I don't suppose you have your courses yet, do you?" she asked in a low voice.

Anna looked blank.

What did Irishwomen call it? "Your monthlies? Have you ever bled?"

"A few times," said Anna, her face clearing.

"Really?" Lib was taken aback.

"In my mouth."

"Oh." Could an eleven-year-old farm child really be so innocent that she didn't know about becoming a woman?

Obligingly, Anna put her finger in her mouth; she brought it out tipped with red.

Lib was abashed that she hadn't examined the girl's gums carefully enough on the first day. "Open wide for a minute." Yes, the tissue was spongy, mauve in patches. She gripped an incisor and wriggled it; slightly loose in its socket? "Here's another riddle for you," she said, to lighten the moment.

A flock of white sheep,
On a red hill.
Here they go, there they go,
Now they stand still.

"Teeth," cried Anna indistinctly.

"Quite right." Lib wiped her hand on her apron.

She realized all at once that she was going to have to warn the girl, even if it was no part of what she'd been hired to do. "Anna, I believe you're suffering from a complaint typical of long ocean voyages, caused by poor diet."

The girl listened, head tilted, as if to a story. "I'm all right."

Lib crossed her arms. "In my educated opinion, you're nothing of the sort."

Anna only smiled.

A surge of anger shook Lib. For a girl blessed with health to embark on this dreadful game—

Kitty brought in the nurse's dinner tray just then, letting in a gust of smoky air from the kitchen.

"Does the fire always have to be kept so high," asked Lib, "even on such a warm day?"

"The smoke does dry the thatch and preserve the timbers," said the maid, gesturing at the low ceiling. "If we were ever to let the fire go out, sure the house would fall down."

Lib didn't bother correcting her. Was there a single aspect of life that this creature didn't see through the dark lens of superstition?

Dinner today consisted of three minuscule fish called roach that the master had netted in the lough. No particular flavour, but a change from oats, at least. Lib took the delicate bones from her mouth and set them on the side of her plate.

The hours passed. She read her novel but kept losing track of the plot. Anna drank two spoonfuls of water and produced a little urine. Nothing that amounted to evidence so far. It rained for a few minutes, drops trickling down the small windowpane. When it cleared, Lib would have liked to go out for a walk, but it struck her: What if eager petitioners were hanging around in the lane in hopes of a glimpse of Anna?

The child lifted her holy cards out of their books and whispered sweet nothings to them.

"I'm very sorry about your candlestick," Lib found herself saying. "I shouldn't have been so clumsy, or taken it out in the first place."

"I forgive you," said Anna.

Lib tried to remember if anyone had ever said that to her so formally. "I know you were fond of it. Wasn't it a gift to mark your confirmation?"

The girl lifted the pieces out of the chest and stroked the crack where the porcelain pieces rested together. "Better not to get too fond of things."

This tone of renunciation chilled Lib. Wasn't it in the nature of children to be graspers, greedy for all of life's pleasures? She remembered the words of the Rosary: *Poor banished children of Eve.* Munchers of any windfalls they could find.

Anna took up the little packet of hair and pushed it back inside the Virgin.

Too dark to be her own. A friend's? Or the brother's?

Yes, Anna might very well have asked Pat for a lock of hair before the ship carried him away.

"What prayers do Protestants say?" the child asked.

Lib was startled by the question. She summoned her forces to give a bland answer about the similarities between the two traditions. Instead, she found herself saying, "I don't pray."

Anna's eyes went wide.

"Nor do I go to church, not for many years now," Lib added. In for a penny, in for a pound.

"More happiness than a feast," the girl quoted.

"I beg your pardon?"

"Prayer brings more happiness than a feast."

"I never found it did much good." Lib felt absurdly embarrassed by her admission. "I had no sense of getting a reply."

"Poor Mrs. Wright," murmured Anna. "Why won't you tell me your first name?"

"Why *poor*?" asked Lib.

"Because your soul must be lonely. That silence you heard, when you tried to pray — that's the sound of God listening." The child's face shone.

A commotion at the front door released Lib from this conversation. A man's voice, booming above Rosaleen O'Donnell's; without being able to make out more than a few words, Lib could tell that he was an English gentleman, and in a temper. Then the sound of the front door shutting.

Anna didn't even lift her eyes from the book she'd picked up, *The Garden of the Soul*.

Kitty came in to check the lamp was prepared. "I heard

tell of one that the vapours caught on fire," she warned Lib, "and cinderized the family in the night!"

"The lamp glass must have been sooty, in that case, so mind you wipe this one well."

"Right, so," said Kitty, with one of her tremendous yawns.

Half an hour later the same angry petitioner was back.

A minute later he was stalking into Anna's room with Rosaleen O'Donnell behind him. A great domed forehead with long silver locks below. He introduced himself to Lib as Dr. Standish, chief of medicine at a Dublin hospital.

"He's brought a note from Dr. McBrearty," said Rosaleen O'Donnell, waving it, "to say could we make an exception and let him in as a *most* distinguished visitor."

"Given that I'm here as a matter of professional courtesy," Standish barked, his accent very clipped and English, "I don't appreciate having my time wasted by being obliged to chase backwards and forwards along these foul boreens for permission to examine a child." His pale blue eyes were fastened on Anna.

She was looking nervous. Afraid this doctor would find out something McBrearty and the nurses hadn't? Lib wondered. Or simply because the man was so severe?

"Can I offer you a cup of tea, Doctor?" asked Mrs. O'Donnell.

"Nothing, thank you."

Said so curtly that she backed out and pulled the door to.

Dr. Standish sniffed the air. "When was this room last fumigated, Nurse?"

"The fresh air from the window, sir—"

"See to it. Chloride of lime, or zinc. But, first, kindly undress the child."

"I've already taken her complete measurements, if you'd like to see them," offered Lib.

He waved her memorandum book away and insisted she strip Anna down till she was stark naked.

The child shuddered on the woven mat, hands drooping by her sides. Angles of shoulder blades and elbows, bulges of calves and belly; Anna had flesh on her, but it had all slid downwards, as if she were slowly melting. Lib looked away. What gentleman would bare a girl of eleven like a plucked goose on a hook?

Standish carried on poking and prodding, tapping Anna with his cold instruments, keeping up a barrage of orders. "Tongue out farther." He put his finger so far down Anna's throat, she gagged. "Does that cause pain?" he asked, pressing between her ribs. "And that? What about this?"

Anna kept shaking her head, but Lib didn't believe her.

"Can you bend over any farther? Breathe in and hold it," said the doctor. "Cough. Again. Louder. When did you last move your bowels?"

"I don't remember," whispered Anna.

He dug into her misshapen legs. "Does that hurt you?"

Anna gave a little shrug.

"Answer me."

"Hurt's not the word for it."

"Well, what word would you prefer?"

"Humming."

"Humming?"

"It seems to hum."

Standish snorted and lifted one of her thickened feet to scrape the sole with a fingernail.

Humming? Lib tried to imagine being swollen up, every cell tight as if ready to burst. Would it feel like a high-pitched vibration, the whole body a tautened bow?

Finally Standish told the child to dress and shoved his instruments back into his bag. "As I suspected, a simple case of hysteria," he threw in Lib's direction.

She was disconcerted. Anna wasn't like any hysteric she'd ever encountered at the hospital: no tics, faints, paralyses, convulsions; no fixed stares or shrieks.

"I've had night-feeders in my wards before, patients who won't eat except when no one's watching," he added. "Nothing to distinguish this one except that she's been indulged to the extremity of half starving herself."

Half starving. So Standish believed Anna was sneaking food but far less than she needed? Or perhaps she'd been getting almost enough until the watch had begun, on Monday morning, but since then, nothing at all? Lib was horribly afraid he might be right about that. But was Anna nearer to starved or nearer to well? How to quantify the quality of being alive?

Tying her drawers at the waist, Anna showed no sign of having heard a word.

"My prescription's very simple," said Standish. "A quart of arrowroot in milk, three times a day."

Lib stared at him, then spelled out the obvious. "She won't take anything by mouth."

"Then drench her like a sheep, woman!"

A slight quiver from Anna.

"Dr. Standish," protested Lib. She knew the staff of asylums and prisons often resorted to force, but—

"If a patient of mine refuses a second meal, my nurses have standing orders to use a rubber tube, above or below."

It took Lib a second to understand what the doctor meant by *below*. She found herself stepping forward, between him and Anna. "Only Dr. McBrearty could give such an order, with the permission of the parents."

"It's just as I suspected when I read about the case in the paper." The words sprayed from Standish's mouth. "In taking up this chit of a girl — and dignifying this charade by setting a formal watch — McBrearty's made himself a laughingstock. No, made his whole unfortunate nation a laughingstock!"

Lib couldn't disagree with that. Her eyes rested on Anna's bent head. "But such unnecessary harshness, Doctor —"

"Unnecessary?" he scoffed. "Look at the state of her: scabby, hairy, and gross with dropsy."

The bedroom door banged behind Standish. A strained silence in the room. Lib heard him bark something at the O'Donnells in the kitchen, then march out to his carriage.

Rosaleen O'Donnell put her head in. "What's happened, in the name of God?"

"Nothing," Lib told her. And held the woman's gaze till she withdrew.

Lib thought Anna might be weeping, but no, the child looked more thoughtful than ever, adjusting her tiny cuffs.

Standish had years, no, decades of study and experience that Lib lacked, that no woman could ever obtain. Anna's downy, scaly skin, the puffy flesh — small matters in themselves, but was he right that they meant she was in actual danger from eating so little? Lib felt an impulse to put her arms around the child.

She restrained it, of course.

She remembered a freckled nurse at Scutari complaining that they weren't allowed to follow *the prompts of the heart* — to take a quarter of an hour, for instance, to sit with a dying man and offer a word of comfort.

Miss N.'s nostrils had flared. *You know what would comfort that man, if anything could? A stump pillow to rest his mangled knee on. So don't listen to your heart, listen to me and get on with your work.*

"What is *fumigated?*" asked Anna.

Lib blinked. "The air can be purified by burning certain disinfectant substances. My teacher didn't believe in it." She took two steps to Anna's bed and began to smoothen the sheets, making every line straight.

"Why not?"

"Because it's the harmful thing that must be taken out of the room, not merely its smell," said Lib. "My teacher even made a joke about it."

"I like jokes," said Anna.

"Well, she said that fumigations are of essential importance to medicine — because they make such an abominable smell, they compel you to open the window."

Anna mustered a tiny laugh. "Did she make lots of jokes?"

"That's the only one I can recall."

"What's the harmful thing in this room?" The child looked from wall to wall as if a bogey might jump out at her.

127

"All that's doing you harm is this fast." Lib's words were like stones thrown down in the quiet room. "Your body needs nourishment."

The girl shook her head. "Not earthly food."

"Every body—"

"Not mine."

"Anna O'Donnell! You heard what the doctor said: *half starving*. You may be doing yourself grievous harm."

"He's looking wrongly."

"No, *you* are. When you see a piece of bacon, say — don't you feel anything?" asked Lib.

The small forehead wrinkled.

"Not the impulse to put it in your mouth and chew, as you did for eleven years?"

"Not anymore."

"Why, what could possibly have changed?"

A long pause. Then Anna said, " 'Tis like a horseshoe."

"A horseshoe?"

"As if the bacon's a horseshoe, or a log, or a rock," she explained. "There's nothing wrong with a rock, but you wouldn't chew it, would you?"

Lib stared at her.

"Your supper, ma'am," said Kitty, walking in with a tray and setting it down on the bed.

Lib's hands shook as she pushed open the door of the spirit grocery that evening. She'd meant to snatch a few words with the nun at the changeover, but her nerves were still jangling too much from her encounter with Dr. Standish.

No carousing farmers in the bar tonight. Lib had made it almost to the staircase when a figure reared up in the doorway. "You didn't tell me who you really were, Nurse Wright."

The scribbler. Lib groaned inwardly. "Still here, Mr. . . . Burke, was it?"

"Byrne," he corrected her. "William Byrne."

Pretending to misremember a name was such a reliable way to annoy. "Good night, Mr. Byrne." She headed up the stairs.

"You might do me the courtesy of staying one minute. I had to hear from Maggie Ryan that it's you who's barred me from the cabin!"

Lib turned. "I don't believe I said anything to mislead you about my presence here. If you jumped to unwarranted conclusions—"

"You don't look or speak like any nurse I've ever met," he protested.

She hid a smile. "Then your experience must have been limited to the old breed."

"Granted," said Byrne. "So when may I talk to your charge?"

"I'm simply protecting Anna O'Donnell from the intrusions of the outside world, including — perhaps above all," Lib added — "Grub Street."

Byrne stepped closer. "Wouldn't you say she's courting the attention of that world by claiming to be a freak of nature as much as any Feejee mermaid at a raree-show?"

Lib flinched at the image. "She's just a little girl."

The taper in William Byrne's hand lit up his copper curls. "I warn you, ma'am, I'll camp outside her window. I'll caper like a monkey, press my nose to the glass, and pull faces till the child begs for me to be let in."

129

"You will not."

"How do you propose to stop me?"

Lib sighed. How she longed for her bed. "I'll answer your questions myself, will that do?"

The man pursed his lips. "All of them?"

"Of course not."

He grinned. "Then my answer's no."

"Caper all you like," Lib told him. "I'll draw the curtain." She went up another two steps, then added, "Making a nuisance of yourself to interfere with the course of this watch will earn you and your newspaper nothing but disrepute. And, no doubt, the wrath of the entire committee."

The fellow's laughter filled the low room. "Haven't you met your employers? They're no pantheon armed with thunderbolts. The quack, the padre, our publican host, and a few of their friends — that's your *entire committee*."

Lib was disconcerted. McBrearty had implied that it was full of *important men*. "My point remains, you'll get more from me than from badgering the O'Donnells."

Byrne's light eyes measured her. "Very well."

"Tomorrow afternoon, perhaps?"

"This minute, Nurse Wright." He beckoned her down with one large hand.

"It's almost ten o'clock," said Lib.

"My editor will have my hide if I don't send something of substance by the next mail. Please!" His voice almost boyish.

To get it over with, Lib came back down and sat at the table. She nodded at his inky notebook. "What have you got so far? Homer and Plato?"

Byrne's smile was lopsided. "Miscellaneous opinions

of fellow travellers denied entrance today. A faith healer from Manchester who wants to restore the girl's appetite by the laying-on of hands. Some medical bigwig twice as outraged as I at being turned away."

Lib winced. The last thing she wanted to discuss was Standish and his recommendations. It occurred to her that if the journalist hadn't seen the Dublin doctor at Ryan's again tonight, that meant Standish must have rattled straight back to the capital after examining Anna.

"One woman suggested the girl might be bathing in oil so that some of it soaks in through her pores and cuticles," said Byrne, "and a fellow assured me that his cousin in Philadelphia's achieved remarkable effects with magnets."

Lib laughed under her breath.

"Well, you've obliged me to scrape the barrel," said Byrne, uncapping his pen. "So why all the secrecy? What are you helping the O'Donnells to hide?"

"On the contrary, this watch is being conducted as scrupulously as possible to uncover any deception," she told him. "Nothing can be allowed to distract us from observing the girl's every move to make sure no food reaches her mouth."

He'd stopped writing and was leaning back against the settle. "Rather a barbaric experiment, no?"

Lib chewed her lip.

"Let's assume the minx has been getting hold of food on the sly somehow ever since the spring, shall we?"

In this village of zealots, Byrne's realistic attitude was a relief.

"But if your watch is so perfect, that means Anna O'Donnell has had nothing to eat for three days now."

Lib swallowed painfully. That was exactly what she'd begun to fear today, but she didn't want to admit it to this fellow. "It's not necessarily perfect yet. I suspect that during the nun's shifts . . ." Was she really going to accuse her fellow nurse, on no evidence? She changed tack. "This watch is for Anna's own good, to disentangle her from her web of deceit." Surely Anna longed to go back to being an ordinary child again?

"By famishing her?" The fellow's mind was as analytical as Lib's.

"I must be cruel, only to be kind," Lib quoted.

He caught the reference. "Hamlet killed three people, or five if you count Rosencrantz and Guildenstern."

Impossible to match wits with a journalist. "They'll speak up if she starts to weaken," she insisted, "one or both of the parents, the maid, whoever's behind this. Especially since I've put a stop to the milking of visitors for cash."

Byrne's eyebrows soared. "They'll speak up, take the blame, and let themselves be hauled before a judge for fraud?"

Lib realized she hadn't thought through the criminal side of the matter. "Well. A hungry child will break down and confess, sooner or later."

But as she said it, she realized with a chill that she didn't believe it. Anna O'Donnell had somehow passed beyond hunger.

Lib lurched to her feet. "I must sleep now, Mr. Byrne."

He raked back his hair. "If you really have nothing to hide, Mrs. Wright, then let me in to see the girl for myself for ten minutes, and I'll sing your praises in my next dispatch."

"I don't like your bargains, sir."

This time he let her go.

Back in her room, Lib tried to sleep. These eight-hour shifts played havoc with the body's rhythms. She heaved herself out of the hollow in her mattress and beat her pillow flat.

It was then, sitting up in the dark, that it occurred to her for the first time: What if Anna wasn't lying?

For a long moment, she set all facts aside. To understand sickness was the beginning of real nursing, Miss N. had taught her; one must grasp the sufferer's mental as well as physical state. So the question was, did the girl believe her own story?

The answer was clear. Conviction shone out of Anna O'Donnell. A *case of hysteria* she might possibly be, but utterly sincere.

Lib felt her shoulders drop. No enemy, then, this soft-faced child; no hardened prisoner. Only a girl caught up in a sort of waking dream, walking towards the edge of a cliff without knowing it. Only a patient who needed her nurse's help, and fast.

CHAPTER THREE

Fast

fast
> to abstain from food
> a period of fasting
> fixed, enclosed, secure, fortified
> constant, steadfast, obstinate

Five a.m., Thursday, when Lib entered the bedroom. By the light of the reeking lamp, she watched Anna O'Donnell sleep. "No change?" she murmured to the nun.

A shake of the coif-covered head.

How could Lib bring up Dr. Standish's visit without expressing her opinions? And what would a nun who believed a little girl could live off *manna from heaven* make of his theory that Anna was a self-starving hysteric?

Sister Michael took up her cloak and bag and left.

The child's face on the pillow was a fallen fruit. Puffier around the eyes this morning, Lib noticed, perhaps from lying flat all night. One cheek scored red by a pillow crease. Anna's body was a blank page that recorded everything that happened to it.

She pulled up one of the chairs and sat staring at Anna from no more than two feet away. The rounded cheek; the rise and fall of the rib cage and belly.

So the girl truly believed herself not to have eaten for four months. But her body told another story. Which had to mean that until Sunday night, someone had been feeding Anna, and she'd then somehow . . . forgotten the fact?

137

Or perhaps never registered it at all. Could the feeding have been done with Anna in a kind of trance? In a deep slumber, could a child swallow food without choking, the way a sleepwalker might fumble through a house, eyes shut? Perhaps when she woke, Anna knew only that she felt sated, as if she'd been fed celestial dew.

But that didn't explain why, by day, four days into this watch, the child showed no interest in food. More than that: despite all the peculiar symptoms that plagued Anna, she remained convinced that she could live without it.

An obsession, a mania, Lib supposed it could be called. A sickness of the mind. Hysteria, as that awful doctor had named it? Anna reminded Lib of a princess under a spell in a fairy tale. What could restore the girl to ordinary life? Not a prince. A magical herb from the world's end? Some shock to jolt a poisoned bite of apple out of her throat? No, something simple as a breath of air: reason. What if Lib shook the girl awake this very minute and said, *Come to your senses!*

But that was part of the definition of madness, Lib supposed, the refusal to accept that one was mad. Standish's wards were full of such people.

Besides, could children ever be considered quite of sound mind? Seven was counted the age of reason, but Lib's sense of seven-year-olds was that they still brimmed over with imagination. Children lived to play. Of course they could be put to work, but in spare moments they took their games as seriously as lunatics did their delusions. Like small gods, children formed their miniature worlds out of clay, or even just words. To them, the truth was never simple.

But Anna was eleven, which was a far cry from seven, Lib argued with herself. Other eleven-year-olds knew when they'd eaten and when they hadn't; they were old enough to tell make-believe from fact. There was something very different about — very wrong with — Anna O'Donnell.

Who was still fast asleep. Framed in the small pane behind her, the horizon was spilling liquid gold. The very idea of terrorizing a delicate child with tubes, pumping food into her body *above or below* —

To shake off these thoughts, Lib picked up *Notes on Nursing.* She noticed a sentence she'd marked on first reading: *She must be no gossip, no vain talker; she should never answer questions about her sick except to those who have a right to ask them.*

Did William Byrne have any such right? Lib shouldn't have been talking to him so frankly in the dining room last night — or at all, probably.

She glanced up and jumped, because the child was looking right at her. "Good morning, Anna." It came out too fast, like an admission of guilt.

"Good morning, Mrs. Whatever-Your-Name-Is."

That was impudence, but Lib found herself laughing. "Elizabeth, if you must know." It had a strange ring to it. Lib's husband of eleven months had been the last to use that name, and at the hospital she was Mrs. Wright.

"Good morning, Mrs. Elizabeth," said Anna, trying it out.

That sounded like some other woman entirely. "No one calls me that."

"Then what do they call you?" asked Anna, getting up on her elbows and rubbing sleep out of one eye.

Lib was already regretting having given her first name, but then, she wouldn't be here for long, so really, what did it matter? "Mrs. Wright, or Nurse, or ma'am. Did you sleep well?"

The girl struggled into a sitting position. *"I have slept and have taken my rest,"* she murmured. "So what do your family call you?"

Lib was disconcerted by this rapid switching between Scripture and ordinary conversation. "I have none left." It was technically true; her sister, if still living, had chosen to go beyond Lib's reach.

Anna's eyes grew huge.

In childhood, Lib remembered, family seemed as necessary and inescapable as a ring of mountains. One never imagined that as the decades went by, one might drift into an unbounded country. It struck Lib now how alone in the world she was.

"But when you were little," said Anna. "Were you Eliza? Elsie? Effie?"

Lib made a joke of it. "What's this, the tale of Rumpelstiltskin?"

"Who's that?"

"A little goblin man who—"

But Rosaleen O'Donnell was hurrying in now to greet her daughter, not so much as glancing at the nurse. That broad back like a shield thrown in front of the child, that dark head bent over the smaller one. Doting syllables; Gaelic, no doubt. The whole performance set Lib's teeth on edge.

She supposed that when a mother had only a solitary child left at home, all her passion was funnelled into that one. Had Pat and Anna had other brothers or sisters? she wondered.

Anna was kneeling beside her mother now, hands pressed together, eyes shut. *"I have sinned exceedingly in thought, word, and deed, through my fault, through my fault, through my most grievous fault."* On each *fault*, the child's closed fist rapped her chest.

"Amen," intoned Mrs. O'Donnell.

Anna began another prayer: *"Maiden mother, meek and mild, take oh take me for thy child."*

Lib considered the long morning ahead. Later on she'd have to keep the girl out of sight in case of would-be visitors. "Anna," she said the moment the mother had gone back into the kitchen, "shall we go out for an early walk?"

" 'Tis barely day."

Lib hadn't even taken Anna's pulse yet, but that would wait. "Why not? Get dressed and put on your cloak."

The girl crossed herself and whispered the Dorothy prayer as she pulled her nightdress over her head. Was that a new bruise on her shoulder blade, greenish brown? Lib made a memorandum of it.

In the kitchen, Rosaleen O'Donnell said it was still dim out and they'd fall into cowpats or break their ankles.

"I'll take perfectly good care of your daughter," said Lib, and pushed the half-door open.

She stepped out, with Anna behind her, and the chickens clucked and scattered. The moist breeze was delicious.

They set off behind the cabin this time, on a faint path between two fields. Anna walked slowly and unevenly, remarking on everything. Wasn't it funny that skylarks were never to be spotted on the ground, only when they shot high up into the sky to sing? Oh, look, that mountain over there with the sun coming up behind it was the one she called her whale.

Lib saw no mountains in this flattened landscape. Anna was pointing to a low ridge; no doubt the inhabitants of the *dead centre* of Ireland saw every ripple as a peak.

Anna sometimes fancied she could actually glimpse the wind; did Mrs. Something-Like-Elizabeth ever think that?

"Call me Mrs. Wright—"

"Or Nurse, or ma'am," said Anna with a giggle.

Full of vitality, Lib thought; how on earth could this child be *half starving?* Someone was still sustaining Anna.

The hedgerows sparkled now. " 'Which is the broadest water,' " Lib asked, " 'and the least jeopardy to pass over?' "

"Is this a riddle?"

"Of course, one I learned when I was a little girl."

"Hm. 'The broadest water,' " Anna repeated.

"You're imagining it like the sea, aren't you? Don't."

"I've seen the sea in pictures."

To grow up on this small island and yet never to have been to its edge, even . . .

"But great rivers with my own eyes," said Anna, boasting.

"Oh yes?" said Lib.

"The Tullamore, and the Brosna too, the time we went to the fair at Mullingar."

Lib recognized the name of the Midlands town where William Byrne's horse had been lamed. Had he stayed on today at Ryan's, in the room across the passage from hers, in hopes of learning more about Anna's case? Or had his satirical dispatches from the scene been enough for the *Irish Times*? "The water in my riddle doesn't look like the widest of rivers, even. Imagine it spread all over the ground, but no danger in crossing it."

Anna wrestled with the thought, and finally shook her head.

"The dew," said Lib.

"Oh! I should have known."

"It's so small, nobody remembers it." She thought of the manna story: *a dew lay round about the camp* and *covered the face of the earth.*

"Another," begged Anna.

"I can't recall another just now," said Lib.

The girl walked in silence for a minute, almost limping. Was she in pain?

Lib was tempted to take her elbow to help her over a rough patch, but no. *Simply to observe,* she reminded herself.

Up ahead was someone she took for Malachy O'Donnell, but as they neared he turned out to be a bent-looking older man. He was cutting black rectangles out of the ground and making a stack; turf for burning, she assumed.

"God bless the work," Anna called to him.

He nodded back. His spade was a shape Lib had never seen before, the blade bent into wings.

"Is that another prayer you're obliged to say?" she asked the child when they'd passed.

"Blessing the work? Yes, otherwise he might be hurt."

"What, he'd be wounded that you didn't think of him?" asked Lib with a touch of mockery.

Anna looked puzzled. "No, he might cut a toe off with the foot slane."

Ah, so it was a sort of protective magic.

The girl was singing now, in her breathy voice.

Deep in thy wounds, Lord,
Hide and shelter me,
So shall I never,
Never part from thee.

The stirring tune didn't fit the morbid words, in Lib's view. The very idea of hiding deep inside a wound, like a maggot—

"There's Dr. McBrearty," said Anna.

The old man was scuttling towards them from the cabin, lapels askew. He took off his hat to Lib, then turned to the child. "Your mother told me I'd find you out taking the air, Anna. Delighted to see you with roses in your cheeks."

She was rather red in the face, but from the exertion of walking, Lib thought; *roses* was stretching a point.

"Still generally well?" McBrearty murmured to Lib.

Miss N. was very stern on the subject of discussing the ill in their hearing. "You go on ahead of us," Lib suggested to Anna. "Why don't you pick some flowers for your room?"

The child obeyed. Lib kept her eyes on her, though. It occurred to her that there might be berries around, unripe nuts, even . . . Might a hysteric — if that's what Anna was — snatch mouthfuls of food without being conscious of what she did?

"I don't quite know how to answer your question," she told the doctor. Thinking of Standish's phrase *half starving*.

McBrearty poked the soft ground with his cane.

Lib hesitated, then made herself say the name. "Did Dr. Standish get a chance to speak to you last night after he left Anna?" She was ready with her best arguments against forcible feeding.

The old man's face screwed up as if he'd bitten into something sour. "His tone was most ungentlemanly. After I did him the politeness of letting him, of all the petitioners, into the cabin to see the girl!"

She waited.

But clearly McBrearty was not going to report the scolding he'd received. "Is her respiration still healthy?" he asked instead.

Lib nodded.

"Heart sounds, pulse?"

"Yes," she conceded.

"Sleeping well?"

Another nod.

"She seems cheerful," he noted, "and her voice is still strong. No vomiting or diarrhoea?"

"Well, I'd hardly expect that in someone who's not eating."

The old man's watery eyes lit up. "So you believe she is indeed living without—"

Lib interrupted him. "I mean, not taking in enough to lead to any kind of voiding. Anna produces no excrement, and very little urine," she pointed out. "This suggests to me that she's getting *some* food — or was until the watch began, more likely — but not sufficient for there to be any waste." Should Lib mention her notion about night-feedings to which Anna had been oblivious all these months? She quailed; it suddenly sounded as implausible as any of the old man's own theories. "Don't you think her eyes are beginning to bulge even more?" she asked. "Her skin's covered with bruises and crusty patches, and her gums bleed. Scurvy, perhaps, I was thinking. Or pellagra, even. Certainly she seems anaemic."

"Good Mrs. Wright." McBrearty gouged the soft grass with his cane. "Are we beginning to stray beyond our remit?" An indulgent father reproving a child.

"I beg your pardon, Doctor," she said stiffly.

"Leave such mysteries to those who've been trained for them."

Lib would have given a lot to know where McBrearty had been trained, and how thoroughly, and whether it had been in this century or the last.

"Your job is simply to observe."

But there was nothing *simple* about such a task; Lib knew that now as she hadn't three days ago.

" 'Tis her!" A screech in the distance. It was coming from a top-heavy wagon parked outside the O'Donnells'. Several of the passengers were waving.

Besieged already, even this early in the day. Where had Anna strayed? Lib's head whipped around till she found the girl, inhaling the scent of some blossom. She couldn't bear the prospect of the fawning, the flattery, the intrusive questions. "I must take her inside, Doctor." She ran over and seized Anna's arm.

"Please—"

146

"No, Anna, you're not to speak to them. We have a rule and we must stick to it."

She hurried the girl towards the cabin, cutting the corner of a field, the doctor at their heels. Anna stumbled and one of her big boots went sideways.

"Hurt?" asked Lib.

A shake of the head.

So Lib pulled her on, around the side of the cabin — why didn't it have a back door? — and through the knot of visitors arguing with Rosaleen O'Donnell, who was floured to the elbows.

"Here she comes, the wee wonder," cried one man.

A woman pushed up close. "If you'd let me take hold of the hem of your dress, sweetheart—"

Lib interposed her shoulder, shielding the child.

"—even a drop of your spit, or a dab of the oil of your fingers to mend this sore on my neck!"

Only when they were all inside and she'd slammed the door behind Dr. McBrearty did Lib realize that Anna was gasping, and not just out of fear of the grabbing hands. The girl was frail, Lib reminded herself. What kind of slapdash nurse would strain her beyond her strength? How Miss N. would have scolded.

"Are you ill, lovey?" demanded Rosaleen O'Donnell.

Anna sank down on the nearest stool.

"Just out of breath, I believe," said McBrearty.

"I'll warm a flannel for you." The mother scraped her hands clean before she hung up a cloth at the fire.

"You got a little chilled on your walk," McBrearty told the girl.

"She's always chilled," Lib muttered. The child's hands

were blue. Lib brought her over to a high-backed chair beside the hearth and chafed the thick fingers between her own — lightly, for fear of hurting them.

When the cloth was warmed, Rosaleen wrapped it tenderly around Anna's throat.

Lib would have liked to feel the cloth first and make sure there was nothing edible hidden in it, but her nerve failed.

"And how are you getting along with Mrs. Wright, my dear?" asked the doctor.

"Very well," Anna told him.

Was the child being polite? All Lib could remember were moments in which she'd been snappish or stern with the girl.

"She's teaching me riddles," added Anna.

"Charming!" The doctor held the child's swollen wrist between his fingers, checking her pulse.

At the table by the back window, beside Kitty, Mrs. O'Donnell paused in the work of slapping oatcakes into shape. "What kind of riddles?"

"Clever ones," Anna told her mother.

"Feeling a little better in yourself now?" McBrearty asked.

She nodded, smiling.

"Well, I'll be off, then. Rosaleen, good day to you," he said with a bow.

"And you, Doctor. God bless you for stopping in."

When the door had shut behind McBrearty, Lib felt flat, grim. He'd barely listened to her; he was ignoring Standish's warnings. Caught up in his own private fascination with the *wee wonder.*

She noticed the empty stool by the door. "I see the strongbox is gone."

"We sent it to Mr. Thaddeus by one of Corcoran's boys, along with the little gloves in the walnut shell," said Kitty.

"Every penny gone to aid and comfort the needy," Rosaleen O'Donnell threw in Lib's direction. "Think of that, Anna. You're storing up riches in heaven."

How Rosaleen basked in the reflected glory. The mother was the genius behind the plot, not just one conspirator among others; Lib was almost sure of that. She averted her gaze now so her hostility wouldn't show.

On the mantel, inches from Lib's face, the new photograph stood beside the old one of the whole family. The little girl looked much the same in both — the same neat limbs, the not-quite-of-this-world expression. As if time didn't pass for Anna; as if she were preserved behind glass.

But the really odd one was the brother, it struck Lib. Pat's adolescent face was similar to his sister's softer one, allowing for the fact that boys parted their hair on the right. But his eyes; something wrong with their glitter. The lips dark, as if rouged. He leaned back on his indomitable mother like a much younger child, or a drunken fop. What was that line in the psalm? *Strange children have faded away.*

Anna spread her hands to warm at the fire, like an elegant fan.

How to find out more about him? "You must miss your son, Mrs. O'Donnell."

A pause. And then: "I do, of course," said Rosaleen O'Donnell. She was cutting up elderly parsnips now, wielding the cleaver with one big gaunt hand. "Ah well. God fits the back for the burden, as they say."

Milking it rather, Lib thought. "Is it long since you've heard from him?"

The cleaver stilled, and Rosaleen O'Donnell stared at her. "He looks down on us."

What, had Pat O'Donnell done well in the New World, then? Too well to bother writing to his plebeian family?

"From heaven." That was Kitty.

Lib blinked.

The slavey pointed upwards to make sure the English-woman understood. "'Twas last November he died."

Lib's hand flew up to cover her mouth.

"He wasn't fifteen," added the slavey.

"Oh, Mrs. O'Donnell," cried Lib, "you must forgive my tactlessness. I didn't realize—" Gesturing at the daguerre-otype, where the boy seemed to watch her with contempt, or was it mirth? It wasn't taken before his death, she real-ized, but after.

Anna, leaning back in the chair, seemed deaf to all this, mesmerized by the flames.

Instead of taking offence, Rosaleen O'Donnell was smiling in a gratified way. "He looks alive to you, ma'am? Well, there's a thing."

Propped up in his mother's lap. Blackened lips, the first indication of decomposition; Lib should have guessed. Had the O'Donnell boy lain in this kitchen for a whole day, or two or three, while his family waited for the photog-raphist?

Rosaleen O'Donnell came up so close that Lib flinched.

She tapped the glass. "A fine bit of brushwork on his eyes, isn't it?"

Someone had painted whites and pupils onto the corpse's closed lids in the print; that was why the gaze was so crocodilian.

Mr. O'Donnell came in then, stamping mud off his boots. His wife greeted him in Gaelic, then switched to English. "Wait till you hear, Malachy. Mrs. Wright thought Pat was still on this side!"

The woman had a talent for taking pleasure from terrible things.

"Poor Pat," said Malachy with an unoffended nod.

"It was the eyes, they tricked her entirely." Rosaleen O'Donnell fingered the glass. "Worth every penny."

Anna's arms lay limp in her lap now, and her eyes reflected the flames. Lib longed to get her out of this room.

"'Twas his stomach that did for him," said Malachy O'Donnell.

Kitty sniffed and wiped one eye on her frayed sleeve.

"Brought up his supper. Couldn't touch another thing."

The man was addressing Lib, so she had to nod.

"The pain took him there, then there, see?" Malachy prodded himself about the navel, then lower down on the right. "Swelled up like an egg." He was speaking more fluently than she'd ever heard him. "In the morning it'd eased, like, so we thought we shouldn't trouble Dr. McBrearty after all."

Lib nodded again. Was the father appealing to her for her professional opinion? For a sort of forgiveness?

"But Pat still felt so faint and cold in himself," said Rosaleen O'Donnell, "we piled all the blankets in the

house on his bed, and put his sister in beside him to warm
him up."

Lib shuddered. Not just at the thing, but at the retelling
of it in the hearing of a sensitive girl.

"He panted a bit, and spoke nonsense, as if he was
dreaming," murmured his mother.

"Gone before breakfast, poor lad," said Malachy
O'Donnell. "No time to send for the priest, even." He
shook his head as if to get rid of a fly.

"Too good for this world," exclaimed Rosaleen.

"I'm so very sorry," said Lib. She turned back to the
daguerreotype so she wouldn't have to look at the parents.
But she found she couldn't bear the shine of those eyes, so
she took Anna by the still-cold hand and went back to the
bedroom.

Her eye fell on the treasure chest. The dark brown hair
in the statuette she'd broken: that had to be the brother's.
Anna's silence worried Lib. What a thing to do to a child,
put her in beside a dying boy as a warming pan. "You must
feel the loss of your brother."

The girl's face contorted. "'Tisn't that. Or — I do, of
course, Mrs. Elizabeth, but that's not it." She stepped up
close to Lib and whispered, "Mammy and Dadda think
he's in heaven. Only, you see, we can't be sure of that.
Never despair, but never presume, they're the two unforgiveable sins against the Holy Ghost. If Pat's in purgatory,
he's burning—"

"Oh, Anna," said Lib, breaking in. "You're distressing
yourself needlessly. He was only a boy."

"But we're all sinners. And he fell sick so fast, he didn't

get absolved in time." Tears plummeted into the girl's collar.

Confession — yes, Catholics clung to the notion of its unique power to wipe all sin away.

Anna wailed so Lib could hardly make out the words: "We have to be cleaned before we're let in."

"Very well, so your brother will be cleaned." Lib's tone absurdly practical, a nursery maid filling a bath.

"By fire, only by fire!"

"Oh, child . . ." This was an alien language and, frankly, one she didn't want to learn. She patted the girl on the shoulder, awkwardly. Felt the knob of bone.

"Don't put this in your paper," said Lib over some kind of stew. (She'd found William Byrne dining in the small room at Ryan's at half past one when she'd come in from her shift.)

"Go on."

Lib decided to take that as a promise. In a low voice: "Anna O'Donnell's mourning her only brother, who died of a digestive complaint nine months ago."

Byrne only nodded and wiped his plate with a crust.

Lib was nettled. "You doubt that's enough to cause mental collapse in a child?"

He shrugged. "My whole country could be said to be in mourning, Mrs. Wright. After seven years of dearth and pestilence, what family was left unbroken?"

She didn't know what to say. "Seven years, really?"

"The potato failed in '45 and only came back fully in '52," he told her.

Discreetly Lib removed a fragment of bone from her

mouth — rabbit, she thought. "Still, what does Anna know of these national questions? She may feel like the only girl who's ever lost a brother." The hymn droned in her head: *So shall I never, never part from thee.* "Perhaps she torments herself with wondering why he was taken and not her."

"She seems depressed in her spirits, then?"

"At times," said Lib uncertainly. "But sometimes quite otherwise: lit up with a secret joy."

"Speaking of secrets, you haven't yet caught her trying to get hold of any food on the sly?"

Lib shook her head. Under her breath: "I've come round to the opinion that Anna truly believes she's living on nothing." She hesitated, but she had to try her idea out on someone. "It's occurred to me that one of the household, taking advantage of the child's delusional state, may have been dosing her in her sleep."

"Oh, come now." William Byrne scraped the red curls out of his face.

"Such a subterfuge would make sense of Anna's conviction that she's not eaten for four months. If she's been quite unconscious while someone has been pouring slop down her throat—"

"Possible. But likely?" He picked up his pencil. "May I air this in my next dispatch?"

"You may not! It's speculation, not fact."

"I'd call it the expert opinion of her nurse."

Through her panic, Lib felt a sting of pleasure that Byrne was taking her seriously. "Besides, I've been strictly enjoined not to express any opinions until I report to the committee on Sunday week."

He threw down his pencil. "So why tantalize me, then, if I can't use a word of it?"

"My apologies," said Lib crisply. "Let's consider the subject closed."

His grin was rueful. "I'm thrown back on reporting gossip, then. And not all of it benevolent. The girl's far from being a universal favourite in these parts, you know."

"You mean some assume she's a liar?"

"Of course, or worse. Last night I stood a mad-eyed labourer a drink, and he shared his conviction that the fairies are behind it."

"What do you mean?"

"The reason Anna doesn't eat is that she's some kind of monstrous changeling disguised as a girl."

The other crowd . . . waiting on her hand and foot. That's what Lib had heard a bearded farmer say the night she'd arrived. He must have meant that Anna had an unseen horde of fairy attendants.

"The fellow even had a remedy to propose. *If 'twas beat, or put to the fire even*" — the brogue Byrne put on was brutally accurate — "*why, then, 'twould go back where it came from!*"

Lib shuddered. It was this sort of drunken ignorance she found *monstrous.*

"Have you ever had a patient remotely like Anna O'Donnell?"

She shook her head. "In private nursing I've encountered specious cases — healthy people who pretend to be in an interesting state of disease. But Anna's the opposite. An underfed child who maintains she's in glowing health."

"Hm. Should hypochondriacs be called pretenders, though?" asked Byrne.

Lib felt abashed, as if she'd been sneering at her employers.

"The mind can bamboozle the body," he pointed out. "Think about itching and one feels an itch. Or yawning—" And he broke off to yawn into his hand.

"Well, but—" Lib had to stop because she was yawning too.

Byrne let out a great guffaw, then quietened and stared into space. "I suppose it's within the bounds of possibility that a practiced mind could command the body to keep going without food, at least for a while."

But wait. At Lib's first encounter with Byrne, he'd called Anna a fraud; at their next, he'd accused Lib of keeping her from eating. Now, having scorned Lib's sleep-feeding idea, he was suggesting the miraculous claims might be true after all? "Don't say you're going over to the O'Donnells' camp."

His mouth twisted. "It's my job to keep an open mind. In India — I was sent to Lucknow to report on the rebellion — it's not unknown for fakirs to make claims of suspended animation."

"Fakers?"

"Fakirs, holy men," he corrected her. "Colonel Wade, formerly agent to the governor-general of the Punjab, he told me he'd watched the digging up of a character called the Fakir of Lahore. Forty days underground — no food, drink, light, little air — and the fellow popped out hale and hearty."

Lib snorted.

Byrne shrugged. "All I can tell you is that this battle-hardened old soldier talked my ear off with such conviction that I was almost inclined to believe him."

"And you a cynical man of the press."

"Am I? I name corruption when I see it," said Byrne. "Does that make me a cynic?"

"I beg your pardon," said Lib, thrown. "I said more than I meant."

"A vice common among men of the press." His smile a darting fish.

Had Byrne claimed his feelings were wounded only to put Lib in the wrong? she wondered dizzily.

"So might Anna O'Donnell be a diminutive Irish girl-yogi?"

"You wouldn't make fun if you knew her." The words burst out of Lib.

The man was on his feet. "I'll accept that invitation at once."

"No, no. The rule against visitors is strict."

"Then how did Dr. Standish from Dublin get around it, may I ask?" His tone was still teasing, but the resentment was audible. "You didn't mention that last night — that you'd let *him* in on his second try."

"The cur!"

William Byrne dropped back into his seat. "A cur let him in?"

"Standish is the cur," said Lib. "All this is in confidence?"

He slapped his memorandum book facedown.

"He recommended I tube-feed her by force."

Byrne winced.

"He was granted entry at Dr. McBrearty's insistence, against my better judgment," Lib added, "but it won't happen again."

"Why, are you altered from gaoler to bodyguard, Elizabeth Wright? Will you stand in the gap and keep off all dragons?"

She didn't answer. How did Byrne know her first name?

"Would I be right in thinking that you rather like the girl?"

"This is my job," Lib snapped. "Your question is irrelevant."

"It's my job to ask questions, all of them."

She gave him a hard look. "Why are you still here, Mr. Byrne?"

"I must say, you know the art of making a fellow traveller feel welcome." He leaned so far back in his chair, it creaked.

"I beg your pardon. But how can this case deserve so many days of your undivided attention?"

"A fair query," said William Byrne. "Before setting off on Monday, I put it to my editor that I could drum up a score of famished urchins on the streets of Dublin. Why trek all the way into the boglands?"

"And what did he say?" asked Lib.

"What I suspected he would: *The one lost sheep, William.*"

After a moment, she got the Gospel reference: the shepherd who left his flock of ninety-nine sheep to go after one stray.

"Journalistic investigations must be narrow," he told

her with a shrug. "Divide a reader's concern among many deserving objects, and there'll be too little left to make him shed a tear for any one."

She nodded. "Nurses are the same. It seems to come naturally, to care more about the individual than the crowd."

One faint auburn eyebrow went up.

"That's why Miss — the lady who trained me," Lib corrected herself, "wouldn't allow us to sit down beside a particular patient and read to him and so on. She said it could lead to attachment."

"Flirting, canoodling, and so forth?"

She refused to blush. "We had no time to waste. She told us, *Do what's needed, and walk on.*"

"Miss Nightingale's an invalid herself now, of course," said Byrne.

Lib stared at him. She hadn't heard anything about her teacher making any public appearances in recent years, but she'd assumed Miss N. was quietly getting on with her mission of hospital reform.

"I'm so sorry," he said, leaning across the table. "You hadn't heard."

Lib struggled to compose herself.

"Was she as great a lady as they say, then?"

"Greater," said Lib, choked. "And still is, invalid or not."

She pushed the remains of her stew aside — unable to finish her meal, for once — and got to her feet.

"Are you itching to be away?" asked William Byrne.

Lib chose to answer that as if he'd meant away from the Irish Midlands, not this cramped dining room. "Well.

It does sometimes seem as if the nineteenth century hasn't reached this part of the world yet."

He grinned.

"Milk for the fairies, wax discs to ward off fire and flood, girls living on air . . . Is there nothing the Irish won't swallow?"

"Fairies aside," said Byrne, "the majority of my countrymen swallow whatever pap our priests feed us."

So he too was a Catholic; that surprised Lib somehow.

He beckoned her closer. She leaned in, just a little. "That's why my money's on Mr. Thaddeus," he murmured. "The O'Donnell girl may be guileless — she may even have slept through months of night-feedings, if you're right — but what of her puppet master?"

Like a blow to the ribs. Why hadn't Lib thought of that? The priest was indeed too glib, too smiling.

But wait. She straightened up. Proceed logically and fair-mindedly. "Mr. Thaddeus claims he's urged Anna to eat from the start."

"*Urged,* only? She's his parishioner, and a fervently pious one. He could command her to go up a mountain on her knees. No, I say the padre's been behind the hoax from the start."

"But with what motive?"

Byrne rubbed his fingers and thumb together.

"The visitors' donations have been given to the needy," said Lib.

"That means to the Church."

Her head was spinning. It was all horribly plausible.

"If Mr. Thaddeus gets Anna's case acknowledged as a miracle and this dreary hamlet as a site of pilgrimage," said Byrne, "there'll be no limit to the profits. The fasting girl's a shrine-building fund!"

"But how could he have managed to feed her secretly by night?"

"No idea," admitted Byrne. "He must be in league with the maid or the O'Donnells. Whom do you suspect?"

Lib demurred. "I really couldn't take it on myself to—"

"Ah, go on, between ourselves. You've been in that household night and day since Monday."

She hesitated, then said, very low, "Rosaleen O'Donnell."

Byrne nodded. "Who was it said that *mother* is a child's word for God?"

Lib had never heard that.

He waggled his pencil between his fingers. "Mind, I can't print a word of this without proof or they'll have me up for libel."

"Of course not!"

"If you'll let me have five minutes with the child, I bet I can weasel out the truth."

"That's impossible."

"Well." Byrne's voice returned to its usual boom. "Sound her out yourself, then?"

Lib didn't like the idea of acting as his snoop.

"At any rate, thanks for your company, Mrs. Wright."

Almost three in the afternoon, and Lib's next shift began at nine. She wanted air, but it was drizzling, and besides, she supposed she needed a nap more. So she went upstairs and took her boots off.

If the potato blight had been such a long catastrophe, ending only seven years ago, it occurred to Lib that a child now eleven must have been born into hunger. Weaned on it, reared on it; that had to shape a person. Every thrifty inch of Anna's body had learned to make do with less. *She's never been greedy or clamoured for treats* — that was how Rosaleen O'Donnell had praised her daughter. Anna must have been petted every time she said she'd had plenty. Earned a smile for every morsel she passed on to her brother or the maid.

But that didn't begin to explain why all the other children in Ireland wanted their dinner, and Anna didn't.

Perhaps what was different was the mother, Lib thought. Like the boastful one in the old tale who'd vaunted her daughter to the world as a spinner of gold. Had Rosaleen O'Donnell noticed her younger child's talent for abstinence and dreamt up a way to turn it into pounds and pence, fame and glory?

Lib lay very still, eyes closed, but light prickled through the lids. Being tired didn't mean one was capable of sleep, just as the need for food wasn't the same as a relish for it. Which brought her back, as everything did, to Anna.

As the last of the evening light drained over the village street, Lib took a right turn down the lane. Rising over the graveyard was a waxing gibbous moon. She thought of the O'Donnell boy in his coffin. Nine months; rotting but not a skeleton yet. Were those his brown trousers the scarecrow wore?

The notice Lib had made for the cabin door was streaked with rain.

Sister Michael was waiting in the bedroom. "Out like a light already," she whispered.

At midday, they'd had only a moment for Lib to report on her shift. This was a rare time when they might talk in private. "Sister Michael—" But Lib realized she couldn't mention her speculations about sleep-feedings because the nun would close up like a box again. No, she'd much better stick to the common ground of their concern for this girl asleep in the narrow bed. "Did you know the child's brother was dead?"

"God rest him," said the nun with a nod, crossing herself.

So why had nobody told Lib? Or, rather, why did she seem to get hold of the wrong end of the stick all the time?

"Anna seems to be fretting over him," she said.

"Naturally."

"No, but — inordinately so." She hesitated. This woman might be riddled with superstition, seeing angels dancing across every bog, but Lib had no one else to talk to who saw the girl at such close quarters. "I think there's something wrong with Anna's mind," she pressed on in a whisper.

The whites of Sister Michael's eyes caught the lamplight. "We weren't asked to look into her mind."

"I'm charting symptoms," Lib insisted. "This brooding over her brother is one."

"You're drawing an inference, Mrs. Wright." The nun held up one rigid finger. "We're not to engage in this kind of discussion."

"That's impossible. Every word we say is about Anna, and how could it not be?"

The nun shook her head violently. "Is she eating or not? That's the only question."

"It's not *my* only question. And if you call yourself a nurse, it can't be yours either."

The nun's cheeks tightened. "My superiors sent me here to serve under Dr. McBrearty. Good night to you." She folded her cloak over her arm and was gone.

Sitting watching Anna's eyelids flicker some hours later, Lib found herself longing for the sleep she should have had that afternoon. But this was an old battle, and like any nurse, she knew she could win if she spoke to herself severely enough.

The body had to be granted something; if not slumber, then food, and if that was unavailable, then stimulus of some sort. Lib set aside her shawl and the hot brick that kept her feet off the floor and walked back and forward across the room, three paces each way.

It struck her that William Byrne must have made inquiries about her, because he knew her full name and who'd trained her. What did Lib know about him? Only that he wrote for a paper she'd never read, had been posted to India, and was a Catholic, if a rather sceptical one. So frank and bluff, yet he'd given away little other than his theory about Mr. Thaddeus — an audacious piece of deduction that now struck Lib as entirely unconvincing. The priest hadn't even been near the cabin since Monday morning. How could she possibly ask Anna, *Is it Mr. Thaddeus who's stopping you from eating?*

She found herself counting the sleeping breaths. Nineteen in one minute, but the count would be different, and the rhythm less regular, if Anna were awake.

Something baking in the crock. Turnips? They'd cook slowly all night, filling the cabin with their starchy aroma.

It was enough to make Lib peckish, even though she'd had a good supper at Ryan's.

What prompted her to look back at the bed? Dark shiny eyes met hers. "How long have you been awake?"

A little shrug from Anna.

"Do you need anything? The pot? Water?"

"No, thank you, Mrs. Elizabeth."

Something about the way Anna formed the words, so politely, almost stiffly. "Is anything hurting you?"

"I don't think so."

"What is it?" Lib moved closer, hovering over the bed.

"Nothing," breathed Anna.

Lib risked it. "Are you hungry at all? Was it the scent of those turnips that roused you?"

A faint, almost pitying smile.

Lib's stomach growled. Hunger was the common ground on which everyone woke. The body an infant stirring to mew, each morning, *Feed me.* But not Anna O'Donnell's, not anymore. *Hysteric, lunatic, maniac;* the words didn't fit her. She was like nothing so much as a little girl who didn't need to eat.

Oh, come, Lib scolded herself. If Anna believed she was one of the queen's five daughters, would that make it so? The child might not feel hunger, but it was still eating away at her flesh, her hair, her skin.

After a stretch of silence so long that she thought perhaps the child was sleeping with her eyes open, Anna said, "Tell me about the little man."

"What little man?" asked Lib.

"The rumpled one."

"Ah, Rumpelstiltskin." She recounted the old tale just

to pass the time. Having to call up the details made her realize how bizarre it was. The girl charged with the impossible task of spinning straw into gold because of her mother's boast. The goblin who helped her. His offer to let her keep her firstborn after all if only she could guess the goblin's outlandish name...

Anna lay still for a while afterwards. It occurred to Lib that the child might be taking the legend as fact. Were all manifestations of the supernatural equally real to her?

"Bet."

"You bet what?" asked Lib.

"Is it Bet, what your family used to call you?"

She chuckled. "Not this foolishness again."

"They couldn't have called you Elizabeth every born day. Betsy? Betty? Bessie?"

"No, no, and no."

"But it comes from Elizabeth, doesn't it?" asked Anna. " 'Tisn't quite another name, like Jane?"

"No, that would be cheating," agreed Lib.

Lib had been her pet name back in the days when she was anyone's pet, the name her younger sister had given her because *Elizabeth* had been too long for her to pronounce. *Lib* was what her whole family had called her, when she'd still had a family, while their parents were still alive and before her sister had said Lib was dead to her.

She laid her hand over Anna's on the grey blanket. The swollen fingers were freezing, so she tucked them in. "Are you glad to have someone with you at night?"

The girl looked confused.

"Not to be alone, I suppose I mean."

"But I'm not alone," said Anna.

"Well, not now." Not since the watch.

"I'm never alone."

"No," agreed Lib. Two gaolers, turn and turnabout, for constant company.

"He comes in to me as soon as I'm asleep."

The bluish lids were fluttering shut already, so Lib didn't ask who *he* was. The answer was obvious.

Anna's breathing was deep again. Lib wondered whether the child dreamt of her Saviour every night. Did he come in the form of a long-haired man, a haloed boy, a baby? What consolations did he bring, what *feasts* that were so much more ambrosial than the earthly kind?

Watching a slumberer was a powerful inducer of sleep; Lib's eyelids were getting heavy again. She stood up, turning her head from side to side to loosen her neck.

He comes in to me as soon as I'm asleep. A strange construction. Perhaps Anna didn't mean Christ after all but some ordinary *he,* a man — Malachy O'Donnell? Mr. Thaddeus, even? — who funnelled liquid into her mouth when she was in an in-between state of drowsy oblivion. Was Anna trying to tell Lib the truth she barely understood herself?

For something to do, Lib looked through the girl's treasure chest. Opened *The Imitation of Christ* carefully, so as not to dislodge the holy cards. *If we were perfectly dead unto ourselves, and not entangled within our own breasts,* she read at the top of a page, *then should we be able to taste divine things.*

The words made her shake. Who'd teach a child to be dead to herself? How many of Anna's most dearly held, mad notions came from these books?

Or from the bright pastel pictures on the cards. So many plants: sunflowers with faces turned towards the light; Jesus perched on the canopy of a tree under which people huddled. Sententious mottoes in Gothic type, describing him as a brother or as a bridegroom. One card showed a steep staircase cut into a cliff face with a looming heart like a setting sun and a cross at the top. The next was even odder: *The Mystic Marriage of Saint Catherine*. A beautiful young woman appeared to be accepting a bridal ring from an infant Jesus perched on his mother's lap.

But the one that troubled Lib most showed a little girl floating on a raft in the shape of a broad cross, stretched out asleep, unaware of the wild waves rising around her. *Je voguerai en paix sous la garde de Marie,* it said. I something in something under the guard of Mary? Only then did Lib notice a sorrowful woman's face in the clouds, watching the little girl.

She closed the book and put it back. Then thought to look at the card again, to see what passage it was marking. She couldn't find anything about Mary, or the sea. *Vessels* was the only word that caught her eye: *For the Lord bestoweth his blessings there, where he findeth the vessels empty.* Empty of what, exactly? Lib wondered. Food? Thought? Individuality? On the next page, near a picture of a bilious-looking angel, *Thou art willing to give me heavenly food and bread of angels to eat.* A few pages farther on, marked with a picture of the Last Supper: *How sweet and pleasant the banquet, when thou gavest thyself to be our food!* Or perhaps that card went with *thou alone art my meat and drink, my love.*

Lib could see how a child could misread such flowery

phrases. If these were Anna's only books, and she'd been kept home from school ever since her illness, mulling over them without proper guidance . . .

Of course some children couldn't grasp what metaphor was. She remembered a girl at school, a stony character with no small talk who for all her scholarliness was idiotic about everyday things. Anna didn't seem like that. What else could you call it but stupidity, though, to take poetic language at face value? Lib felt like shaking the child awake again: *Jesus is not* actual *meat, you dunderhead!*

No, not a dunderhead. Anna had excellent wits; they'd just gone astray.

One of the nurses at the hospital had a cousin, Lib remembered now, who'd become convinced that the commas and full stops of the *Daily Telegraph* contained coded messages for him.

Almost five in the morning when Kitty put her head in and watched the sleeping girl for a long moment.

Perhaps Anna was Kitty's last surviving cousin, it struck Lib now. The O'Donnells never mentioned any other relations. Did Anna ever confide in her cousin?

"Sister Michael's here," said the slavey.

"Thank you, Kitty."

But it was Rosaleen O'Donnell who came in next.

Leave her be, Lib wanted to say. But she held her tongue while Rosaleen bent down to rouse her daughter with a long embrace and murmured prayers. Like something out of grand opera, the way she barged in to make a show of her maternal feelings twice a day.

The nun came in and nodded a greeting, her mouth sealed shut. Lib picked up her things and left.

Outside the cabin, the slavey was pouring an iron bucket of water into a gigantic tub that stood over a fire.

"What are you doing, Kitty?"

"Wash day."

The laundry tub was set too near the dung heap for Lib's liking.

"It'd be Monday, usually, not Friday," said Kitty, "only 'tisn't Monday Lá Fhéile Muire Mór?"

"I beg your pardon?"

"The Blessed Virgin Mary's feast."

"Ah, really?"

Kitty rested her hands on her hips, staring at Lib. "'Twas on the fifteenth of August that Our Lady was taken up."

Lib couldn't bring herself to ask what that meant.

"Lifted up bodily to heaven." Miming it with the bucket.

"She died?"

"She did not," Kitty scoffed. "Didn't her loving son spare her that?"

There was no talking to this creature. With a nod, Lib turned towards the village.

Lib walked back to the spirit grocery in the dregs of the darkness, a nibbled-looking moon low on the horizon. Before she lurched up the stairs to her bed above the grocery, she remembered to beg Maggie Ryan to keep some breakfast for her.

She woke at nine, having slept just enough to befuddle herself but not enough to clear her head. Rain was tapping the roof like the fingers of a blind man.

No sign of William Byrne in the dining room. Could he have gone back to Dublin already, even though he'd urged Lib to find out more about the possible involvement of the priest in the hoax?

The girl served her cold griddle cakes. Cooked — Lib deduced from the faint crunch — directly on the embers. Did the Irish hate food? She was about to ask after the journalist, then was struck by how such a question might sound.

Lib thought of Anna O'Donnell, waking up even emptier on the fifth day. Suddenly sickened, she pushed her plate away and went up to her room.

She read for several hours — a volume of miscellaneous essays — but found she was retaining nothing.

Lib set off down a lane behind the spirit grocery despite the rain pattering on her umbrella; anything to be outside. A few disconsolate cows in a field. The soil seemed to be getting poorer as she walked towards the only elevated land, Anna's whale, a long ridge with one thick end and one pointed one. She followed a path until it petered out in bogland. She tried to stick to the higher, drier-looking areas, purpled with heather. She saw something move out of the corner of her eye; a hare? There were depressions full of what looked like hot cocoa and others glinting with dirty water.

To avoid soaking her boots, Lib jumped from one mushroom-shaped hummock to the next. Occasionally she swung her umbrella point downwards and poked the ground to check its firmness. She picked her way along a wide ribbon of sedge grass for a while, though it made her nervous to hear a trickling below, an underground stream, perhaps; was the whole landscape honeycombed?

A bird with a curved bill stalked past and sent up a high-pitched complaint. Small white tufts nodded in ones and twos across the wet ground. When Lib bent down to look at a curious lichen, it proved to have horns, like those of a minuscule deer.

A chopping sound came from a great gouge in the ground. When Lib approached and peered in, she saw the hole was half full of brown water, and there was a man in it up to his chest, clinging by one hooked elbow to a sort of rudimentary ladder. "Wait!" she cried.

He gawked up at Lib.

"I'll be back with help as soon as I can," she told him.

"I'm grand, missus."

"But—" She gestured at the engulfing water.

"Just taking a bit of a rest."

Lib had misunderstood again. Her cheeks scorched.

He swung his weight and gripped the ladder with his other arm now. "You'll be the English nurse."

"That's right."

"Don't they cut turf over there?"

Only then did she recognize the winged spade hanging from his ladder. "Not in my part of the country. May I ask, why do you go down so low?"

"Ah, the scraw at the top's no good." He gestured at the rim of the hole. "Just moss for bedding animals and dressing wounds, like."

Lib couldn't imagine inserting this rotting matter into any wound, even on a battlefield.

"For turves for burning, you have to dig down the length of a man or two."

"How interesting." Lib was trying to seem practical, but she sounded more like a silly lady at a party.

"Are you lost, missus?"

"Not at all. Just getting my constitutional. Exercise," she added, in case the turf cutter was unfamiliar with the word.

He nodded. "Have you a slice of bread in your pocket?"

She stepped back, discomfited. Was the fellow a beggar? "I do not. Nor any money either."

"Ah, money's no good. You want a bit of bread to keep off the other crowd when you're out walking."

"The other crowd?"

"The little folk," he said.

More fairy nonsense, evidently. Lib turned to go.

"You'll have been up the green road?"

Another supernatural reference? She turned back. "I'm afraid I don't know what that means."

"Sure you're on it, nearly."

Looking the way the turf cutter pointed, Lib was startled to spot a path. "Thank you."

"How's the girleen doing?"

She almost answered with an automatic *Well enough* but stopped herself in time. "I'm not at liberty to discuss the case. Good day."

Up close, the *green road* was a proper cart track paved with crushed rock that began all at once in the middle of the bog. Perhaps it led here from the next village, and the final section — the one that would bring it all the way down to the O'Donnells' village — hadn't been built yet?

Nothing particularly green about it, yet the name promised something. Lib set out at a brisk pace on the soft verge where occasional flowers bloomed.

Half an hour later, the track had zigzagged up the side of the low rise and down again without any obvious reason. Lib clicked her tongue with irritation. Was a straight path to walk too much to ask? Finally it seemed to turn back on itself, disheartened, and the surface began to break up. The so-called road petered out as arbitrarily as it had begun, its stones swallowed up by weeds.

What a rabble, the Irish. Shiftless, thriftless, hopeless, hapless, always brooding over past wrongs. Their tracks going nowhere, their trees hung with putrid rags.

Lib stomped all the way back. The wet had slanted under her umbrella and misted her cloak. She was determined to have a word with the fellow who'd set her on that pointless course, but when she got to that bog hole, all it contained was water. Unless she'd confused it with another one? Beside the great bite out of the earth, turf sods lay on drying racks in the rain.

On the way down to Ryan's, she spotted what she thought was a tiny orchid. Perhaps she could pick it for Anna. She stepped onto an emerald patch to reach the flower and too late felt the moss give way underfoot.

Thrown headlong, Lib found herself groveling face-down in slime. Although she got up on her knees almost at once, she was soaked through. When she hauled up her skirt and set one foot down, it sank through the peat. Like a creature caught in a snare, she clawed her way out, panting.

Staggering back down the lane, Lib was just relieved

that the spirit grocery was close by so she wouldn't have to walk the length of the village street in this state.

Her landlord, in the doorway, raised his bushy eyebrows.

"Treacherous, your bogs, Mr. Ryan." Her skirt dripped. "Do many drown in them?"

He snorted, which brought on a coughing fit. "Only if they're soft in the head," he said when he could speak again, "or loaded with drink on a moonless night."

By the time Lib had dried herself off and put on her spare uniform, it was five past one. She strode as fast as she could to the O'Donnells'. She'd have run if it hadn't been beneath the dignity of a nurse. To be twenty minutes late for her shift, after all her insistence on high standards . . .

Where the laundry tub had stood this morning was an ashy puddle with a four-footed wooden dolly laid down beside it. Sheets and clothes were draped over bushes and pegged on a rope strung between the cabin and a crooked tree.

In the good room, sipping tea with a buttered scone on his plate, sat Mr. Thaddeus. Outrage swelled up in Lib.

But then, he didn't count as a visitor, she told herself, being the parish priest and a member of the committee. And at least Sister Michael was sitting right beside Anna. Undoing her cloak, Lib caught the nun's eye and mouthed an apology for her lateness.

"My dear child," the priest was saying, "to answer your question, 'tis neither up nor down."

"Where, then?" asked Anna. "Does it float between?"

"Purgatory should not be considered an actual place as much as time allotted for cleansing the soul."

"How long a time, though, Mr. Thaddeus?" Anna, sitting up very straight, was as pale as milk. "I know 'tis seven years for every mortal sin we commit, because they offend against the seven gifts of the Holy Ghost, but I don't know how many Pat committed, so I can't do the sum."

The priest sighed but didn't contradict the child.

Lib was revolted by this mathematical mumbo jumbo. Was it Anna who was suffering from religious mania or her whole nation?

Mr. Thaddeus put down his cup.

Lib watched his plate for any crumb to fall. Not that she could really imagine Anna palming and swallowing it if it did.

"'Tis a process more than a fixed period," he told Anna. "In the eternity of the Almighty's love, there is no time."

"But I don't think Pat's in heaven with God yet."

Sister Michael's fingers slid over Anna's.

Watching, Lib hurt for the girl. As there'd been only two of them, the siblings must have clung together through the worst of times.

"Those in purgatory are not permitted to pray, of course," said the priest, "but we may pray for them. To expiate their sins, to make amends—'tis like pouring water on their flames."

"Oh, but I have, Mr. Thaddeus," Anna assured him, eyes huge. "I've made a novena for the Holy Souls, nine days every month for nine months. I've said Saint Gertrude's Prayer in the graveyard, and read Holy Scripture, and adored the Blessed Sacrament, and prayed for the intercession of all the saints—"

He held up one palm to hush her. "Well, then. That's half a dozen acts of reparation already."

"But that might not be enough water to put out Pat's flames."

Lib almost pitied the flailing priest.

"Don't picture it as an actual fire," he urged Anna, "so much as the soul's painful sense of its unworthiness to come into God's presence, its self-punishment, you see?"

The child let out one harsh sob.

Sister Michael cupped the child's left hand in both of hers. "Come," she murmured. "Didn't Our Lord say, *Be not afraid*?"

"That's right," said Mr. Thaddeus. "Leave Pat to Our Heavenly Father."

A tear raced down Anna's swollen face, but she swiped it away.

"Ah, God love her, the tender dote," whispered Rosaleen O'Donnell behind Lib in the doorway. Kitty hovered at her elbow.

Being part of this audience made Lib suddenly uneasy. Could the whole scene have been staged by the mother and the priest? And what about Sister Michael — was she comforting the girl or luring her further into the maze?

Mr. Thaddeus clasped his hands. "Will we pray, Anna?"

"Yes." The girl flattened her hands together. "*I adore thee, O most precious cross, adorned by the tender, delicate and venerable members of Jesus my Saviour, sprinkled and stained with his precious blood. I adore thee, O my God, nailed to the cross for love of me."*

It was the Dorothy prayer! *Adore thee* and *adorned by,* not *Dorothy* — that's what Lib had been hearing over the past five days.

After the brief satisfaction of having solved the puzzle, she felt flat. Just another prayer; what was so special about it?

"Now, to the matter that's brought me here, Anna," said Mr. Thaddeus. "Your refusal to eat."

Was the priest trying to absolve himself of all blame in the Englishwoman's hearing? *Then make her eat that plump scone this minute,* Lib urged him silently.

Anna said something, very low.

"Speak up, my dear."

"I don't *refuse,* Mr. Thaddeus," she said. "I just don't eat."

Lib watched those serious, puffy eyes.

"God sees into your heart," said Mr. Thaddeus, "and he's moved by your good intentions. Let's pray that you'll be granted the grace to take food."

The nun was nodding.

The grace to take food! As if it were some miraculous power, when every dog, every caterpillar, was born with it.

The three prayed together silently for a few minutes. Then Mr. Thaddeus ate his scone, blessed the O'Donnells and Sister Michael, and took his leave.

Lib led Anna back to her bedroom. She could think of nothing to say, no way to refer to the conversation without insulting the child's faith. All across the world, she told herself, people placed their trust in amulets or idols or magic words. Anna could believe whatever she liked for all Lib cared, if only she'd eat.

She opened *All the Year Round* and tried to find any article that looked remotely interesting.

Malachy came in for a few words with his daughter. "Which are these, now?"

Anna introduced him to the flowers in her jar: bog asphodel, bog bean, cross-leaved heath, purple moor grass, butterwort.

His hand absentmindedly followed the curve of her ear.

Did he notice the thinning hair? Lib wondered. The scaly patches, the down on her face, the distended limbs? Or was Anna always the same in her father's eyes?

No knocks at the cabin door that afternoon; perhaps the constant rain kept the curious at bay. Anna seemed muted after her encounter with the priest. She sat with a hymnbook open in her lap.

Five days, thought Lib, staring so hard her eyes prickled. Could a stubborn child possibly last five days on sips of water?

Kitty brought Lib's tray in at a quarter to four. Cabbage, turnips, and the inevitable oatcakes — but Lib was hungry, so she set to as if it were the finest of spreads. The oatcakes were slightly blackened this time, and raw in the middle. But she forced them down. She'd cleared half her plate by the time she even remembered Anna, not three feet away, muttering what Lib still thought of as the Dorothy prayer. That was what hunger could do: blind you to everything else. The wad of oats rose in Lib's throat.

A nurse she'd known at Scutari had passed some time on a plantation in Mississippi and said the most dreadful thing was how quickly one stopped noticing the collars and chains. One could grow used to anything.

Lib stared at her plate now and imagined seeing it as Anna claimed she saw it: *a horseshoe, or a log, or a rock.* Impossible. She tried again, picturing the vegetables in a detached way, as if in a frame. Now this was only a photograph of a greasy plate, and after all, one wouldn't put one's tongue to an image or take a bite out of a page. Lib added a layer of glass, then another frame and another sheet of glass, boxing the thing away. *Not for eating.*

But the cabbage was an old friend; its hot, savoury scent spoke to her. She forked it into her mouth.

Anna watched the rain, face almost pressed to the smeary window.

Miss N. held passionate views on the importance of sunshine to the sick, Lib remembered. Like plants, they shrank without it. Which made her think of McBrearty and his arcane theory about living off light.

The skies finally cleared around six, and Lib decided there was little risk of visitors this late, so she took Anna out for a turn around the farmyard, wrapped up well in two shawls.

The girl held out her swollen hand to a brown butterfly that jerked about and wouldn't light on it. "Isn't that cloud over there exactly like a seal?"

Lib squinted at it. "You've never seen a real seal, I think, Anna."

"Real in a picture, I have."

Children would like clouds, of course: formless, or, rather, ever-shifting, kaleidoscopic. This little girl's inchoate mind had never been put in order. No wonder she'd fallen prey to an ambition as fantastical as a life free of appetite.

When they came back in, a tall, bearded man was smoking on a stool in the best chair. He turned to beam at Anna.

"You let a stranger in the minute my back was turned?" Lib asked Rosaleen O'Donnell in a sharp whisper.

"Sure John Flynn's no stranger." The mother didn't lower her voice. "He has a fine big farm up the road, and doesn't he often stop in of an evening to bring Malachy the paper?"

"No visitors," Lib reminded her.

The voice that emerged from that beard was very deep. "I'm a member of the committee that's paying your wages, Mrs. Wright."

Wrong-footed again. "I beg your pardon, sir. I didn't realize."

"Will you have a drop of whiskey, John?" Mrs. O'Donnell went for the little bottle kept for visitors in the nook beside the fire.

"I won't, not at the minute. Anna, how are you this evening?" asked Flynn in a soft voice, beckoning the child closer.

"Very well," Anna assured him.

"Aren't you marvellous?" The farmer's eyes looked glassy, as if he were seeing a vision. One massive hand stretched out as if he wanted to stroke the child's head. "You give us all hope. The very thing we need in these depressed times," he told her. "A beacon shining across these fields. Across the whole benighted island!"

Anna stood on one leg, squirming.

"Would you say a prayer with me?" he asked.

"She needs to get out of these damp things," said Lib.

"Whisper one for me, then, when you're going to sleep," he called as Lib hurried the child towards the bedroom.

"I will of course, Mr. Flynn," said Anna over her shoulder.

"Bless you!"

So poky and dim in there without the lamp. "It'll be dark soon," said Lib.

"*He that followeth me walketh not in darkness,*" quoted Anna, undoing her cuffs.

"You may as well put your nightclothes on now."

"All right, Mrs. Elizabeth. Or is it Eliza, maybe?" Fatigue made the girl's grin lopsided.

Lib concentrated on Anna's tiny buttons.

"Or is it Lizzy? I like Lizzy."

"It's not Lizzy," said Lib.

"Izzy? Ibby?"

"Iddly-diddly!"

Anna spilled over with laughter. "I'll call you that, then, Mrs. Iddly-Diddly."

"You will not, you goblin girl," said Lib. Were the O'Donnells and their friend Flynn wondering at all this mirth coming through the wall?

"I will so," said Anna.

"Lib." The word came out of her on its own, like a cough. "Lib's what I was called." Rather regretting telling her already.

"Lib," said Anna with a satisfied nod.

It was sweet to hear it. Like childhood days, when Lib's sister still looked up to her, when they'd thought they'd always have each other.

She pushed the memories to arm's length. "What about you, have you ever had a nickname?"

Anna shook her head.

"You could be Annie, perhaps. Hanna, Nancy, Nan . . ."

"Nan," said the girl, sounding out the syllable.

"You like Nan best?"

"But she wouldn't be me."

Lib shrugged. "A woman can change her name. On marriage, for instance."

"You were married, Mrs. Lib."

She nodded, wary. "I'm a widow."

"Are you sad all the time?"

Lib was disconcerted. "I knew my husband less than a year." Did that sound cold?

"You must have loved him," said Anna.

She couldn't answer that. She called up Wright in her mind; his face was a blur. "Sometimes, when disaster strikes, there's nothing to be done but begin all over again."

"Begin what?"

"Everything. A whole new life."

The girl absorbed that notion in silence.

They were half blinded when Kitty carried in the flaring lamp.

Later, Rosaleen O'Donnell came in with the *Irish Times* that John Flynn had left. Here was the photograph of Anna that Reilly had taken on Monday afternoon but changed into a woodcut, all the lines and shades cruder. The effect unnerved Lib, as if her days and nights in this cramped cabin were being translated into a cautionary tale. She confiscated the folded page before Anna could see it.

"There's a long piece below." The mother was quivering with gratification.

While Anna was brushing her hair, Lib went over to the lamp and skimmed the article. This was William Byrne's first dispatch, she realized, the one quoting Petronius, thrown together on Wednesday morning when he didn't have any solid information about the case at all. She couldn't disagree about *provincial ignorance*.

The second paragraph was new to her.

Of course, abstention has long been a distinctly Irish art. As the old Hibernian maxim goes, *Leave the bed sleepy, leave the table hungry.*

This wasn't news, Lib thought, only chat; the flippant tone left a bad taste in her mouth.

Those metropolitan sophisticates who have shed their Gaelic may need to be reminded that in our ancient tongue, Wednesday is designated by a word that means "first fast," Friday by "second fast." (On both these days, tradition holds that impatient infants are to be let cry three times before getting the bottle.) The word for Thursday, by delightful contrast, means "the day between fasts."

Could that all be true? She didn't trust this joker; Byrne had erudition enough but played it for laughs.

Our forefathers had a custom of (in the Hibernian idiom) *fasting against* an offender or debtor, that is, starving conspicuously outside his door. Saint Patrick himself is said to have fasted against his Maker on his namesake mountain in Mayo, with noted success: he shamed the Almighty into granting him the right to judge the Irish in the Last Days. In India, too, protest by means of doorstep fasting has become so prevalent that the Viceroy is proposing to ban it. As to whether little Miss O'Donnell is expressing some juvenile grievance by passing up four months of breakfasts, dinners, and suppers, this correspondent has not yet been able to determine.

Lib wanted to throw the paper in the fire. Had the fellow no heart? Anna was a child in trouble, not a joke for the summertime entertainment of newspaper readers.

"What does it say about me, Mrs. Lib?"

She shook her head. "It's not about you, Anna."

To distract herself, Lib glanced at the headlines in thick black, matters of world importance. The general election; union of Moldavia and Wallachia; Veracruz besieged; ongoing volcanic eruption in Hawaii.

No use. Lib didn't care about any of it. Private nursing was always narrowing, and the peculiarity of this particular job had intensified the effect, shrinking her world to one small chamber.

She folded the paper into a tight stick and left it on her tea tray by the door. Then she checked every surface again, not because she still believed there was some hidden cache that Anna crept out to eat during the nun's shifts, but just for something to do.

In her nightdress, the child sat knitting wool stockings. Could Anna have some unvoiced *grievance* after all? Lib wondered.

"Time to get into bed." She beat the pillows into shape so they'd keep the girl's head up at the correct angle. She made her notes.

Dropsy no better.
Gums ditto.
Pulse: 98 beats per minute.
Lungs: 17 respirations per minute.

When the nun came in for her shift, Anna was already dozing.

Lib found she had to speak, even though the woman resisted her every overture. "Five days and four nights, Sister, and I've seen nothing. Please tell me, for our patient's sake, have you?"

A hesitation, and then the nun shook her head. Even more quietly: "Perhaps because there's been nothing to see."

Meaning what — that there'd been no surreptitious feeding because Anna was indeed a living wonder who thrived on a diet of prayer alone? A fug of the ineffable filled this cabin — this whole country — and it turned Lib's stomach.

She spoke as tactfully as she could. "I have something to say. It's not about Anna so much as us."

That hooked the nun. After a long moment, she said, "Us?"

"We're here to observe, aren't we?"

Sister Michael nodded.

"Yet to study something can mean interfering with it. If one puts a fish in a tank or a plant in a pot for purposes of observation, one changes its conditions. However it is that Anna's been living over the past four months — everything's different now, wouldn't you agree?"

The nun only put her head to one side.

"Because of us," Lib spelled out. "The watch has altered the situation that's being watched."

Sister Michael's eyebrows soared, disappeared behind the band of white linen.

Lib pressed on. "If by any chance there's been some subterfuge going on in this house over the past months, our surveillance must have put an end to it, beginning on Monday. So there's a very real possibility that you and I are the ones preventing Anna from getting nourishment now."

"We're doing nothing!"

"We're watching, every minute. Haven't we pinned her like a butterfly?" The wrong image; too morbid.

The nun shook her head, not once but over and over.

"I hope I'm wrong," said Lib. "But if I'm right, if the child's had nothing for five days now..."

Sister Michael didn't say *That couldn't be* or *Anna needs no food.* Her only reply was "Have you noted some serious change in her condition?"

"No," Lib admitted. "Nothing I can put my finger on."

"Well, then."

"Well, then, what, Sister?" Was *God in his heaven* and *all right with the world*? "What do we do?"

"What we were hired to do, Mrs. Wright. No more, no less." And with that, the nun sat down and opened her holy book like a barricade.

This farm woman who'd ended up in the House of Mercy was no doubt a good soul, Lib thought in exasperation. And probably intelligent in her own way, if only she could let her mind roam beyond the boundaries prescribed by her superiors and their master in Rome. *We vow to be of use,* Sister Michael had boasted, but what real use was she here? Lib thought of what Miss N. had told a nurse she'd sent back to London after only a fortnight at Scutari: *At the front, anyone who's not useful is an impediment.*

In the kitchen, the Rosary had begun. The O'Donnells, John Flynn, and their maid were on their knees already as Lib passed through, all of them chanting, *"Give us this day our daily bread."*

Didn't these people hear what they were saying? What about Anna O'Donnell's daily bread?

Lib shoved the door open and went out into the night.

Sleep led her, over and over, back to the base of that cliff pictured on the holy card, the one with the cross looming at its highest point and the gigantic red heart beneath it, pulsing. Lib had to mount the staircase hacked into the rock face. Her legs strained and shook under her, and no matter how many steps she climbed, she never got any nearer the top.

This was Saturday morning, she realized when she woke in the dark.

When she reached the cabin, she saw the washing stretched on the bushes, looking wetter than ever after yesterday's rain.

Sister Michael was by the bedside watching the rise and fall of the small chest under the tangled blanket. Lib's eyebrows lifted in a silent question.

The nun shook her head.

"How much water has she taken?"

"Three spoons," whispered Sister Michael.

Not that it mattered; it was only water.

The nun collected her things and went out without another word.

A square of light moved slowly across Anna: right hand, chest, left hand. Did children of eleven generally sleep so long? Lib wondered. Or was it because Anna's system was running on no fuel?

Just then Rosaleen O'Donnell came in from the kitchen, and Anna blinked awake. Lib moved away to the dresser to allow the morning greeting.

The woman stood between her daughter and the pale lemony sun. As Rosaleen leaned over to engulf the child in her usual embrace, Anna put her hand up flat against her mother's expanse of bony chest.

Rosaleen O'Donnell froze.

Anna shook her head, wordless.

Rosaleen O'Donnell straightened up and put her fingers to the girl's cheek. On the way out, she gave Lib a venomous look.

Lib felt shaken; she'd done nothing. Was it her fault if

the girl had finally had enough of being fawned over by her hypocrite of a mother? Whether Rosaleen O'Donnell was behind the hoax or had merely turned a blind eye to it, at the very least she was standing by now while her daughter began her sixth day of fasting.

Refused mother's greeting, Lib noted in her memorandum book. Then wished she hadn't, because this record was supposed to be limited to medical facts.

On her way back to the village that afternoon, Lib pushed open the rusty gate of the cemetery. She was curious to see Pat O'Donnell's grave.

The headstones were not as ancient as she'd expected; she could find no inscriptions earlier than 1850. She supposed it had to be the soft ground that made so many of them list, and the damp air that furred them with moss.

Have mercy on . . . In fond memory . . . In affectionate remembrance of . . . Here lies the body . . . Sacred to . . . In memory of his first wife, who departed this life . . . Erected for the posterity of . . . Also of his second wife . . . Pray for the soul of . . . Who died exulting in her Saviour in sure and certain hope of the Resurrection. (Really, thought Lib, who ever died exultingly? Whatever fool penned that phrase had never sat by a bed with his ears pricked for the last rasp.)

Aged fifty-six years . . . Twenty-three years . . . Ninety-two years . . . Thirty-nine years. Thanks be to God, who gave her the victory. Lib noticed a little carving on almost every grave: *IHS,* in a sort of sunburst. She had a vague memory that this stood for *I Have Suffered.* There was one incongruous plot with no headstone, wide enough for twenty coffins side by side; who lay in there? Then she realized it must be a mass grave, full of the nameless.

Lib shivered. By trade, she was on intimate terms with death, but this was like walking into her enemy's house.

Whenever she saw a reference to a young child, she averted her eyes. *Also a son and two daughters . . . Also three children . . . Also their children who died young . . . Aged eight years . . . Aged two years and ten months.* (Those broken parents, counting every month.)

The angels saw the opening flower,
And swift with joy and love,
They bore her to a fairer home,
To bloom in fields above.

Lib found her nails digging into the flesh of her palms. If Earth was such unworthy soil for God's best specimens, why did he perversely plant them there? What could possibly be the point of these short, blighted lives?

Just as she was about to abandon the search, she found the boy.

PATRICK MARY O'DONNELL
3 DECEMBER 1843–21 NOVEMBER 1858
ASLEEP IN JESUS

She stared at the plainly chiselled words, trying to feel what they meant to Anna. Pictured a warm-fleshed, lanky boy in his cracked boots and muddy trousers, all the restless energy of fourteen.

Pat's was the sole O'Donnell grave, which suggested that

he'd been the one hope of passing on Malachy's surname, in this village at least. And also that if Mrs. O'Donnell had had other pregnancies since Anna, they hadn't made it to birth. Lib suspended her dislike of the woman for a moment and considered what Rosaleen O'Donnell had been through; what had hardened her. *Seven years of dearth and pestilence,* as Byrne had put it with a biblical ring. A boy and his little sister, and little or nothing to feed them during the *bad time.* Then, after Rosaleen had come through those terrible years, to lose her almost-grown son overnight . . . Such a wrench might have worked a strange alteration. Instead of clinging to her last child all the more, perhaps Rosaleen had found her heart frost-burnt. Lib could understand that, a sensation of having no more left to give. Was that why the woman made an uncanny cult of Anna now, apparently preferring her daughter to be more saint than human?

A breeze cut through the churchyard, and Lib wrapped her cloak around her. Shutting the squealing gate, she turned right, past the chapel. Apart from the small stone cross above the slates, the chapel struck her as little different from any of the neighbouring houses, and yet what power Mr. Thaddeus wielded from its altar.

By the time she reached the village, the sun was out again and everything sparkled. A ruddy-faced woman caught her by the sleeve as she turned onto the street.

Lib recoiled.

"Beg pardon, missus. I just wondered, how's the little girl?"

"I can't say." In case she hadn't made herself understood, she added, "It's a matter of confidentiality."

Did the woman know the word? It wasn't clear from her stare.

This time Lib went right, in the direction of Mullingar, merely because she hadn't walked that way before. She had no appetite and couldn't bear to enclose herself in her room at Ryan's yet.

The metallic clattering of a horse's hooves behind her. Only as the rider caught up to Lib did she recognize the broad shoulders and rusty curls. She nodded, expecting William Byrne to touch his hat and canter on.

"Mrs. Wright. What a pleasure to run into you." Byrne slid out of the saddle.

"I need my daily stroll" was all she could think to say.

"And Polly and I our ride."

"Is she mended, then?"

"Quite, and enjoying country life." He slapped the glossy flank. "What about you, have you happened on any *sights* yet?"

"Not one, not even a stone circle. I've just been in the graveyard," Lib mentioned, "but there was nothing of historic interest there."

"Well, it used to be against the law for us to bury our own, so the older Catholic graves would all be in the Protestant cemetery in the next town over," he told her.

"Ah. Forgive my ignorance."

"Gladly," said Byrne. "It's harder to excuse your resistance to the charms of this lovely landscape," he said with a flourish of the hand.

Lib pursed her lips. "One endless, waterlogged mire. I fell headlong into it yesterday, and I thought I might never get out of it again."

He grinned. "All you need to fear is quaking bog. It looks like solid land but it's really a floating sponge. If you step onto that, you'll rip right through to the murky water below."

She made a face. She was rather enjoying talking about anything other than the watch.

"Then there's a moving bog," he went on, "which is something like an avalanche—"

"This is pure invention, now."

"I swear," said Byrne, "after heavy rain the whole top of the land can peel off, hundreds of acres of peat sliding faster than a man can run."

Lib shook her head.

Hand on heart. "On my journalistic honour! Ask anyone around here."

She cast a sidelong glance, imagining a brown wave rolling towards them.

"Extraordinary stuff, bog," said Byrne. "The soft skin of Ireland."

"Good for burning, I suppose."

"What is, Ireland?"

Lib burst out laughing at that.

"You'd set a match to the whole place, I suspect, if it could be dried out first," he said.

"You're putting words in my mouth."

William Byrne smirked. "Did you know that peat possesses the eerie power of keeping things as they were at the moment of immersion? Troves of treasure have been pulled out of these bogs — swords, cauldrons, illuminated books — not to mention the occasional body in a remarkable state of preservation."

Lib winced. "You must be missing the more urbane pleasures of Dublin," she said, to change the subject. "Have you family there?"

"My parents, and three brothers," said Byrne.

That wasn't what Lib had meant, but she supposed she had her answer: the man was a bachelor. Of course, he was still young.

"The fact is, Mrs. Wright, I work like a dog. I'm the Irish correspondent for a number of English papers, and in addition I churn out stern unionism for the *Dublin Daily Express,* Fenian fervour for the *Nation,* Catholic pieties for the *Freeman's Journal*—"

"A ventriloquist dog, then," said Lib. That made him chuckle. She thought of Dr. McBrearty's letter about Anna, which had begun the whole controversy. "And for the *Irish Times,* satirical comment?"

"No, no. *Moderate* views on national questions and matters of general interest," said Byrne in the quavering tone of a dowager. "Then, in spare moments, of course, I study for the bar."

His wit made his boasting bearable. Lib was thinking of the article she'd wanted to toss in the fire yesterday evening. She supposed the man was only doing his job with the means at hand, as she did hers. If he wasn't allowed even to set eyes on Anna, what could he write but erudite flippancies?

She was too warm now; she undid her cloak and carried it over one arm, letting the air go through her tweed dress.

"Tell me, do you ever bring your young charge out for a walk?" asked Byrne.

Lib gave him a repressive look. "Oddly rippled, these fields."

"They'd have been lazy beds," he told her. "The seed potatoes were set in a line, and the peat was folded on top of them."

"But they're grassed over."

He shrugged. "Well, fewer mouths to feed around here since the famine."

She thought of that mass grave in the churchyard. "Wasn't some kind of potato fungus to blame?"

"There was more to it than a fungus," said Byrne, so vehemently that Lib took a step away. "Half the country wouldn't have died if the landlords hadn't kept shipping away the corn, seizing cattle, rack-renting, evicting, torching cabins . . . Or if the government at Westminster hadn't thought it the most prudent course of action to sit on their arses and let the Irish starve." He wiped a sheen off his forehead.

"*You* didn't starve, though, personally?" she asked, punishing him for his coarseness.

He took it well, with a wry grin. "A shopkeeper's son rarely does."

"You were in Dublin during those years?"

"Until I turned sixteen and got my first job as a special correspondent," he said, pronouncing the term with light irony. "Meaning an editor consented to send me off into the eye of the storm, at my father's expense, to describe the effects of the failure of the potato. I tried to keep my tone neutral and make no accusations. But by my fourth report it seemed to me that to do nothing was the deadliest sin."

Lib watched Byrne's taut face.

He was staring far down the narrow road. "So I wrote that God may have sent the blight, but the English made the famine."

She was thrown. "Did the editor print that?"

Byrne put on a funny voice, eyes bulging. "*Sedition!* he cried. That's when I decamped to London."

"To work for those same English villains?"

He mimed a stab to the heart. "What a knack you have for finding the sore spot, Mrs. Wright. Yes, within a month I was devoting my God-given talents to debutantes and horse races."

She dropped the mockery. "You'd done your best."

"Briefly, yes, at sixteen. Then I shut my mouth and took the pieces of silver."

A quiet between the two of them as they walked. Polly paused to nibble a leaf.

"Are you a man of belief still?" asked Lib. A shockingly personal question, but she felt as if they were past trivialities.

Byrne nodded. "Somehow all the miseries I've seen haven't quite shaken that out of me. And you, Elizabeth Wright — quite godless?"

Lib drew herself up. He made it sound as if she were some crazed witch invoking Lucifer on the moors. "What entitles you to assume—"

He interrupted. "You asked the question, ma'am. True believers never ask."

The man had a point. "I believe in what I can see."

"Nothing but the evidence of your senses, then?" One ruddy eyebrow tilted.

"Trial and error. Science," she said. "It's all we can rely on."

"Was it being widowed that did that?"

Blood boiled up from her throat to her hairline. "Who's been giving you information about me? And why must it always be presumed that a woman's views are based on personal considerations?"

"The war, then?"

His intelligence cut to the quick. "At Scutari," said Lib, "I found myself thinking, *If the Creator can't prevent such abominations, what good is he?*"

"And if he can but won't, he must be a devil."

"I never said that."

"Hume did," said Byrne.

She didn't know the name.

"A long-dead philosopher," he told her. "Finer minds than yours have reached the same impasse. It's a great puzzle."

The only sounds the tread of their boots on the dried mud and the soft clopping of Polly's hooves.

"So what possessed you to go to the Crimea in the first place?"

Lib half smiled. "A newspaper article, as it happens."

"Russell, in the *Times*?"

"I don't know the individual—"

"Billy Russell's a Dubliner like myself," said Byrne. "Those dispatches of his from the front changed everything. Made it impossible to turn a blind eye."

"All those men rotting away," said Lib, nodding, "and no one to help."

"What was the worst of it?"

Byrne's bluntness made her flinch. But she answered, "The paperwork."

"How so?"

"To get a soldier a bed, say, one took a coloured slip to the ward officer and then to the purveyor to have it countersigned, whereupon — and only then — the commissariat would issue the bed," Lib told him. "For a liquid or meat diet, or medicine, or even for an urgently required opiate, one had to bring a different-coloured form to a doctor and persuade him to find the time to make requisition of the relevant steward and have it countersigned by two other officers. By which point, the patient would very likely be dead."

"Christ." He didn't apologize for swearing.

Lib couldn't remember the last time anyone had listened to her with such attention. "*Unwarranted items* was the commissariat term for those things that, by definition, couldn't be supplied because the men were supposed to have brought their own in their knapsacks: shirts, forks, and so forth. But in some cases the knapsacks had never been unloaded from the ships."

"Bureaucrats," murmured Byrne. "A phalanx of cold-blooded little Pilates, washing their hands of it all."

"We had three spoons to feed a hundred men." Only on the word *spoons* did her voice wobble. "There were rumours of a hoard in some supply cupboard, but we never did find it. Finally Miss Nightingale thrust her own purse into my hand and sent me to the market to buy a hundred spoons."

The Irishman half laughed.

That day, Lib had been in too much of a hurry to ask

herself why, out of all of them, Miss N. had sent her. She realized now that it hadn't been a matter of nursing skills but of reliability. It occurred to Lib what an honour it was to have been chosen for that errand — better than any medal pinned on her cloak.

They walked in silence, very far from the village now. "Perhaps I'm a child, or a fool, that I still believe," said William Byrne. "*There are more things in heaven and earth, Horatio,* et cetera."

"I didn't mean to imply—"

"No, I admit it: I can't face horror without the shield of consolation."

"Oh, I'd take consolation if I could get it," said Lib under her breath.

Their footfalls, and Polly's, and a bird making a clinking sound in the hedge.

"Haven't people in all times and places cried out to their Maker?" asked Byrne. Sounding, for a moment, pompous and young.

"Which only proves we wish for one," muttered Lib. "Doesn't the very intensity of that longing make it all the more likely that it's only a dream?"

"Oh, that's cold."

She sucked her lip.

"What about our dead?" asked Byrne. "The sense that they're not quite gone, is that mere wishful thinking?"

Memory seized Lib like a cramp. The weight in her arms; sweet pale flesh, still warm, not moving. Blinded by tears, she stumbled forward, trying to escape him.

Byrne caught up to her and took her elbow.

She couldn't explain herself. She bit down on her lip and tasted blood.

"I'm so very sorry," he said, as if he understood.

Lib shook him off, folded her arms around herself. Tears raced down the oilproof cloth of the cloak over her arm.

"Forgive me. Talk's my trade," he said. "But I should learn to shut my mouth."

Lib tried to smile. She feared the effect was grotesque.

For a few minutes, while they walked, Byrne kept his mouth shut, as if to prove he knew how.

"I'm not myself," Lib said hoarsely at last. "This case has . . . unsettled me."

He only nodded.

Of all people to whom she shouldn't blab — a reporter. Yet who else in the world would understand? "I've watched the girl until my eyes hurt. She doesn't eat, yet she's alive. More alive than anyone I know."

"She's half swayed you, then?" he asked. "Almost won you over, hardheaded as you are?"

Lib couldn't tell how much of this was sardonic. All she could say was "I just don't know what to make of her."

"Let me try, then."

"Mr. Byrne—"

"Consider me a fresh pair of eyes. If I say so myself, I know how to talk to people. Perhaps I can tease some truth out of the girl."

Eyes down, she shook her head. Oh, the man knew how to talk to people, that was undeniable; he had a knack for teasing information out of those who should have known better.

"Five days I've been hanging around here," he said, steelier, "and what have I to show for it?"

The blood swept up from Lib's throat. Of course the journalist would consider all this time making conversation with the English nurse a waste and a bore. Not beautiful, not brilliant, no longer young; how could Lib have forgotten that she was only a means to an end?

She was under no obligation to exchange another word with this provocateur. She spun around and strode back in the direction of the village.

CHAPTER FOUR

Vigil

vigil
   a devotional observance
   an occasion of keeping awake for a purpose
   a watch kept on the eve of a festival

The laundry was gone from the bushes, and the cabin smelled of steam and hot metal; the women must have been ironing all afternoon. No Rosary this evening, it seemed. Malachy O'Donnell was smoking a pipe, and Kitty was encouraging the hens into their cupboard. "Is your mistress out?" Lib asked her.

" 'Tis her Female Sodality on Saturdays," said Kitty.

"What's that?"

But the slavey was running after one recalcitrant bird.

Lib had more urgent questions that had occurred to her as she'd lain awake this afternoon. Somehow, out of the whole crew, Kitty was the one she was most inclined to trust, for all that the young woman's head was crammed with fairies and angels. In fact, Lib rather wished she'd taken more trouble to cultivate the maid's friendship from the first day. She went a few steps closer now. "Kitty, do you by any chance remember the last food your cousin ate before her birthday?"

"I do, of course; sure how could I forget?" Kitty's tone was ruffled. Bent in two, shutting the dresser, she added something that sounded like *Toast*.

"Toast?"

"The Host, she said," Malachy O'Donnell threw over his shoulder. "The body of Our Lord, ah, under the species of bread."

Lib pictured Anna opening her mouth to receive that tiny baked disc that Roman Catholics believed to be the actual flesh of their God.

Arms crossed, the maid nodded at her master. "Her very first Holy Communion, bless the girl."

" 'Twas no earthly food she wanted for her last meal, was it, Kitty?" he murmured, eyes on the fire again.

" 'Twas not."

Her last meal; like a condemned prisoner. So Anna had taken the Host for the first and only time, then shut her mouth. What strange distortion of doctrine could have impelled her? Lib wondered. Had Anna somehow picked up the notion that now she'd been granted divine nourishment, she'd no further need for the earthly kind?

The father's face hung, uneven in the flicker of the flames. Some adult had been keeping Anna alive all these months, Lib reminded herself: Could it have been Malachy? She could hardly credit that.

Of course, there was a grey zone between innocent and guilty. What if the man had discovered the trick — his wife's or their priest's or both — but by then, his little pet's fame had already spread so far, he hadn't been able to bring himself to interfere?

In the bedroom, beside the sleeping girl, Sister Michael was already doing up her cloak. "Dr. McBrearty put his head in this afternoon," she whispered.

Had everything Lib had told him sunk in at last? "What instructions did he give?"

"None."

"But what did he say?"

"Nothing in particular." The nun's expression was unreadable.

Of all the doctors under whom Lib had served, this affable old man was the most difficult.

The nun left, and Anna slept on.

The night shift was so quiet, Lib had to keep pacing to ward off sleep herself. At one point she picked up the toy from Boston. The songbird was on one side, the cage on the other, yet when Lib twirled its strings as fast as she could, her senses were tricked and two incompatible things became one: a vibrating, humming caged bird.

Past three, Anna blinked awake.

"Can I do anything for you?" asked Lib, leaning over her. "Make you more comfortable?"

"My feet."

"What about them?"

"I don't feel them," whispered Anna.

The tiny toes under the blanket were icy to the touch. Such poor circulation in someone so young. "Here, climb out for a minute to get the blood moving again." The girl did, slowly and stiffly. Lib helped her to cross the room. "Left, right, like a soldier."

Anna managed a clumsy march on the spot. Her eyes were on the open window. "Lots of stars tonight."

"There are always just as many, if only we could see them," Lib told her. She pointed out the Plough, the North Star, Cassiopeia.

"Do you know them all?" asked Anna, marvelling.

"Well, just our constellations."

"Which ones are ours?"

"Those easily seen from the Northern Hemisphere, I mean," said Lib. "They're different in the South."

"Really?" The girl's teeth were chattering, so Lib helped her back into bed.

Wrapped in flannels, the brick was still hoarding heat from the fire in which it had sat all evening. She tucked it under the child's feet.

"But it's yours," said the girl, shuddering.

"I don't need it on a mild summer night. Do you feel the warmth yet?"

Anna shook her head. "I'm sure I will, though."

Lib looked down at the small figure lying as straight as a Crusader on a tomb. "Go back to sleep, now."

Still, Anna's eyes stayed wide. She whispered her Dorothy prayer, the one she said so often that Lib barely noticed it anymore. Then she sang some hymns, barely above a whisper.

> The night is dark,
> And I am far from home,
> Lead thou me on.

On Sunday morning Lib should have been catching up on her sleep, but the clanging church bells made that impossible. She lay awake, stiff-limbed, going through everything she'd learned about Anna O'Donnell. So many peculiar symptoms, but they didn't constitute anything

Lib recognized as a disease. She would have to speak to Dr. McBrearty again, and this time pin him down.

At one o'clock, the nun reported that the girl had been distressed at not being allowed to go to mass but had agreed to recite the liturgy for the day in her missal with Sister Michael instead.

For their walk, Lib set a very slow pace so as not to overtire Anna as she had the other day. She scanned the horizon before they set out to make sure there were no gawkers nearby.

They picked their way across the farmyard, their boots slithering. "If you were looking stronger," she said, "we might have gone a half a mile that way" — pointing west — "as far as a very curious hawthorn I've found with strips of cloth tied all over it."

Anna nodded with enthusiasm. "The rag tree at our holy well."

"It didn't have what I'd call a well, exactly, just a tiny pool." Lib remembered the tarry whiff of the water; perhaps it had some mildly disinfectant power? Then again, there was no use looking for a seed of science in a superstition. "Are the rags some kind of offering?"

"They're for dipping in the water and rubbing on a sore or an ache," said Anna. "After, you tie the rag on the tree, see?"

Lib shook her head.

"The badness stays on the rag, and you leave it behind. Once it rots away, what was ailing you will be gone too."

Meaning that time heals all ills, Lib supposed. A cunning legend, this one, because it would take so long for cloth to disintegrate, the sufferer's complaint would be almost sure to be cured by then.

Anna stopped to stroke a vivid cushion of moss on a wall, or perhaps to catch her breath. A pair of birds picked at red currants in the hedge.

Lib pulled a bunch of the gleaming globes and held them up close to the child's face. "Do you remember the taste of these?"

"I think so." Anna's lips were just a hand span from the currants.

"Doesn't your mouth water?" asked Lib, her voice seductive.

The girl shook her head.

"God made these berries, didn't he?" *Your* God, Lib had almost said.

"God made everything," said Anna.

Lib crushed a red currant between her own teeth and juice flooded her mouth so fast it almost spilled. She'd never tasted anything so dazzling.

Anna picked one small red ball from the bunch.

Lib's heart thudded loud enough to hear. Was this the moment? As easy as that? Ordinary life, as close as these dangling berries.

But the girl held out her palm quite flat, the currant in the middle, and waited till the bravest of the birds dived for it.

On the way back to the cabin, Anna moved slowly, as if she were walking through water.

*

Lib was so tired, stumbling back to the spirit grocery after nine that Sunday evening, she felt sure she'd sleep as soon as her head touched the pillow.

Instead her mind sprang to life like a buzzing hornet. It weighed on her that she might have misjudged William Byrne yesterday afternoon. What had he done but ask, one more time, for an interview with Anna? He hadn't actually insulted Lib; it was she who'd leapt to conclusions so touchily. If he really found her company so tedious, wouldn't he have kept their conversations brief and focused on Anna O'Donnell?

His room was just across the passage, but he probably hadn't gone to bed yet. Lib wished she could talk to him — as an intelligent Roman Catholic — about the child's last meal having been Holy Communion. The fact was, she was getting desperate for someone else's opinion of the girl. Someone whose mind Lib trusted; not Standish with his hostility, McBrearty with his fey hopefulness, the blinkered nun or bland priest, the besotted and probably corrupt parents. Someone who could tell Lib if she was losing her grip on reality.

Let me try, Byrne said again in her head. Teasingly, charmingly.

Two things could be true at once. He was a journalist, paid to dig up the story, but might he not also truly want to help?

One week exactly since Lib had arrived from London. So full of confidence she'd been — misplaced confidence in her own acuity, it had turned out. She'd thought to be back at the hospital by now, putting Matron in her place. Instead she was trapped here, in these same greasy-feeling

211

sheets, no nearer to understanding Anna O'Donnell than she'd been a week ago. Only more muddled, and exhausted, and troubled by her own part in these events.

Before dawn on Monday, Lib slid a note under Byrne's door.

When she arrived at the cabin, precisely at five, Kitty was still stretched out on the settle. The maid said there'd be no work done today except what was needful, given that it was a Holy Day of Obligation.

Lib paused; this was a rare chance to speak to Kitty on her own. "You're fond of your cousin, I think?" she asked under her breath.

"Sure why wouldn't I be fond of the little dote?"

Too loud. Lib put her finger to her lips. "Has she ever intimated" — she reached for a simpler word — "hinted to you as to why she won't eat?"

Kitty shook her head.

"Have you ever urged her to eat something?"

"I've done nothing." Sitting up, the slavey blinked in fright. "Get away with your accusations!"

"No, no, I only meant —"

"Kitty?" Mrs. O'Donnell's voice, from the outshot.

Well, she'd made an utter hash of that. Lib slipped into the bedroom at once.

The child was still sleeping, under three blankets. "Good morning," whispered Sister Michael, showing Lib the bare record of the night.

Sponge bath given.
2 tsp. water taken.

212

"You look tired, Mrs. Wright."

"Is that so?" snapped Lib.

"You've been seen tramping all over the county."

Lib had been seen alone, did the nun mean? Or with the journalist? Were the locals talking? "Exercise helps me sleep," she lied.

When Sister Michael had left, Lib studied her own notes for a while. The velvety white pages seemed to mock her. The numbers didn't add up; they failed to tell any tale except that Anna was Anna and like no one else. Fragile, plump-faced, bony, vital, chilly, smiling, tiny. The girl continued to read, sort her cards, sew, knit, pray, sing. An exception to all rules. A miracle? Lib shied from the word, but she was beginning to see why some might call it that.

Anna's eyes were wide, the hazel flecked with amber. Lib leaned over. "Are you well, child?"

"More than well, Mrs. Lib. 'Tis the Feast of Our Lady's Assumption."

"So I understand," said Lib. "When she was lifted up to heaven, am I correct?"

Anna nodded, squinting at the window. "The light's so bright today, with coloured halos around everything. The scent of that heather!"

The bedroom seemed dank and musty to Lib, and the purple tufts in the jar had no fragrance. But children were so open to sensation, and especially this child.

Monday, August 15, 6:17 a.m.
Reports having slept well.
Temperature in armpit still low.

Pulse: 101 beats per minute.
Lungs: 18 respirations per minute.

The readings went up and down, but on the whole they were creeping upwards. Dangerously? Lib couldn't be sure. It was doctors who were taught to form these judgments. Though McBrearty seemed unfit for the task.

The O'Donnells and Kitty came in early to tell Anna that they were off to the chapel. "To offer the first fruits?" Anna asked, eyes lit.

"Of course," said her mother.

"What's that, exactly?" asked Lib, to be civil.

"Bread made with the first pull of the wheat," said Malachy, "and, ah, a bit of oats and barley thrown in too."

"Don't forget there'll be bilberries offered too," Kitty put in.

"And a few new potatoes no bigger than the top of your thumb, God bless them," said Rosaleen.

From the smeary window, Lib watched the party set off, the farmer a few steps behind the women. How could they care about their festival in the second week of this watch? Did it mean they'd nothing on their consciences, she wondered, or that they were monsters of callousness? Kitty hadn't sounded callous earlier; worried for her cousin, more like. But so nervous of the English nurse, she'd misunderstood Lib's question and thought she was being accused of feeding the girl in secret.

Lib didn't take Anna out till ten o'clock this morning because that was the time she'd specified in her note. It was a beautiful day, the best since her arrival; a proper sun, as clear as that of England. She tucked the child's arm in hers and set a very cautious pace.

Anna was moving in what struck Lib as an odd way, with her chin stuck out. But the girl showed a relish for everything. Snuffed at the air as if it were attar of roses instead of cows and chickens. Stroked every mossy rock that they passed.

"What's the matter with you today, Anna?"

"Nothing. I'm happy."

Lib looked at her askance.

"Our Lady's pouring such a great deal of light on everything, I can nearly smell it."

Could eating little or nothing open the pores? Lib wondered. Sharpen the senses?

"I see my feet," said Anna, "but as if they belong to somebody else." Looking down at her brother's worn boots.

Lib tightened her grip on the girl.

A black-jacketed silhouette at the end of the path, out of sight of the cabin: William Byrne. He lifted his hat and unleashed his curls. "Mrs. Wright."

"Ah, I believe I know this gentleman," remarked Lib as casually as she could. Thinking, did she know him at all, really? The committee could dismiss her for arranging this interview if any of its members heard about it. "Mr. Byrne, this is Anna O'Donnell."

"Good morning, Anna." He shook her hand. Lib saw him eyeing the bloated fingers.

She began with bland nothings about the weather, her mind skittering along underneath. Where could the three walk to run the lowest risk of being spotted? How soon would the family come back from mass? She steered Byrne and Anna away from the village and took a cart track that looked little used.

"Is Mr. Byrne a visitor, Mrs. Lib?"

Startled by the child's question, she shook her head. She couldn't have Anna reporting to her parents that the nurse had broken her own rule.

"I'm in these parts just for a little while, to see the sights," said Byrne.

"With your children?" asked Anna.

"Sadly, I have none, as yet."

"Have you a wife?"

"Anna!"

"That's all right," Byrne told Lib, and he turned back to Anna. "No, my dear. I very nearly had one once, but at the last minute, the lady changed her mind."

Lib looked away, at a stretch of bog studded with shining puddles.

"Oh," said Anna sorrowfully.

Byrne shrugged. "She's settled in Cork, and good riddance to her."

Lib liked him for that.

Byrne found out that Anna loved flowers, which was a very great coincidence, he told her, because he did too. He broke off a red stem of dogwood with one last white bloom and gave it to her.

"At the mission," she told him, "we learned that the cross was made of dogwood, so the tree only grows short and twisted now because of being sorry."

He bent right down to hear her.

"The flowers are like a cross, see? Two long petals, two

short," said Anna. "And those brown bits are the nail prints, and that's the crown of thorns in the middle."

"Fascinating," said Byrne.

Lib was glad she'd risked this meeting after all. Before, he'd been able only to crack jokes about the case; now he was getting a sense of the real girl.

Byrne told a story of a Persian king who'd halted his army for days just to admire a plane tree. He broke off to point out a grouse running by, gingery body vivid against the grasses. "See its red eyebrows, like mine?"

"Redder than yours." Anna laughed.

He'd been to Persia himself, he told her, and Egypt too.

"Mr. Byrne is quite a traveller," said Lib.

"Oh, I've thought of going farther," he said.

She looked sideways at him.

"Settling in Canada, perhaps, or the States, even Australia or New Zealand. Wider horizons."

"But to sever all your connections, professional as well as personal . . ." Lib fumbled for words. "Wouldn't it be like a little death?"

Byrne nodded. "I believe emigration generally is that. The price of a new life."

"Would you like to hear a riddle?" Anna asked him suddenly.

"Very much," he told her.

She repeated the ones about the wind, paper, and flame; she turned to Lib only to confirm one or two words. Byrne failed to guess any of them and rapped himself on the skull on hearing the answer every time.

He tested Anna on birdsongs next. She correctly identified the melodic sobbing of a curlew and a drumming made by the wings of what she called a bog bleater, which turned out to be an Irishism for snipe.

Finally Anna admitted that she was a little tired. Lib gave her a searching look and felt her forehead, which was still stone cool, despite the sunshine and exertion.

"Would you like a little rest here to fortify you for the walk back?" asked Byrne.

"Yes, please."

He took off his coat with a flap of the tails and spread it out on a large flat rock for the child.

"Sit down," said Lib, crouching to pat the brown lining, still warm from his back.

Anna subsided onto it and stroked the satin with one finger.

"I'll have my eye on you all the time," Lib promised the girl. Then she and Byrne stepped away.

The two of them drifted till they reached a broken wall. They stood close enough that Lib could feel the heat coming off his shirtsleeve like a vapour. "Well?"

"Well what, Mrs. Lib?" His voice was oddly tight.

"What do you make of her?"

"She's delightful." Byrne spoke so quietly that she had to lean in to make it out.

"Isn't she?"

"A delightful dying child."

Lib was suddenly winded. She looked over her shoulder at Anna, a tidy figure on one edge of the man's long jacket.

"Are you blind?" asked Byrne, still as softly as if he were saying something kind. "The girl's wasting away in front of you."

She was almost stuttering. "Mr. Byrne. How, how —"

"I suppose that's exactly it: you're too close up to see it."

"How can you — what makes you so sure?"

"I was sent to study famine when I was only five years older than her," he reminded her in the quietest of snarls.

"Anna isn't . . . her belly's round," Lib argued weakly.

"Some starve fast, some slow," said Byrne. "The slow kind swell up, but it's only water, there's nothing there." He kept his eyes on the green field. "That waddle, the ghastly fuzz on her face. And have you smelled her breath lately?"

Lib tried to remember. That wasn't one of the measurements she'd been taught to record.

"It goes vinegary as the body turns on itself; eating itself up, I suppose."

Lib looked over and saw that the child had crumpled like a leaf. She ran.

"I didn't faint," Anna kept insisting as William Byrne carried her home, blanketed in his jacket. "I was just resting." Eyes looking as deep as bog holes.

Lib's throat was constricted with fright. *A delightful dying child.* He was right, damn the man.

"Let me in," Byrne told Lib outside the cabin. "You can tell the parents I happened to be passing and came to your aid."

"Get away from here." She wrenched Anna out of his arms.

Only when he'd turned towards the lane did Lib dip her nose to the girl's face and inhale. There it was: a faint, awful fruitiness.

*

When Lib woke that Monday afternoon to the rattling of rain on Ryan's roof, she was groggy. A rectangle of white at the base of the door confused her eye; she thought it was light, and only when she dragged herself out of bed did it turn into a page. Handwritten, hastily but without mistakes.

A chance and fleeting encounter with the Fasting Girl herself has at last given this correspondent an opportunity to form a personal opinion on this most heated of controversies, as to whether she is being used to perpetrate a nefarious fraud upon the public.

First, it must be said that Anna O'Donnell is an exceptional maiden. Despite having received only a limited education at the village's National School, under a teacher who is obliged to supplement his income by cobbling, Miss O'Donnell speaks with sweetness, composure and candour. As well as the piety for which she is known, she displays great feeling for nature, and a sympathy striking in one so young. The Egyptian sage wrote some five millennia ago, Wise words are rarer than emeralds, yet they come from the mouths of poor slave girls.

Second, it falls to this correspondent to give the lie to the reports of Anna O'Donnell's health. Her stoical character and elevated spirits may obscure the truth, but the lurching walk and strained posture, the chill, distended fingers, the sunken eyes, and above all the sharp-scented breath known as the odour of famine, all testify to her state of malnutrition.

Without speculating on what covert devices may have been used to keep Anna O'Donnell alive for four months until the watch commenced on the eighth of August, it may be said — rather, must be said, without equivocation — that the child is now in grave peril, and that her watchers must beware.

Lib balled up the page so tightly that it disappeared in her fist. How it bit, every word of it.

In her memorandum book, she'd logged so many warning signs — why had she resisted the obvious conclusion that the girl's health was in decline? Arrogance, Lib supposed; she'd held firmly to her own judgment and overestimated her knowledge. Wishful thinking, too, as bad as what she'd seen in the families of those she'd nursed. Because Lib wanted the girl kept from harm, all week she'd indulged in fantasies about unconscious night-feedings or inexplicable powers of mind that bore the girl up. But to an outsider such as William Byrne, it was clear as day that Anna was just starving.

Her watchers must beware.

Lib's guilt should have made her grateful to the man. So why, picturing his handsome face, did she feel incensed?

She pulled the pot out from underneath the bed and retched up the boiled ham she'd had for dinner.

The sun went down just before she reached the cabin that evening, and the moon came up full, a swollen white globe.

Lib hurried in past the O'Donnells and Kitty, who were sitting over cups of tea, with barely a word of greeting. She had to alert the nun. It struck her that Dr. McBrearty might perhaps hear the truth better from Sister Michael if the nun could possibly be persuaded to tackle him.

But for once, she found Anna lying flat in the bed and the Sister of Mercy sitting on the edge, the child so engrossed in a story the nun was telling that she didn't even look over at Lib.

"A hundred years old, and in awful pain all the time," Sister Michael was saying. Her eyes slid to Lib and then back to Anna. "The old woman confessed that when she was a little girl at mass, she'd taken Holy Communion but hadn't closed her mouth in time, and the Host had slipped out onto the floor. She'd been too ashamed to tell a soul, you see, so she'd left it there."

Anna sucked in her breath.

Lib had never heard her fellow nurse so voluble.

"Now, do you know what he did, that priest?"

"When it fell out of her mouth?" asked Anna.

"No, the priest to whom the woman was making her confession, when she was a hundred years old. He went back to that same church, and it was in ruins," said Sister Michael, "but there was a bush blooming right out of the broken stones of the floor. He searched among the roots, and what did he find but the Host itself, as fresh as the day it fell from the little girl's mouth nearly a century before."

Anna made a small marvelling sound.

Lib was hard-pressed not to grab the nun by the elbow

and yank her out of the room. What kind of story was this to tell Anna?

"He carried it back and put it on the old woman's tongue, and the curse was broken, and she was released from her pain."

The child fumbled the sign of the cross. *"Eternal rest grant unto her, O Lord, and let perpetual light shine upon her, may she rest in peace."*

Released from her pain meant she'd died, Lib realized. Only in Ireland would this count as a happy ending.

Anna blinked up at her. "Good evening, Mrs. Lib. I didn't see you there."

"Good evening, Anna."

Sister Michael stood up and gathered her things. She came over and murmured in Lib's ear, "Highly excited all afternoon, singing one hymn after another."

"And you thought such a lurid tale would calm her?"

The nun's face closed up inside its frame of linen. "I don't think you understand our stories, ma'am."

That was fighting talk for Sister Michael. And the nun glided from the room before Lib could say what she'd been waiting to say all afternoon: that in her view — she couldn't mention Byrne, obviously — Anna was in real danger.

She busied herself arranging the lamp, the can of burning fluid, the wick scissors, the water glass, the blankets, everything ready for the night. She got out her memorandum book and lifted Anna's wrist. *A delightful dying child.* "How are you feeling?"

"Quite content, Mrs. Lib."

Anna's eyes were sunken, Lib could see now, engulfed by the swollen tissue. "But in your body, I mean."

"Floating," said the girl after a long moment.

Dizziness? wrote Lib. "Anything else troubling you?"

"The floating doesn't trouble me."

"Is there anything else that's different today, then?" Metallic pencil ready.

Anna leaned forward as if confiding a great secret. "Like bells, far off."

Ringing in ears, Lib wrote.

Pulse: 104 beats per minute.
Lungs: 21 respirations per minute.

The girl's movements were definitely slower, Lib saw, now that she was looking for evidence; her hands and feet a little colder and bluer than a week ago. But her heart was going faster, like the wings of a small bird. The blood was hectic in Anna's cheeks tonight. Her skin was as rough as a nutmeg grater in places. She smelled a little sour, and Lib would have liked to give her a sponge bath, but she feared to chill her even more.

"*I adore thee, O most precious cross . . .*" Anna whispered the Dorothy prayer, staring up at the ceiling.

Lib suddenly lost patience. "Why recite that one so very often?" Expecting Anna to tell her again that it was *private*.

"Thirty-three."

"I beg your pardon?"

"Just thirty-three times a day," said Anna.

Lib's mind reeled. That was more than once an hour, but allowing for sleep, that meant more than twice in every waking hour. What would Byrne ask if he were here;

how would he unravel the story? "Was it Mr. Thaddeus who said you had to do that?"

Anna shook her head. "That's how old he was."

It took a moment for Lib to understand. "Christ?"

A nod. "When he died and was resurrected."

"But why must you say that particular prayer thirty-three times a day?"

"To get Pat out of —" She broke off.

In the open door, Mrs. O'Donnell stood, holding out her arms.

"Good night, Mammy," said the girl.

That stony face; Lib could feel the woman's grief from here. Or was it fury at being denied as small a thing as an embrace? Didn't a child owe the mother who'd borne her that much?

Rosaleen turned away and thumped the door shut behind her.

Yes, fury, Lib decided; not only against the girl who was keeping her mother at arm's length but against the nurse who was witnessing it.

It occurred to her that Anna might — without even being conscious of it — be trying to make the woman suffer. *Fasting against* a mother who'd turned her into a sort of fairground attraction.

Through the wall, the call and moaning response of the Rosary went up. Anna hadn't asked to take part in it tonight, Lib noticed; another sign that her strength was beginning to drain away.

The child curled up on her side now. Why did people say *sleep like a baby* to mean someone slumbering peacefully? Lib wondered. Babies often sprawled like broken things or wound themselves into balls as if to go back in time and return to the long oblivion from which they'd been dragged.

She tucked the blankets around Anna and added a fourth, because the girl was still shivering. She stood and waited till Anna dropped off to sleep and the chanting from next door came to an end.

"Mrs. Wright." Sister Michael again, in the doorway.

"Still here?" asked Lib, relieved to get another chance to talk to her.

"I stayed for the Rosary. Might I —"

"Come in, come in." This time Lib would explain everything clearly enough to win over the nun.

Sister Michael shut the door carefully. "The legend," she said under her breath, "the old story I was telling Anna."

Lib frowned. "Yes?"

"It's about confession. The girl in the story wasn't being punished for letting the Host fall," said the nun, "but for keeping her mistake a secret all her life."

This was theological hairsplitting, and Lib had no time for it. "You're speaking in riddles."

"When the old woman confessed it at last, you see, she laid her burden down," the nun whispered, eyes turning towards the bed.

Lib blinked. Could these hints mean that the nun thought Anna had a terrible secret to confess — that the girl was no miracle after all?

She tried to recall their brief conversations of the past week. Had the nun ever actually said that she believed Anna to be living without food?

No; blinkered by prejudice, Lib had just assumed she thought that. Sister Michael had kept her own counsel or uttered anodyne generalities.

Lib stepped up very close to her now and murmured, "You've known all along."

Sister Michael's hands flew up. "I was only—"

"You're as familiar with the facts of nutrition as I. We've both known from the start that this must be a hoax."

"Not *known*," whispered Sister Michael. "We know nothing for sure."

"Anna's sinking fast, Sister. Weaker every day, colder, more numb. Have you smelled her breath? That's her stomach consuming itself."

The nun's prominent eyes glistened.

"You and I must dig out the truth," said Lib, gripping her wrist. "Not just because we've been charged with that task, but because the child's life depends on it."

Sister Michael turned on her heel and fled from the room.

Lib couldn't pursue her; she was shackled here. She groaned to herself.

But in the morning the nun would have to come back, and Lib would be ready for her.

Anna was awake on and off that night. She turned her head or curled the other way. Six days left till the end of the watch. No, Lib corrected herself, that was only if Anna lasted six more days. How long could a child cling to life on sips of water?

A delightful dying child. It was as well that Lib knew the truth, she told herself; now she could act. But for

Anna's sake, she had to proceed with the greatest care, without displaying arrogance or losing her temper again. *Remember,* she told herself, *you're a stranger here.*

A fast didn't go fast; it was the slowest thing there was. *Fast* meant a door shut fast, firmly. A fastness, a fortress. To fast was to hold fast to emptiness, to say no and no and no again.

Anna was staring torpidly at the shadows the lamp projected on the walls.

"Is there anything you want?"

A shake of the head.

Strange children have faded away, and have halted from their paths. Lib sat and watched the girl. Blinked with dry eyes.

When the nun put her head in the door just after five in the morning, Lib leapt up so fast, a muscle in her back twanged. She shut the door almost in the face of Rosaleen O'Donnell. "Listen, Sister." Barely voicing the words. "We must tell Dr. McBrearty that the child's killing herself by degrees out of an excess of grief for her brother. It's time to call off the watch."

"We did accept this charge," said the nun faintly, as if each syllable were coming up from a deep hole in the earth.

"But did you ever think we'd reach this point?" Lib gestured at the sleeper in the bed.

"Anna's a very special girl."

"Not so special that she can't die."

Sister Michael writhed. "I'm under a vow of obedience. Our orders were very clear."

"And we've been following them to the letter, as tor- turers do."

Lib watched the nun's face register that blow. Suspicion seized her. "Do you have other orders, Sister? From Mr. Thaddeus, perhaps, or your superiors at the convent?"

"What do you mean?"

"Have you been told to see nothing and hear nothing and say nothing, no matter what you really think is going on in this cabin?" Almost snarling. "Told to testify to a miracle?"

"Mrs. Wright!" The nun's face was livid.

"I beg your pardon if I'm wrong." Lib's tone was sullen, but she did believe the woman. "Then why won't you speak to the doctor with me?"

"Because I'm only a nurse," said Sister Michael.

"I was taught the full meaning of that word," Lib raged. "Weren't you?"

The door opened with a bang. Rosaleen O'Donnell. "May I say good morning to my child, at least?"

"Anna's still asleep," said Lib, turning to the bed.

But the girl's eyes were wide open. How much had she heard?

"Good morning, Anna," said Lib, her voice uneven.

The girl looked quite insubstantial, a drawing on old parchment. "Good morning, Mrs. Wright. Sister. Mammy." Her smile radiating weakly in all directions.

At nine — Lib had waited as long as she could, for manners' sake — she walked to McBrearty's house.

"The doctor's out," said the housekeeper.

"Out where?" Too shaky with fatigue to phrase it more politely.

"Is it the O'Donnell girl, is she not well?"

Lib stared at the woman's pleasant face under her starched cap. *Anna hasn't had a proper meal since April,* she wanted to scream, *how can she be well?* "I must speak to him on a matter of urgency."

"He's been called to the bedside of Sir Otway Blackett."

"Who's that?"

"A baronet," said the woman, clearly shocked that Lib didn't know, "and a resident magistrate."

"Where's his seat?"

The housekeeper stiffened at the notion of the nurse pursuing the doctor there. It was miles out; Mrs. Wright had much better come back later.

Lib let herself sway just enough to hint that she might collapse on the doorstep.

"Or you could wait in my parlour below, I suppose," said the woman.

Doubtful as to the status of a Nightingale, Lib could tell, unsure whether it might be more suitable to put her in the kitchen.

Lib sat over a cup of cold tea for an hour and a half. If only she had the backing of that wretched nun.

"The doctor's returned, and he'll see you now." That was the housekeeper.

Lib leapt to her feet so fast, she saw black.

Dr. McBrearty was in his study, moving papers about in a desultory way. "Mrs. Wright, how good of you to come."

Calm was crucial; a strident female voice caused men's ears to close. She remembered to begin by asking after the baronet.

"An aching head; nothing serious, thank goodness."

"Doctor, I'm here out of grave concern for Anna's welfare."

"Oh, dear."

"She fainted yesterday. Her pulse is speeding up, yet her circulation's getting so sluggish she can hardly feel her feet," said Lib. "Her breath—"

McBrearty held up one hand to stop her. "Mm, I've been giving little Anna a great deal of thought and applying myself most diligently to the historical record in search of illumination."

"The historical record?" repeated Lib, dazed.

"Did you know — well, why would you? — in the Dark Ages, many saints were visited with a complete loss of appetite for years, for decades, even. *Inedia prodigiosa*, it was called, the prodigious fast."

So they had a special name for it, this freakish spectacle, as if it were as real a thing as a stone or a shoe. Dark Ages, indeed; they weren't over. Lib thought of the Fakir of Lahore. Did every country have such tall tales of preternatural survival?

The old man went on with animation. "They aspired to be like Our Lady, you see. In her infancy she was said to have suckled only once a day. Saint Catherine, now — after she forced herself to swallow a bit of food, she'd poke a twig down her throat and sick it back up."

With a shiver, Lib thought of hair shirts and spiked belts and monks whipping themselves raw in the streets.

"They meant to put down the flesh and raise up the spirit," he explained.

But why does it have to be one or the other? Lib wondered. *Aren't we both?* "Doctor, these are modern times, and Anna O'Donnell is only a child."

"Granted, granted," he said. "But might some physiological mystery lie behind those old tales? The persistent chilliness you've mentioned, say — I've formed a tentative hypothesis about that. Might her metabolism not be altering to one less combustive, more of a reptilian than mammalian nature?"

Reptilian? she wanted to scream.

"Every year, don't men of science discover apparently inexplicable phenomena in far-flung corners of the globe? Perhaps our young friend represents a rare type that may become common in future times." McBrearty's voice shook with excitement. "One that may offer hope for the whole human race."

Was the man mad? "What hope?"

"Freedom from need, Mrs. Wright! If it were within the bounds of possibility for life to endure without food . . . why, what cause would there be to fight over bread or land? That could put an end to Chartism, socialism, war."

How convenient for all the tyrants of the world, Lib thought; whole populations meekly subsisting on nothing.

The doctor's expression was beatific. "Perhaps nothing is impossible to the Great Physician."

It took Lib a moment to understand whom he meant. Always God — the real tyrant in this part of the world. She made an effort to answer in the same terms. "Without the food he's provided for us," she said, "we die."

"Until *now,* we've died. Until now."

And Lib saw it clearly at last, the pitiful nature of an old man's dream.

"But about Anna." She had to bring McBrearty back to the point. "She's failing fast, which means she must have been getting food until we thwarted it. We're to blame."

He frowned, fumbling with the arms of his glasses. "I don't see how that follows."

"The child I met last Monday was vigorous," said Lib, "and now she's barely able to stand. What can I deduce but that you must call off the watch and bend all your efforts to persuading her to eat?"

His papery hands shot up. "My good woman, you overstep your mark. You've not been called upon to *deduce* anything. Though your protectiveness is only natural," he added more gently. "I suppose the duties of a nurse, especially with a patient so young, must stimulate the dormant maternal capacity. Your own infant didn't live, I understand?"

Lib looked away so he couldn't read her face. It was an old wound the doctor had prodded, but he'd done it without warning, and she was dizzy with pain. With outrage too; had Matron really been obligated to share Lib's history with the man?

"But you mustn't allow your personal loss to distort your judgment." McBrearty waved one crooked finger, almost playfully. "Given free rein, this kind of motherly anxiety can lead to irrational panic, and a touch of self-aggrandizement."

Lib swallowed and made her voice as soft and womanly as she could. "Please, Doctor. Perhaps if you were to call your committee together, and warn them of the deterioration in Anna's condition—"

He cut her off with a gesture. "I'll pop in again this very afternoon, will that set your mind at rest?"

Lib lurched to the door.

She'd botched this interview. She should have brought McBrearty around gradually to the point where he thought it was his idea — and his duty — to abort the watch, just as he'd begun it. Since she'd come to this country eight days ago, Lib had made one blunder after another. How ashamed of her Miss N. would have been.

At one o'clock she found Anna in bed with hot bricks pushing up the blankets all around her feet.

"She needed a wee nap after we went around the yard," murmured Sister Michael, fastening her cloak.

Lib couldn't speak. This was the first time the child had taken to her bed in the middle of the day. She examined the tiny puddle in the chamber pot. A teaspoonful, at most, and very dark. Could that be blood in the urine?

When Anna roused from her doze, she and Lib chatted about the sunshine. Her pulse was 112, the highest Lib had recorded. "How do you feel, Anna?"

"Pretty well." Barely audible.

"Is your throat dry? Will you take some water?"

"If you like." Anna sat up and took a sip.

A tiny trail of red marked the spoon.

"Open your mouth, would you please?" Lib peered in, tilting Anna's jaw towards the light. Scarlet brimmed around several of the teeth. Well, at least the bleeding was coming from the gums rather than the stomach. One of the molars was at an odd angle. Lib nudged it with her nail, and it tilted sideways. When she tugged it out, between finger and thumb, she saw it wasn't a milk tooth but one of the permanent ones.

Anna blinked at the tooth, and then at Lib. As if daring the nurse to say something.

Lib slipped it into the pocket of her apron. She'd wait to show it to McBrearty. She'd follow her orders, keep gathering information to strengthen her case, and bide her time — but not much longer.

The child was dark around the lips and under the eyes. Lib noted everything down in her book. The simian fuzz on the cheeks had thickened, and it was coming in on the neck. A cluster of brown marks around the collarbone, scaly. Even where the skin was still pale, it was turning bumpy, like sandpaper. Anna's pupils seemed more dilated than usual too, as if the black holes had been growing day by day, swallowing up the light brown. "How are your eyes? Can you see as you used to?"

"I see what I need to see," said Anna.

Weakening sight, Lib added to her memoranda. "Is there anything else . . . do you hurt anywhere?"

" 'Tis just" — Anna made a vague gesture around her middle — "passing through."

"Passing through you?"

"Not me." So softly that Lib wasn't sure she'd heard right.

The pain wasn't Anna? The girl through whom the pain was passing wasn't Anna? Anna wasn't Anna? Perhaps the girl's brain was beginning to be drained of force. Perhaps Lib's was too.

The child turned the pages of her Book of Psalms and occasionally muttered lines aloud. *"Thou that liftest me up from the gates. Deliver me out of the hands of my enemies."*

Lib didn't know whether Anna could still make out the print or if she was reciting from memory.

"Save me from the lion's mouth, and my lowness from the horns of unicorns."

Unicorns? Lib had never pictured these storybook creatures as predators.

Anna reached up to place the book on her dresser. Then slid down in the bed, gratefully, as if it were night again.

In the silence, Lib thought of offering to read her something. Children often preferred to be told stories rather than read them, didn't they? Lib couldn't think of any. Not even any songs. Anna usually sang to herself; when had the singing stopped?

The girl's eyes moved from wall to wall, as if she were looking for a way out. Nothing to rest on but four corners and her nurse's strained face.

Lib called to the maid from the door, holding out the jar. "Kitty, fresh bedding, please, and could you fill this with a few flowers?"

"Which ones, now?"

"Anything colourful."

Kitty came back in ten minutes with a pair of sheets and a handful of grasses and flowers. She turned her head sideways to consider the little girl in the bed.

Lib scrutinised the slavey's broad features. Was that just tenderness, or was it guilt? Could it be that Kitty knew how Anna had been fed until recently, even if she hadn't done it herself? Lib tried to think how to phrase the question without alarming the maid; how to persuade the maid to give up whatever information she possessed, if it might save Anna.

"Kitty!" Rosaleen O'Donnell's cry was irritated.

"Coming." The slavey hurried off.

Lib helped Anna up and onto a chair so she could change the bedding.

Anna huddled over the jar, arranging the stems. One was dogwood; Lib's fingers itched to tear up its cruciform bloom, the brown marks of the Roman nails.

The child stroked an unremarkable leaf. "Look, Mrs. Lib, even the little teeth have tinier little teeth all over them."

Lib thought of the fallen molar in her apron. She pulled the new sheets very tight and smooth. (*A crease can score skin as surely as a whip,* Miss N. always said.) She tucked Anna back into bed and covered her with three blankets.

Dinner, at four, was some kind of fish stew. Lib was wiping her plate with oat bread when Dr. McBrearty bustled in. She got up so fast that she almost knocked over her chair, oddly ashamed to be caught eating.

"Good day, Doctor," the girl croaked, struggling up, and Lib raced to put another pillow behind her.

"Well, Anna. You've a good colour on you this afternoon."

Could the old man really be mistaking that hectic flush for health?

He was gentle with the girl, at least, examining her as he chitchatted about the unusually fine weather. He kept referring to Lib in a mollifying way as *our good Mrs. Wright here*.

"Anna just lost a tooth," said Lib.

"I see," he said. "Do you know what I've brought you, child, kindly lent by Sir Otway Blackett himself? A bath chair, on wheels, so you can take the air without over-tiring yourself."

"Thank you, Doctor."

After another minute, he took his leave, but Lib followed him to just outside the bedroom door.

"Fascinating," he murmured.

The word struck her dumb.

"The swelling of the limbs, the darkening skin, that blue tint to her lips and nails . . . I do believe Anna's altering at a systemic level," he confided in her ear. "It stands to reason that a constitution powered by something other than food would operate differently."

Lib had to look away so McBrearty wouldn't see her rage.

The baronet's chair was parked just inside the front door: a bulky thing in worn green velvet with three wheels and a folding hood. Kitty was standing at the long table, red eyes dripping as she chopped onions.

"But I still see no real, imminent risk in the absence of a plunging temperature or a constant pallor," McBrearty went on, rubbing his side-whiskers.

Pallor! Had the man studied medicine by reading French novels? "I've known men on their deathbeds look yellow or red more than white," Lib told him, her voice rising despite her efforts.

"Have you really? But Anna has no fits either, you

notice, and no delirium," he wound up. "It goes without saying, of course, that you must send for me if she shows any sign of serious exhaustion."

"She's already bedridden!"

"A few days' rest should do her a world of good. I wouldn't be surprised if she rallied by the end of the week."

So McBrearty was twice the idiot she'd thought him. "Doctor," said Lib, "if you won't call off this watch—"

The hint of threat in her tone made his face close up. He snapped, "For one thing, such a step would require the unanimous consent of the committee."

"Then ask them."

He spoke in Lib's ear, making her jump. "If I were to propose that we abort the watch on the grounds that it's jeopardizing the child's health by preventing some secret method of feeding, how would that look? It would be tantamount to a declaration that my old friends the O'Donnells are vile cheats!"

Lib whispered back, "How will it look if your old friends let their daughter die?"

McBrearty sucked in his breath. "Is this how Miss Nightingale taught you to speak to your superiors?"

"She taught me to fight for my patients' lives."

"Mrs. Wright, be so good as to let go of my sleeve."

Lib hadn't even realized she was gripping it.

The old man tugged it away and headed out of the cabin.

Kitty's mouth hung open.

When Lib hurried back into the bedroom, she found Anna asleep again, the snub nose letting out the lightest of snores. Still oddly lovely, despite everything wrong with her.

By rights Lib should have been packing her bag and asking for the driver with the jaunting car to take her to the station at Athlone. If she believed this watch to be indefensible, she should have no further part in it.

But she couldn't leave.

At half past ten that Tuesday night, at Ryan's, Lib tiptoed across the passage and tapped on William Byrne's door.

No answer.

What if he'd returned to Dublin by now, revolted by what Lib was letting happen to Anna O'Donnell? What if another guest came to the door; how could she explain herself? Suddenly she saw this as others would: a desperate woman outside a man's bedroom.

She'd wait to the count of three, and then —

The door was flung open. William Byrne, wild-haired and in his shirtsleeves. "You."

Lib blushed so fast it hurt her face. The only mercy was that he wasn't in his nightshirt. "Please excuse me."

"No, no. Is something the matter? Won't you—" His eyes veered to the bed and back.

His small chamber or hers, both equally impossible for a conversation. Lib couldn't ask him to come downstairs; that would attract even more attention at this time of night.

"I owe you an apology. You're entirely right about Anna's state," she whispered. "This watch is an abomin-ation." The word came out too loud; she'd bring Maggie Ryan running up the stairs.

Byrne nodded, without triumph.

"I've spoken to Sister Michael but she won't take a single step without the express permission of her masters," Lib told him. "I've urged Dr. McBrearty to halt the watch and concentrate on dissuading the child from starving herself, but he accused me of irrational panic."

"Thoroughly rational, I'd call it."

Byrne's calm voice made Lib feel slightly better. How necessary this man's conversation had become to her, and so quickly.

He leaned into the door frame. "Do you take a vow? Like that old Hippocratic oath for doctors, to heal and never kill?"

"Hypocrites' oath, more like!"

That made Byrne grin.

"We have none," she told him. "As a profession, nursing is in its infancy."

"Then for you it's a matter of conscience."

"Yes," said Lib. Only now did it sink in. Never mind *orders*; there was a deeper duty.

"And more than that, I think," he said. "You care for your nursling."

Byrne wouldn't have believed her if she'd denied it. "I suppose I'd be back in England by now if I didn't."

Better not to get too fond of things, Anna had said the other day. Miss N. warned against personal affection as much as she did against romance. Lib had been taught to watch for attachments in any form and root them out. So what had gone wrong this time?

He asked, "Have you ever put it to Anna plain and simple that she must eat?"

Lib struggled to remember. "I've certainly raised the issue. But on the whole I've tried to remain objective, neutral."

"The time for neutrality's passed," said Byrne.

Footsteps on the stairs; someone coming up.

Lib fled into her room and shut the door with the softest of pulls so as not to make a sound.

Hot cheeks, a thumping head, icy hands. If Maggie Ryan had caught the English nurse talking to the journalist so late at night, what would she have thought? And would she have been wrong?

Everybody was a repository of secrets.

Lib's state was horribly predictable. She'd have spotted the danger earlier if she hadn't been so preoccupied with Anna. Or perhaps she wouldn't have, because it was a new one for her. She'd never felt this for her husband, or for any other man.

How much younger than Lib was Byrne, with his zestful energy and his milky skin? She could hear Miss N. sum it up: *One of those yearnings that spring up like weeds in the dry soil of a nurse's life.* Had Lib no respect for herself at all?

She was groggy with fatigue, but it took her a long time to fall asleep.

Lib was on the green road again, hand in hand with a boy who was somehow a brother of hers. In the dream, the grass gave way to a wilderness of marsh, and the path grew faint. She couldn't keep up; she was mired in the wet tangle, and despite her protests this brother loosed her hand and went ahead of her. When she could no longer make out his calls or distinguish them from those of the birds overhead, she found he'd marked the way with crusts of bread. But faster than she could follow, the birds carried them away in their sharp mouths. Now there was no sign of a path at all, and Lib was alone.

On Wednesday morning, Lib's face looked haggard in the mirror.

She got to the cabin before five. The bath chair had been shifted outside the cabin door, its velvet damp with dew.

She found Anna sunk in sleep, her face scored with pillow creases. The chamber pot held only a blackish trickle.

"Mrs. Wright," Sister Michael began, as if to justify herself.

Lib looked her in the eye.

The nun hesitated, then went out without another word.

In the night, she'd decided on her tactics. She'd choose the weapon most likely to shake the girl: Holy Writ. She took the whole stack of Anna's pious volumes into her lap now and started skimming them, marking passages with strips torn out of the back page of her memorandum book.

When the girl woke a little later, Lib wasn't ready yet, so she put the books back in the treasure box. "I have a riddle for you."

Anna managed a smile and a nod.

Lib cleared her throat.

I've seen you where you never were,
And where you never will be,

And yet you in that very same place
May still be seen by me.

"A mirror," said Anna almost at once.

"You're getting too clever," Lib told her. "I'm running out of riddles." On impulse, she held the hand mirror up to Anna's face.

The child flinched. Then considered her reflection steadily.

"See what you look like these days?" asked Lib.

"I see," said Anna. And she crossed herself and clambered out of bed.

But she was wobbling so much that Lib made her sit down right away. "Let me change your nightdress." She took the fresh one out of the drawer.

The child struggled with the tiny buttons, so Lib had to undo them. Lifting the nightdress over Anna's head, she sucked in her breath at the extent of the brown patches on the skin, the reddish-blue spots that were like a scattering of coins now. New bruises too, in odd places, as if invisible assailants had been beating the girl in the night.

When Anna was dressed and wrapped in two shawls to stop her shivering, Lib prevailed on her to take a spoonful of water. "Another tick, please, Kitty," she called from the door.

The maid was elbow-deep in a bucket of dishes. "We've no others, but the colleen's welcome to mine."

"What will you do?"

"I'll find something by bedtime. It doesn't matter." Kitty's tone was desolate.

Lib hesitated. "Very well, then. Could I have something soft, too, to put on top?"

The maid wiped her eyebrow with a scarlet forearm. "A blanket?"

"Softer than that," said Lib.

She pulled the three blankets off the bed and shook them so hard they made a dull slap. *Piled all the blankets in the house on his bed,* Rosaleen O'Donnell had said. This must have been Pat's bed, it occurred to Lib; there was no other except in the outshot where the parents slept. She ripped off the grimy bottom sheet, baring the tick. Her eyes traced the indelible stains. So Pat had died right here, cooling in his little sister's warm grip.

In the chair, Anna seemed folded up into almost nothing, like the Limerick gloves in their walnut shell. Lib heard voices arguing in the kitchen.

Rosaleen O'Donnell bustled in a quarter of an hour later with Kitty's tick as well as a sheepskin she'd borrowed from the Corcorans. "Quiet this morning, sleepyhead?" She held her daughter's misshapen hands in hers.

How could this woman think *sleepy* was the word for such lethargy? Lib wondered. Couldn't she see that Anna was melting away like a halfpenny taper?

"Ah, well. A mother understands what a child doesn't say, as the proverb has it. Here's Dadda now."

"Good morning, pet," said Malachy from the doorway.

Anna cleared her throat. "Good morning, Dadda."

He came over to stroke her hair. "How are you today?"

"Well enough," she told him.

He nodded as if convinced.

The poor lived for the day, was that it? Lib wondered.

Lacking control over their circumstances, they learned not to borrow trouble by looking any farther down the road?

Or else this pair of criminals knew exactly what they were doing to their daughter.

When they'd left, Lib made the bed again, with the two mattresses and then the sheepskin under the bottom sheet. "Hop back in now and rest some more."

Hop: a ludicrous word for the way Anna was crawling into bed.

"Soft," the girl murmured, patting the spongy surface.

"It's to prevent bedsores," Lib explained.

"How did you begin again, Mrs. Lib?" The words came low and gravelly.

Lib put her head to one side.

"When you were widowed. *A whole new life,* you said."

She was ruefully impressed that the girl could rise above her own suffering and take an interest in Lib's past. "There was a dreadful war in the east, and I wanted to help the sick and wounded."

"And did you?"

Men had spewed, soiled, sprayed, seeped, died. Lib's men, those Miss N. had assigned to her. They'd died sometimes in her arms but more often while she was obliged to be in another room stirring gruel or folding bandages. "I believe I helped some of them. Somewhat." Lib had been there, at least. She'd tried. How much did that count? "My teacher said this was the kingdom of hell, and it was our job to haul it a little closer to heaven."

Anna nodded, as if that went without saying.

Wednesday, August 17, 7:49 a.m., Lib noted down. *Tenth day of watch.*

Pulse: 109 beats per minute.
Lungs: 22 breaths per minute.
Unable to walk.

She took out the books again and worked through them until she had what she needed. Lib expected Anna to ask her what she was doing, but no. The girl lay still, eyes on the dust motes dancing in the rays of morning light.

"Would you like another riddle?" asked Lib at last.

"Oh yes."

Two bodies have I,
Though both joined in one.
The stiller I stand,
The faster I run.

" 'The stiller I stand,' " repeated Anna in a murmur. " 'Two bodies.' "

Lib nodded, waited. "Do you give up?"

"Just a minute."

Lib eyed the second hand of her watch going around. "No answer?"

Anna shook her head.

"An hourglass," said Lib. "Time falling like sand through the glass, and nothing can slow it."

The child looked back at Lib, unshaken.

Lib drew her chair very close to the bed. Time for

battle. "Anna. You've convinced yourself that God has chosen you, out of all the people in the world, not to eat?"

Anna took a breath to speak.

"Hear me out, please. These holy books of yours, they're full of instructions to the contrary." Lib opened *The Garden of the Soul* and found the line she'd marked. *"Look upon your meat and drink as medicines, necessary for your health.* Or here, in the Psalms." She flipped to the right page. *"I am smitten as grass, and my heart is withered, because I forgot to eat my bread.* And what about this: *Eat, and drink, and be merry?* Or this line that I hear you say all the time: *Give us this day our daily bread."*

"Not actual bread," muttered Anna.

"It's actual bread that an actual child needs," Lib told her. "Jesus shared the loaves and fishes with the five thousand, didn't he?"

Anna swallowed slowly, as if she had a stone in her throat. "He was merciful because they were weak."

"Because they were human, you mean. He didn't say, *Ignore your stomachs and keep listening while I preach.* He gave them dinner." Lib's voice shook with wrath. "At the Last Supper he broke bread with his followers, didn't he? What did he tell them, what were the exact words?"

Very low. *"Take ye and eat."*

"There!"

"Once he'd consecrated it, the bread wasn't bread anymore, it was *him,*" said Anna in a rush. "Like manna." She stroked the leather binding of the Psalms as if the book were a cat. "For months I was fed on manna from heaven."

"Anna!" Lib tugged the volume away from her, too

hard, and it thumped onto the floor, scattering its cargo of precious cards.

"What's all the commotion?" Rosaleen O'Donnell put her face around the door.

"Nothing," said Lib, on her knees, heart pounding as she snatched up the tiny pictures.

A terrible pause.

Lib wouldn't look up. She couldn't afford to meet the woman's eye in case her feelings showed.

"All right, pet?" Rosaleen asked her daughter.

"Yes, Mammy."

Why didn't Anna say the Englishwoman had thrown down her book and was bullying Anna to break her fast? Then the O'Donnells would no doubt lodge a complaint against Lib, and she'd be sent packing.

Anna said nothing else, and Rosaleen withdrew.

Once the two were alone again, Lib stood and put the book back in the child's lap, the cards in a small pile on top. "I'm sorry they're out of place."

"I know where they all go." Her thick fingers still deft, Anna tucked each one back where it belonged.

Lib reminded herself that she was quite prepared to lose this job. Hadn't William Byrne been cashiered at sixteen for the seditious truths he'd told about his famished countrymen? That had probably been the making of the man. Not so much the loss itself as his surviving it, realizing that it was possible to fail and start again.

Anna took a long breath, and Lib heard the faintest of crackles. Fluid in the lungs, she registered. Which meant there was little time left.

I've seen you where you never were, and where you never will be.

"Will you listen to me, please?" *Dear child,* she almost added, but that was the mother's soft language; Lib had to speak plainly. "You must see that you're getting worse."

Anna shook her head.

"Does this hurt?" Lib leaned down and pressed where the belly was roundest.

Agony shot across the child's face.

"I'm sorry," said Lib, only half sincerely. She tugged Anna's cap off. "Look how much hair you're losing every day."

"The very hairs of your head are all numbered," the girl whispered.

Science was the most magical force Lib knew. If anything could break the spell that held this girl — "The body's a kind of engine," she began, trying to summon up Miss N.'s most teacherly tone. "Digestion is the burning of fuel. Denied fuel, the body will destroy its own tissues." She sat down and laid her palm on Anna's belly again, gently this time. "This is the stove. The food you had the year you were ten, the amount you grew that year as a consequence — it's all been used up in the past four months. Think of what you ate at nine, at eight. Burnt to cinders already." Time rolled backwards sickeningly. "When you were seven, six, five. Every meal your father toiled to put on the table, every bite your mother cooked, is being consumed now by the desperate fire inside you." Anna at four, three, before she'd formed her first sentence. At two, toddling; one. All the way back to her first day, her first suck of mother's milk. "But the engine can't run much longer without proper fuel, do you see?"

Anna's calm was a layer of unbreakable crystal.

"It's not just that there's less of you every day," Lib told her, "it's that all your workings are winding down, beginning to seize up."

"I'm not a machine."

"*Like* a machine, that's all I mean. No insult to your Creator," Lib told her. "Think of him as the most ingenious of engineers."

Anna shook her head. "I'm his child."

"Could I speak to you in the kitchen, Mrs. Wright?" Rosaleen O'Donnell, in the doorway, long arms akimbo.

How much had the woman heard? "This is not a convenient time."

"I must insist, ma'am."

Lib stood up with a short sigh.

She'd be breaking the rule about leaving Anna alone in the room, but what did it matter now? She couldn't imagine the child leaning out of bed to scrape crumbs out of some hidey-hole, and, frankly, if that were to happen, Lib would be glad. *Cheat me, hoodwink me, so long as you eat.*

She shut the door behind her so Anna wouldn't hear a word.

Rosaleen O'Donnell was alone, looking out the smallest kitchen window. She turned and brandished a newspaper. "John Flynn got hold of this in Mullingar this morning."

Lib was taken aback. So this wasn't about the things she'd been saying to the girl just now. She looked at the paper, folded open to an inside page. The banner at the top identified it as the *Irish Times,* and her eye immediately picked out Byrne's article reporting on Anna's decline. *A chance and fleeting encounter with the Fasting Girl herself . . .*

"How did this blaggard come to have a chance encounter with my child, may I ask?" demanded Rosaleen.

Lib weighed how much to admit.

"And where did he get this nonsense about her being *in grave danger?* I caught Kitty bawling into her apron this morning because she heard you say something to the doctor about a *deathbed.*"

Lib decided to go on the attack. "What would you call it, Mrs. O'Donnell?"

"The cheek of you!"

"Have you looked at your daughter lately?"

"Oh, 'tis you who knows better than the girl's own physician, is it? You, who couldn't even tell a dead child from a living one?" Rosaleen scoffed, gesturing at the photograph on the mantel.

That stung. "McBrearty imagines your daughter to be turning into something like a lizard. This is the dotard you're trusting with her life."

The woman's fists were clenched, white knobs in red. "If you hadn't been appointed by the committee, I'd have you out of my house this minute."

"What, so that Anna can die all the faster?"

Rosaleen O'Donnell rushed at her.

Startled, Lib stepped aside to evade the blow.

"You know nothing about us!" the woman roared.

"I know Anna's too famished to get out of bed."

"If the child's . . . struggling somewhat, 'tis only from the nervous strain of being watched like a prisoner."

Lib snorted. She moved in closer to the woman, her whole body stiff. "What kind of mother would let it come to this?"

Rosaleen O'Donnell did the last thing Lib was expecting: she burst into tears.

Lib stared at her.

"Didn't I try my best?" the woman wailed, water scudding down the lines of her face. "Sure isn't she flesh of my flesh, my last hope? Didn't I bring her into the world and rear her tenderly, and didn't I feed her as long as she'd let me?"

For a moment Lib glimpsed how it must have been. That day in spring when the O'Donnells' good little girl had turned eleven — and then, with no explanation, had refused to eat another bite. For her parents, perhaps it had been a horror as overwhelming as the illness that had carried off their boy the autumn before. The only way Rosaleen O'Donnell could have made sense of these cataclysms was to convince herself that they were part of God's plan. "Mrs. O'Donnell," she began, "let me assure you—"

But the woman fled, ducking into the little outshot behind the sack curtain.

Lib went back to the bedroom, shaking. It confused her, to feel such sympathy for a woman she loathed.

Anna showed no sign of having heard the quarrel. She lay propped up on pillows, absorbed in her holy cards.

Lib tried to collect herself. She looked over Anna's shoulder at the picture of the girl floating on a cross-shaped raft. "The sea's quite a different thing from a river, you know."

"Bigger," said Anna. She touched one fingertip to the card as if to feel the wet.

"Infinitely bigger," Lib told the girl, "and while a river moves only one way, the sea seems to breathe, in and out, in and out."

Anna inhaled, straining to fill her lungs.

Lib checked her watch: almost time. *Noon* was all she'd put on the note that she'd slipped under Byrne's door before dawn. She didn't like the look of those slate-grey clouds, but it couldn't be helped. Besides, Irish weather turned every quarter of an hour.

At exactly twelve, the clamour of the Angelus went up in the kitchen. She was counting on it as a distraction. "Shall we take a little walk, Anna?"

Rosaleen O'Donnell and the maid were on their knees — *"The angel of the Lord declared unto Mary"* — as Lib hurried by to collect the invalid chair from outside the front door. *"Now and at the hour of our death, amen."*

She pushed it through the kitchen, back wheel squeaking.

Anna had managed to clamber out of bed and kneel beside it. *"Be it done to me according to thy word,"* she was chanting. Lib covered the chair with one blanket, then helped the girl into it and added three more, tucking in her thickened feet. She wheeled her rapidly past the praying adults and out the door.

The summer was beginning to turn already; some of those yellow starry flowers on their long stalks were darkening to bronze. A mass of cloud split as if along a seam, and light spilled through. "Here's the sun," croaked Anna, head back against the padding.

Down the track Lib hurried, bumping the chair through ruts and over stones. She turned onto the lane and there was William Byrne, just a few feet away.

He didn't smile. "Unconscious?"

Only now did Lib see that Anna had slid down in the chair and was lying with her head to one side. She flicked the girl's cheek lightly and the nearer eyelid flickered, to her relief. "Just dozing," she told him.

Byrne had no small talk today. "Well, have your arguments done any good?"

"They roll over her like water," she admitted, turning the chair away from the village and pushing it along to keep the girl asleep. "This fast, it's Anna's rock. Her daily task, her vocation."

He nodded grimly. "If she keeps going downhill so quickly—"

What was coming?

Byrne's eyes were dark, almost navy blue. "Will you — would you consider forcing her?"

Lib made herself picture the procedure: holding Anna down, pushing a tube down her throat, and dosing her. She looked up, met his burning gaze. "I don't think I could. It's not a matter of squeamishness," she assured him.

"I know what it would cost you."

That wasn't it either, or not all of it. She couldn't explain.

They walked for a minute; two. It struck Lib that the

three of them could have been mistaken for a family taking the air.

Byrne began again, in a brisker tone. "Well, it turns out the padre's not behind the hoax after all."

"Mr. Thaddeus? How can you be sure?"

"O'Flaherty the schoolteacher says it may have been McBrearty who talked them all into forming this committee, but it was the priest who insisted they mount a formal guard on the girl, with seasoned nurses."

Lib puzzled over that. Byrne was right; why would a guilty man have wanted Anna watched? Perhaps she'd been too quick to go along with Byrne's suspicions of Mr. Thaddeus because of her wariness of priests.

"Also I found out more about this mission Anna mentioned," said Byrne. "Last spring, Redemptorists from Belgium swooped down—"

"Redemptorists?"

"Missionary priests. The pope sends them out all over Christendom, like bloodhounds, to round up the faithful and sniff out unorthodoxy. They hammer the rules into the heads of country folk, put the fear of God back into their souls," he told her. "So. For three weeks, thrice daily, these Redemptorists harrowed the bog men in these parts." His finger swung across the motley-coloured land. "According to Maggie Ryan, one sermon was a real barnstormer: hellfire and brimstone raining down, children screeching, and such urgent queues for confession afterwards that a fellow fell under the crowd and got his ribs stove in. The mission wound up with a massive Quarantore—"

"A what?" asked Lib, lost again.

"Forty hours, it means — the length of time Our Lord spent in the tomb." Byrne put on a heavy brogue. "Do you know nothing, you heathen?"

That made her smile.

"For forty hours the Blessed Sacrament was exposed in all the chapels within walking distance, with a mob of the faithful shoving along the lanes to prostrate themselves before it. The whole hullabaloo culminated in the confirmation of all eligible boys and girls."

"Including Anna," Lib guessed.

"The day before her eleventh birthday."

Confirmation: the moment of decision. *The end of being a child* was how Anna had described it. Placed on her tongue, the sacred Host — her God in the guise of a little disc of bread. But how could she have formed the dire resolution to make that her last meal? Could she have misunderstood something the foreign priests had said as they wound the crowd up to a fever pitch?

Lib felt so nauseated, she had to stop for a moment and lean on the bath chair's leather handles. "What was it about, the sermon that caused such a riot, did you learn?"

"Oh, fornication, what else?"

The word made Lib angle her face away.

"Is that an eagle?" The thin voice startled them.

"Where?" Byrne asked Anna.

"Away up there, over the green road."

"I think not," he told the child, "just the king of all crows."

"I walked that so-called green road the other day," said Lib, making conversation. "A long and rambling waste of time."

"An English invention, as it happens," said Byrne.

She looked sideways at him. Was this one of his jokes?

"It was the winter of '47, when Ireland was chest-deep in snow for the first time in her history. Because charity was considered *corrupting*," he said ironically, "the starving were invited to go on the Public Works instead. In these parts, that meant building a road from nowhere to nowhere."

Lib frowned at him, jerking her head towards the girl.

"Oh, I'm sure she's heard all the stories." But he bent to look at Anna.

Asleep again, head limp in the corner of the chair. Lib tucked the loosening blankets around her.

"So the men picked stones out of the ground and hammered them apart for a pittance a basket," he went on in a low voice, "while the women toted the baskets and fitted the pieces together. The children—"

"Mr. Byrne," Lib protested.

"You wanted to know about the road," he reminded her.

Did he resent her for the mere fact of her being English? she wondered. If he knew the feelings she was harbouring for him, would he respond with contempt? Pity, even? Pity would be worse.

"But I'll be brief. Whoever was struck down by cold or hunger or fever and didn't get up was buried by the verge, in a sack, just a couple of inches under."

Lib thought of her boots going along the soft, flowered edge of the green road. Bog never forgot; it kept things *in a remarkable state of preservation*. "No more," she begged, "please."

A merciful silence between them, at last.

Anna twitched, and turned her face against the thread-bare velvet. One drop of rain, then another. Lib clawed at the black canopy of the bath chair with its rusty hinges, and Byrne helped her unfold it over the sleeping child a moment before the rain slammed down.

She couldn't sleep in her room at Ryan's, couldn't read, couldn't do anything but fret. She knew she should have some supper, but her throat felt sealed up.

At midnight the lamp was burning low on Anna's dresser, and the child was a handful of dark hair across the pillow, her body hardly interrupting the plane of the blankets. All evening Lib had talked to the child — *at* the child — until she was hoarse.

Now she sat close to the bed making herself think of a tube. A very narrow, flexible, greased one, no wider than a straw, snaking between the girl's lips, so slowly, so very gently that Anna might possibly even sleep on. Lib imagined trickling fresh milk down that tube into the child's stomach, just a little at a time.

Because what if Anna's obsession was the *result* of her fast as much as its cause? After all, who could think straight on an empty stomach? Perhaps, paradoxically, the child could learn to feel normal hunger again only once she had some food in her. If Lib tube-fed Anna, really, she'd be fortifying the girl. Tugging Anna back from the brink, giving her time to come to her senses. It wouldn't be using force so much as taking responsibility; Nurse Wright, alone out of all the grown-ups, brave enough to do what was needed to save Anna O'Donnell from herself.

Lib's teeth pressed together so hard they ached.

Didn't adults often do painful things to children for their own good? Or nurses to patients? Hadn't Lib debrided burns and picked shrapnel out of wounds, dragging more than a few patients back into the land of the living by rough means? And after all, lunatics and prisoners survived force-feeding several times a day.

She pictured Anna waking, beginning to struggle, choking, retching, her eyes wet with betrayal. Lib holding the girl's small nose, pressing her head down on the pillow. *Lie still, my dear. Let me. You must.* Pushing in the tube, inexorable.

No! So loud in her head, Lib thought for a moment she'd shouted it.

It wouldn't work. That was what she should have told Byrne this afternoon. Physiologically, yes, she supposed slop forced down Anna's throat would supply her with energy, but it wouldn't keep her alive. If anything, it would speed her withdrawal from the world. Crack her spirit.

Lib counted the breaths for a full minute on her watch. Twenty-five, too many, dangerously fast. But still so perfectly regular. For all the thinning hair, the dun patches, the sore at the corner of the mouth, Anna was beautiful as any sleeping child.

For months I was fed on manna from heaven. That's what she'd said this morning. *I live on manna from heaven,* she'd told her Spiritualist visitors last week. But today, Lib noticed, it had come out differently, in a wistful past tense: *For months I was fed on manna from heaven.*

Unless Lib had heard it wrong? Not *for* months. *Four* months, was that it? *Four months I was fed on manna from heaven.* Anna had started her fast four months ago, in April, and subsisted on manna — whatever secret means of nourishment she meant by that — until the arrival of the nurses.

But no, this made no sense, because then she should have begun to show the effects of a complete fast no more than a couple of days later. Lib hadn't noticed any such deterioration until Byrne had alerted her to it on Monday of this second week. Could a child really have gone seven days before flagging?

Lib flicked back through her memorandum book now, a series of telegraphic dispatches from a distant battlefront. Every day during the first week had been much the same until —

Refused mother's greeting.

She stared at the neat words. Saturday morning, six days into the watch. Not a medical notation at all; Lib had jotted it down simply because it was an unexplained change in the child's behaviour.

How could she have been so blind?

Not just a greeting twice a day; an embrace in which the big bony woman's frame had blocked the child's face from view. A kiss like that of a great bird feeding her nestling.

Lib broke Miss N.'s rule and shook the girl awake.

Anna blinked, cringing away from the harsh light of the lamp.

Lib whispered, "When you were fed on manna, who—" Not *who gave it to you,* because Anna would say that manna came from God. "Who brought it to you?"

261

She was expecting resistance, denial. Some elaborate cover story about angels.

"Mammy," murmured Anna.

Had the girl always been ready to answer so candidly the moment she was asked? If only Lib had been a little less contemptuous of pious legends, she might have paid more attention to what the child was trying to tell her.

She remembered the way Rosaleen O'Donnell had sidled in for the permitted embrace morning and evening, smiling but oddly silent. So full of chatter at other times, but not when she came to hug her daughter. Yes, Rosaleen always kept her mouth shut tight until after she'd bent down to wrap her whole body around Anna.

Lib moved closer to the small ear. "She passed it from her mouth to yours?"

"By a holy kiss," said Anna, nodding, with no sign of shame.

Fury shot through Lib's veins. So the mother had chewed food to pap in the kitchen, then fed Anna right in front of the nurses, making sport of them twice a day. "What does manna taste like?" she asked. "Milky, or porridge-like?"

"Like heaven," said Anna, as if the answer were obvious.

"She told you it was from heaven?"

Anna looked confused by the question. "That's what manna is."

"Does anyone else know? Kitty? Your father?"

"I don't think so. I've never spoken of it."

"Why?" asked Lib. "Did your mother forbid you? Threaten you?"

"It's private."

A secret exchange, too sacred to be put into words. Yes, Lib could imagine a woman of strong character persuading her little girl of that. Especially such a girl as Anna, growing up in a world of mysteries. The young placed such trust in the grown-ups into whose hands they were consigned. Had the feeding begun on Anna's eleventh birthday or perhaps developed gradually long before that? Was it a sort of sleight of hand, the mother reading the daughter the manna story from the Bible and confounding her with mystical obscurities? Or had both parties contributed something unspoken to the invention of this deadly game? After all, the girl was brighter than the mother, and better read. Families all had their peculiar ways that couldn't be discerned by outsiders.

"So why tell me?" Lib demanded.

"You're my friend."

The way the girl's chin tilted up then. It broke Lib's heart. "You don't take the manna anymore, do you? Not since Saturday."

"I don't need it," said Anna.

Didn't I feed her as long as she'd let me? Rosaleen had wailed. Lib had heard the woman's grief and remorse and still not understood. The mother had set Anna up on a pedestal to shine like a beacon to the world. She'd had every intention of keeping her daughter alive indefinitely with this covert supply of food. It was Anna who'd put an end to it, one week into the watch.

Had the child had any sense of what the consequence would be? Did she grasp it now?

"What your mother spat into your mouth" — Lib

spoke with deliberate crudity — "that was food from the kitchen. Those doses of mush are what's been keeping you alive all these months."

She paused for some reaction, but the child's eyes had gone unfocused.

Lib seized her thick wrists. "Your mother lied, don't you see? You need food like everyone else. There's nothing special about you." The words were coming out all wrong, a rain of abuse. "If you won't eat, child, you'll die."

Anna looked right at her, then nodded and smiled.

CHAPTER FIVE

Shift

shift
 a change, an alteration
 a period of working time
 an expedient, means to an end
 a movement, a beginning

Thursday came scorching, the August sky a terrible blue. When William Byrne walked into the dining room at noon, Lib was alone, staring into her soup. She looked up and tried to smile at him.

"How's Anna?" he asked, sitting down across from her, his knees against her skirt.

She couldn't answer.

He nodded at her bowl. "If you aren't sleeping, you need to keep up your strength."

The spoon made a metallic scraping when Lib lifted it. She brought it almost to her lips, then put it down with a small splash.

Byrne leaned over the table. "Tell me."

Lib pushed away her bowl. Watching the door for the Ryan girl, she explained about the *manna from heaven* delivered under cover of an embrace.

"Christ," he marvelled. "The audacity of the woman."

Oh, the relief of unburdening herself. "Bad enough that Rosaleen O'Donnell's been making her child subsist on two mouthfuls a day," said Lib. "But for the past five days,

Anna's refused to take the manna, and her mother hasn't said a word."

"I suppose she doesn't know how to speak up without condemning herself."

A qualm struck her. "You can't publish any of this, not yet."

"Why not?"

How could Byrne have to ask? "I'm aware that it's in the nature of your profession to broadcast everything," she snapped, "but what matters is saving the girl."

"I know that. And what of your profession? For all the time you've spent with Anna, how far have you got?"

Lib put her face in her hands.

"I'm sorry." Byrne grabbed her fingers. "I spoke out of frustration."

"It's perfectly true."

"Still, forgive me."

Lib slid her hand out of his, the skin still burning.

"Believe me," he said, "it's for Anna's sake that the hoax should be shouted to the four winds."

"But a public scandal won't do anything to make her eat!"

"How can you be sure?"

"Anna's quite alone in this now." Lib's voice lurched. "She seems to welcome the prospect of death."

Byrne thrust his curls out of his face. "But why?"

"Perhaps because your religion's filled her head with morbid nonsense."

"Perhaps because she's mistaken morbid nonsense for true religion!"

"I don't know why she's doing this," admitted Lib,

"except that it has something to do with missing her brother."

He frowned in puzzlement. "Have you told the nun about the manna yet?"

"There was no opportunity this morning."

"What about McBrearty?"

"I've told no one but you."

Byrne looked at Lib in a way that made her wish she hadn't blurted that out. "Well. I say you should share your discovery with the whole committee tonight."

"Tonight?" she echoed, confused.

"Haven't you and Sister been called in? At ten o'clock, they're gathering in the back room here" — he jerked his head towards the peeling wallpaper — "at the doctor's behest."

Perhaps McBrearty had taken in something of what Lib had told him yesterday after all. "No," she said, sardonic, "we're only the nurses, why would they want to hear from us?" She leaned her chin on her knotted hands. "Perhaps if I went to him now and told him about the manna trick—"

Byrne shook his head. "Better to march into the meeting and announce to the whole committee that you've succeeded in the task for which they hired you."

Success? It felt more like a hopeless failure. "But how will that help Anna?"

His hands flailed. "Once the watch is over, she'll have room — time — out of the public eye. A chance to change her mind."

"She's not keeping up her fast to impress the readers of

the *Irish Times,*" Lib told him. "It's between her and your greedy God."

"Don't blame him for the follies of his followers. All he asks us to do is live."

The two of them eyed each other.

Then a grin lit Byrne's face. "D'you know, I've never met a woman — a person — quite as blasphemous as you."

As he watched Lib, a slow heat spread right through her.

Sun in her eyes. Lib's uniform was glued to her sides already. By the time she reached the cabin, she'd decided she had to go to this committee meeting tonight, invited or not.

Silence as she let herself in the door. Rosaleen O'Donnell and the maid were plucking a scrawny chicken at the long table. Had they been working in tense quiet or had they been talking — perhaps about the English nurse — until they'd heard her come in?

"Good day," said Lib.

"Good day," they both said, eyes on the carcass.

Lib looked at Rosaleen O'Donnell's long back and thought: *I've found you out, you fiend.* There was almost a sweetness to it, this sense of holding in her hand the one weapon that could demolish the woman's shoddy imposture.

Not yet, though. There'd be no going back from that point; if Rosaleen threw her out of the cabin, Lib would have no more chances to change Anna's mind.

In the bedroom, the child lay curled up, facing the

window, ribs rising and falling. Her cracked mouth gulped air. Nothing at all in the chamber pot.

The nun's face was drawn. *Worse,* she mouthed as she gathered her cloak and bag.

Lib put a hand on her arm to stop her from leaving. "Anna confessed," she said in the nun's ear, barely voicing the words.

"To the priest?"

"To me. Until last Saturday, the mother was feeding her chewed-up food under cover of kisses and convincing the girl that it was manna."

Sister Michael blanched, and crossed herself.

"The committee will be at Ryan's at ten this evening," Lib went on, "and we must speak to them."

"Has Dr. McBrearty said so?"

Lib was tempted to lie. Instead she said, "The man's delusional. He thinks Anna's turning cold-blooded! No, we must make our report to the rest of the committee."

"On Sunday, as instructed."

"Three more days is too long! Anna may not last," she whispered, "and you know it."

The nun averted her face, big eyes blinking.

"I'll do the talking, but you must stand with me."

Haltingly: "My place is here."

"Surely you can find someone else to watch Anna for an hour," said Lib. "The Ryan girl, even."

The nun shook her head.

"Instead of spying on Anna, we should all be doing everything we can to induce her to eat. To live."

The smoothly wimpled head kept swinging like a bell. "Those aren't our orders. 'Tis all dreadfully sad, but—"

"Sad?" Lib's voice too loud, scathing. "Is that the word?"

Sister Michael's face crumpled in on itself.

"Good nurses follow rules," Lib growled, "but the best know when to break them."

The nun fled from the room.

Lib took a long, ragged breath and sat down beside Anna.

When the child woke, her heartbeat was like a violin string vibrating just under the skin. *Thursday, August 18, 1:03 p.m. Pulse at 129, thready,* Lib noted down, her hand as legible as ever. *Straining for breath.*

She called Kitty in and told her to gather all the pillows in the house.

Kitty stared, then rushed off to do it.

Lib banked them up behind Anna so the girl could lie almost upright, which seemed to ease her breathing a little.

"Thou that liftest me up from the gates," murmured Anna, eyes shut. *"Deliver me out of the hands of my enemies."*

How gladly Lib would have done that if she'd known how, delivered Anna, set her free from her bonds. The way a message was delivered, or a blow, or a baby. "More water?" She offered the spoon.

Anna's eyelids flickered but didn't open; she shook her head. *"Be it done to me."*

"You may not feel thirst, but you need to drink all the same."

The lips clung together stickily as they opened and let in a spoonful of water.

It would be easier to talk frankly outdoors. "Would you like to go out in the chair again? It's a lovely afternoon."

"No, thank you, Mrs. Lib."

Lib put that down too: *Too weak to be wheeled in chair.* Her memorandum book wasn't just to supplement her memory anymore. It was evidence of a crime.

"This boat's big enough for me," mumbled Anna.

Was that a whimsical metaphor for the bed, the child's one inheritance from her brother? Or was her brain becoming affected by her fast? Lib wrote, *Slight confusion?* Then it struck her that perhaps she'd misheard *bed,* slurred, as *boat.*

"Anna." She took one of the bloated hands between her two. Cold, like a china doll's. "You know of the sin called self-murder."

The hazel-brown eyes opened, but angled away from her.

"Let me read you something from *The Examination of Conscience,*" said Lib, snatching up the missal and finding the page she'd marked yesterday. *"Have you done anything to shorten your life, or to hasten death? Have you desired your own death, through passion or impatience?"*

Anna shook her head. Whispering: *"I will fly and be at rest."*

"Are you sure of that? Don't suicides go to hell?" Lib forced herself on. "You won't be buried with Pat, even, but outside the wall of the churchyard."

Anna turned her cheek to her pillow like a small child with an earache.

Lib thought of the first riddle she'd ever told the girl:

I neither am nor can be seen. She leaned closer and whispered: "Why are you trying to die?"

"To give myself." Anna corrected her instead of denying it. She began muttering her Dorothy prayer again, over and over: "*I adore thee, O most precious cross, adorned by the tender, delicate and venerable members of Jesus my Saviour, sprinkled and stained with his precious blood.*"

By the last light of the afternoon, Lib helped the child into a chair so she could air the bedclothes and smoothen the sheets. Anna sat with her knees up under her chin. She hobbled to the pot but produced only a dark drip. Then back to bed, moving like an old woman, the old woman she'd never grow up to be.

Lib paced as the child dozed. Nothing to do but call for more hot bricks, because all the heat of the day couldn't stop Anna's shivers.

The slavey's eyes were rimmed with scarlet a quarter of an hour later when she brought four bricks in — still ashy from the fire — and tucked them under Anna's blankets. The child was deep in slumber now.

"Kitty," said Lib, before she knew she was going to speak. Her pulse hammered. If she was wrong — if the maid was as bad as Mrs. O'Donnell and in on the plot with her — then this attempt would do more harm than good. How to begin? Not with accusation, or even information. Compassion — that's what Lib needed to rouse in the young woman. "Your cousin's dying."

Water brimmed in Kitty's eyes at once.

"All God's children need to eat," Lib told her. She lowered her voice further. "Until a few days ago, Anna's been kept alive by means of a wicked trick, a criminal swindle

274

practiced on the whole world." She regretted *criminal*, because fear was flaring in the maid's eyes now. "Do you know what I'm about to tell you?"

"Sure how could I know that?" asked Kitty, with the look of a rabbit scenting a fox.

"Your mistress" — *Aunt?* Lib wondered now. *Cousin of some sort?* — "Mrs. O'Donnell, has been feeding the child from her own mouth, pretending to kiss her, you see?" It struck her that Kitty might blame the girl. "In her innocence, Anna thought she was receiving holy manna from heaven."

The wide eyes narrowed all of a sudden. A guttural sound.

Lib leaned forward. "What did you say?"

No answer.

"It must be a shock, I know—"

"You!" No mistaking the syllable this time, or the fury contorting the maid's face.

"I'm telling you so you can help me save your little cousin's life."

A pair of hard hands seized her face, then clamped over her mouth. "Shut your lying gob."

Lib staggered backwards.

"Like a sickness you came into this house, spreading your poison. Godless, heartless, have you no shame?"

The child in the bed shifted then, as if disturbed by the voices, and both women froze.

Kitty dropped her arms. Took two steps to the bed and bent down, planted the lightest of kisses on Anna's temple. When she straightened up, her face was striped with tears.

The door banged behind her.

You tried, Lib reminded herself, standing very still.

This time she couldn't tell what she'd done wrong. Perhaps it was inevitable that Kitty would have blindly sided with the O'Donnells; they were all she had in the world — family, home, the only means of earning her crust.

Better to have tried than to have done nothing? Better for Lib's conscience, she supposed; for the starving girl, it made no difference.

She threw out the shrunken flowers and tidied the missal back into its box.

Then on an impulse she took it out again and leafed through it once more, looking for the Dorothy prayer. Out of all the formulae there were, why did Anna recite that one thirty-three times a day?

Here it was — the Good Friday Prayer for the Holy Souls as Revealed to Saint Bridget. The text told Lib nothing new: *I adore thee, O most precious cross, adorned by the tender, delicate and venerable members of Jesus my Saviour, sprinkled and stained with his precious blood.* She squinted at the notes in minute print below. *If said thirty-three times fasting on a Friday three souls will be released from purgatory, but if on Good Friday the harvest will be thirty-three souls.* An Easter bonus, multiplying the reward by eleven. Lib was about to shut the book when she belatedly registered one word: *fasting.*

If said thirty-three times fasting.

"Anna." She bent and touched the girl's cheek. "Anna!"

She blinked up at Lib.

"Your prayer, *I adore thee, O most precious cross.* Is that why you won't eat?"

Anna's smile was the oddest thing: joyful, with a dark edge.

At last, thought Lib, *at last.* But there was no satisfaction in it, only a heavy grief.

"Did he tell you?" asked Anna.

"Who?"

Anna pointed at the ceiling.

"No," said Lib, "I guessed it."

"When we guess," said the girl, "that's God telling us things."

"You're trying to get your brother into heaven."

Anna nodded with a child's certainty. "If I say the prayer, fasting, thirty-three times every day—"

"Anna," Lib wailed. "To say it fasting — I'm sure that means skipping only *one* meal on *one* Friday to save three souls, or thirty-three if it's Good Friday." Why was she granting these absurd figures credence by repeating them like something from a clerk's ledger? "The book never says to stop eating entirely."

"Souls need a lot of cleaning." Anna's eyes glistened. "Nothing's impossible to God, though, so I won't give up, I'll just keep saying the prayer and begging him to fetch Pat into heaven."

"But your fasting—"

"That's to make amends." She strained for breath.

"I've never heard of such a ludicrous and horrible bargain," Lib told her.

"Our Heavenly Father doesn't make bargains," said Anna reprovingly. "He hasn't promised me anything. But maybe he'll have mercy on Pat. And on me too, even," she added. "Then Pat and I can be together again. Sister and brother."

There was a weird plausibility to the scheme, a sort of dream logic that would make sense to an eleven-year-old. "Live first," Lib urged her. "Pat will wait."

"He's waited nine months already, burning." Cheeks still chalk-dry, Anna let out a sob.

Had the child not enough liquid left to make tears anymore? Lib wondered. "Think how your father and mother would miss you" was all she could say. Had Rosaleen O'Donnell had any idea where it would lead when she began the awful game of make-believe?

Anna's face twisted. "They'll know Pat and I are safe above." She corrected herself: "If 'tis God's will."

"In the wet ground, that's where you'll be," said Lib, her heel thumping the packed-earth floor.

"That's only the body," said the girl with a hint of scorn. "The soul just—" She wriggled.

"What? What does it do?"

"Drops the body, like an old coat."

It occurred to Lib that she was the only one in the world who knew for sure that this child meant to die. It was like a leaden cape on Lib's shoulders.

"Your body — every body is a marvel. A wonder of creation." She fumbled for the right words; this was a foreign language. No use speaking of pleasure or happiness to this tiny zealot, only duty. What was it Byrne had said? "The day you first opened your eyes, Anna, God asked just one thing: that you live."

Anna looked back at her.

"I've seen infants born dead. Others who've suffered

for weeks or months before they've given up the fight," said Lib, her voice cracking despite herself, "and no rhyme or reason to it."

"His plan," wheezed Anna.

"Very well, then; it must also be his plan for you to survive." Lib pictured the wide famine grave in the churchyard. "Hundreds of thousands — perhaps millions of your compatriots died when you were a tiny child. That means it's your sacred task to keep going. To keep breathing, to eat like the rest of us, to do the daily work of living."

She could see only the tiniest shift of the child's jaw, saying no, always no.

A vast weariness took hold of Lib. She drank half a glass of water, sat down, and stared into space.

At eight that evening, when Malachy O'Donnell came in to say good night, Anna was fast asleep. He hovered, patches of sweat under his arms.

With a great effort, Lib roused herself. As he moved towards the door, she seized her chance. "I must tell you, Mr. O'Donnell," she whispered, "your daughter doesn't have long."

Terror glinted in his eyes. "The doctor said—"

"He's wrong. Her heart's racing, her temperature's dropping, and her lungs are filling up with fluid."

"The creature!" He stared down at the small body outlined by the blankets.

It was on the tip of Lib's tongue now to blurt out the whole story of the manna. But it was a grave thing to come between man and wife, and risky, because how could Malachy possibly take the Englishwoman's word against Rosaleen's? If Kitty had been outraged by Lib's accusation

279

against her mistress, wouldn't Malachy be also? After all, Lib had no hard evidence. She couldn't bring herself to wake Anna and try to force her to repeat the story to her father, and besides, she very much doubted she'd succeed.

No. What mattered was not the truth, but Anna. Stick to what Malachy could see for himself, now Lib had ripped the veil off. Tell him just enough to wake the protective father in him. "Anna means to die," she said, "in hopes of getting your son out of purgatory."

"What?" Wildly.

"As a sort of exchange," said Lib. Was she rendering it right, this nightmarish story? "A sacrifice."

"God save us," muttered Malachy.

"When she wakes, won't you tell her she's wrong?"

His big hand was covering his face. His words were muffled.

"I beg your pardon?"

"Sure there's no telling Anna."

"Don't be absurd. She's a child," Lib pointed out. "Your child."

"She has twice my wits and more," said Malachy. "I don't know where we got her."

"Well, you're going to lose her if you don't act fast. Be firm with her. Be her father."

"Only her earthly one," said Malachy, mournful. "He's the only one she'll hear," he said, jerking his head towards the sky.

The nun was in the doorway; nine o'clock. "Good evening, Mrs. Wright."

Malachy hurried out, leaving Lib baffled. These people! Only when she was putting on her cape did she remember the wretched meeting. "I mean to address the committee tonight," she reminded Sister Michael.

A nod. The nun hadn't brought any substitute with her to the cabin, Lib realized, which meant she was adamant in her refusal to come to the meeting.

"A pot of boiling water for steam might ease Anna's breathing," said Lib on her way out.

She waited in her upstairs room, belly clenched. It was not just nerves at the thought of barging into a meeting of her employers but an awful ambivalence. If Lib persuaded the committee that the purpose of the watch had been accomplished — told them all about the manna hoax — then they might very well discharge Lib on the spot, with their thanks. In which case, she doubted she'd even get a chance to say good-bye to Anna before setting off for England. (She pictured the hospital and somehow couldn't imagine taking up her old life there again.)

The personal loss was irrelevant, Lib told herself; every nurse had to bid farewell to every patient, one way or another. But what about Anna; who'd look after her then, and would anyone or anything persuade her to give up her doomed fast? Lib was aware of the irony: she hadn't enticed the girl to eat so much as a crumb yet, but she was convinced that she was the only one who could. Was she arrogant to the point of delusion?

To do nothing was the deadliest sin; that was what Byrne had said about his reports on the famine.

Lib checked her watch. A quarter past ten; the committee should be gathered by now, even if the Irish were always late. Standing up, she neatened her grey uniform and smoothened down her hair.

Behind the grocery shop, she waited outside the meeting room until she recognized some of the voices: the doctor's and the priest's. Then she tapped at the door.

No answer. Perhaps they hadn't heard her. Was that a woman's voice? Had Sister Michael managed to come to the meeting after all?

When Lib let herself in, the first person she saw was Rosaleen O'Donnell. Their eyes locked. Malachy, behind his wife. Both of them looked shaken at the sight of the nurse.

Lib bit her lip; she hadn't expected the parents to be here.

A short, long-nosed man in old brocade was in the big chair with a carved back, presiding over a table improvised from three trestles. Sir Otway Blackett, she guessed; a retired officer, from his bearing. She recognized the *Irish Times* on the table; were they discussing Byrne's piece?

"And this is?" inquired Sir Otway.

"The English nurse, come without being asked," said big John Flynn in the next chair along.

"This is a private meeting, Mrs. Wright," said Dr. McBrearty.

Mr. Ryan — her host — jerked his head at Lib as if to say she should go back upstairs.

The one stranger to her was a greasy-haired man who had to be O'Flaherty, the schoolteacher. Lib looked from face to face, refusing to be cowed. She'd begin on firm ground with what was charted in her memorandum book.

"Gentlemen, excuse me. I thought you should hear the very latest news of Anna O'Donnell's health."

"What *news?*" scoffed Rosaleen O'Donnell. "Sure I left her sleeping peacefully not half an hour ago."

"I've already given my report, Mrs. Wright," said Dr. McBrearty scoldingly.

She turned on him. "Have you told the committee that Anna's so swollen up with dropsy, she can no longer walk? She's faint and freezing, and her teeth are falling out." Lib flipped through her notes, not because she needed them but to show that all this was a matter of record. "Her pulse is higher every hour, and her lungs crackle because she's beginning to drown from within. Her skin's covered in crusts and bruises, and her hair comes out in handfuls like an old—"

Belatedly she noticed that Sir Otway was holding up one palm to stop her. "We take your point, ma'am."

"I've always said the whole thing's a nonsense." It was Ryan the publican who broke the silence. "Come on, now — who can live without food?"

If the man really had been so sceptical from the start, Lib would have liked to ask, why had he agreed to help sponsor this watch?

John Flynn turned to him. "Hold your tongue."

"I'm a member of this committee, as good as you."

"Surely we need not stoop to squabbling," said the priest.

"Mr. Thaddeus," said Lib, taking a step towards him, "why haven't you told Anna to end her fast?"

"I believe you've heard me do so," said the priest.

"The gentlest of suggestions! I've discovered that she's

starving herself in the demented hope of saving her brother's soul." She looked from one man to another to make sure they registered this. "Apparently with the blessing of her parents." Lib flung an arm towards the O'Donnells.

Rosaleen burst out: "You ignorant heretic!"

Oh, the pleasure of finally speaking her mind. Lib turned on Mr. Thaddeus. "You represent Rome in this village, so why don't you command Anna to eat?"

The man bristled. "The relationship between priest and parishioner is a holy one, ma'am, that you're in no way qualified to understand."

"If Anna won't listen to you, can't you call in a bishop?"

His eyes bulged. "I won't — mustn't — entangle my superiors or the Church as a whole in this case."

"What do you mean, *entangle*?" demanded Flynn. "Won't it be to the Church's glory when Anna's proved to be living by spiritual means only? Couldn't this little girl be Ireland's first saint canonized since the thirteenth century?"

Mr. Thaddeus's hands sprang up in front of him like a fence. "That process has not even begun. Only after extensive testimony has been gathered and all other possible explanations have been ruled out may she send a delegation of commissioners to investigate whether an individual's holiness has worked a miracle. Until then, in the absence of any proof, she must be scrupulous to keep her distance."

She; that meant the Church, Lib realized. She'd never heard the genial priest speak so coldly, as if reading from a manual. *Absence of any proof.* Was he hinting to the whole group that the O'Donnells' claims were spurious?

Perhaps Lib had at least one backer among these men. For all that he was a family friend, she remembered, it was Mr. Thaddeus who'd pressed the committee to fund a thorough investigation. The priest's plump features twitched, as if he knew he'd said too much.

John Flynn was leaning forward, red-faced, pointing at him. "You're not fit to do up her little shoe!"

Big boot, Lib corrected him; Anna's feet had long ago swelled too much for anything but her dead brother's boots. To these men the girl was a symbol; she had no body anymore.

Lib had to take advantage of this moment of crisis. "I have something else to report, gentlemen, something of a grave and urgent nature, which I hope excuses my coming here uninvited." She didn't look in Rosaleen O'Donnell's direction, in case the woman's hawkish stare made Lib lose her nerve. "I have discovered by what means the child has been —"

A creak; the door of the room flapped open, then almost shut again, as if admitting a ghost. Then a black shape appeared in the gap, and Sister Michael backed in, pulling the wheeled chair with her.

Lib was speechless. She'd urged the nun to come. But with Anna?

The tiny girl lay askew in the baronet's chair, bundled up in blankets. Her head lay at an odd angle but her eyes were open. "Daddy," she murmured. "Mammy. Mrs. Lib. Mr. Thaddeus."

Malachy O'Donnell's cheeks were wet.

"Child," said Mr. Thaddeus, "we hear you're under the weather."

This was Irish euphemism at its worst.

"I'm very well," said Anna in the smallest of voices.

Lib knew all at once that she couldn't tell them about the manna. Not here, not now. Because it was only hearsay, after all, secondhand reporting of the word of a child. Rosaleen O'Donnell would shriek that the Englishwoman had made up the whole blasphemous story out of spite. The members of the committee would turn to Anna and demand to know whether it was true. And what then? For Lib to force the girl to choose between her nurse and Rosaleen was too risky; what child wouldn't side with her own mother? Besides, it would be unconscionably cruel.

Changing tack, she nodded at the nun and walked to the wheeled chair. "Good evening, Anna."

A slow smile from the girl.

"May I take off your blankets so these gentlemen can see you better?"

A tiny nod. Wheezing, yawning to catch a breath.

Lib unveiled the child, then pushed the chair up close to the table so the candlelight illuminated her white nightdress. So the committee could see her in all her grotesque disproportion: The hands and lower legs of a giant grafted onto the frame of an elf. The sunken eyes, the limpness, the hectic colour, the blue fingers, the weird marks on ankles and neck. Anna's wrecked body was a more articulate testament than any Lib could offer. "Gentlemen, my fellow nurse and I have found ourselves overseeing the slow execution of a child. Two weeks was an arbitrarily chosen period, was it not? I beg that the watch be called off tonight and all efforts bent to saving Anna's life."

For a long moment, not a word. Lib watched McBrearty. His faith in his theories was shaken, she could tell; his papery lips quivered.

"We've seen enough, I believe," said Sir Otway Blackett.

"Yes, you may take Anna home now, Sister," said McBrearty.

Meek as ever, the nun nodded and wheeled the chair out. O'Flaherty hopped up to hold the door open for them.

"And you may leave us, Mr. and Mrs. O'Donnell."

Rosaleen looked mutinous but went out with Malachy.

"And Mrs. Wright—" Mr. Thaddeus gestured for her to go as well.

"Not till this meeting's over," she told him through her teeth.

The door closed behind the O'Donnells.

"I'm sure we all concur on the necessity of being quite certain before deviating from our agreed course of action and curtailing the watch?" asked the baronet.

Hemming and hawing along the table. "I suppose there's only a couple of days in it," said Ryan.

Nods all around.

They didn't mean that Sunday was only three days away so they might as well end the watch now, Lib registered dizzily. They meant to keep it going till Sunday. Hadn't they *seen* the child?

The baronet and John Flynn maundered on about procedure and burdens of proof.

"After all, the watch is the only way to find out the truth once and for all," McBrearty was reminding the committee. "For the sake of science, for the sake of mankind—"

Lib couldn't bear anymore. She raised her voice and pointed at the doctor. "You'll be struck off the Medical Register." Bluffing; she had no idea what it took to get a physician banned from practicing. "All of you — your negligence could be considered *criminal*. Failure to provide the necessities of life to a child," she said, improvising as she moved her accusing finger from one man to the next. "Conspiracy to pervert the course of justice. Complicity in a suicide."

"Ma'am," barked the baronet, "may I remind you that you have been employed for a not ungenerous daily consideration for an agreed period of a fortnight? Your final testimony as to the matter of whether you've observed the girl take any nourishment will be required of you on Sunday."

"Anna will be dead by Sunday!"

"Mrs. Wright, restrain yourself," the priest urged her.

"She's in breach of the terms of her hire," Ryan pointed out.

John Flynn nodded. "If there were more than three days left, I'd propose we replace her."

"Quite so," said the baronet. "Dangerously unbalanced."

Lib stumbled to the door.

In her dream, scratching. Rats swarmed down the long ward, filling the walkway, leaping from cot to cot, lapping at fresh blood. Men cried out, but above their voices it was the scratching Lib heard, the furious friction of claws on wood—

No. The door. A scratching at her door, upstairs at

Ryan's. Somebody who didn't want to wake anyone but Lib.

She clambered out of bed, fumbled for her dressing gown. Opened the door a crack. "Mr. Byrne!"

He didn't apologize for disturbing her. They considered each other in the shaky light of his candle. Lib shot a look at the dark hollow of the staircase; someone could come up at any time. She beckoned him into her room.

Byrne stepped in without hesitation. He smelled warm, as if he'd been riding today. Lib gestured at the single chair, and he took it. She chose a perch on her rumpled bed far enough from the man's legs but near enough so they'd be able to talk in low voices.

"I heard about the meeting," he began.

"From which of them?"

He shook his head. "Maggie Ryan."

Lib felt a ridiculous pang that he was on such intimate terms with the maid.

"She caught only the odd snatch of what was said, but her sense of it was that they all came down on you like a wolf pack."

Lib almost laughed.

She told him everything: Anna's perverse hope to expiate her brother's juvenile sins by making a burnt offering of herself. Lib's guess that the priest had brought her to this country in hopes that the watch would expose the fact that there was no miracle and save his precious Church from the embarrassment of a false saint. The committee members and their pigheaded refusal to deviate from their plan.

"Forget them," said Byrne.

Lib stared at him.

"I doubt any of them can talk the girl out of her madness now. But you — she likes you. You have influence."

"Not enough," protested Lib.

"If you don't want to see her stretched out in a box, use that influence."

For a moment Lib pictured the child's treasure chest, and then she realized that he meant a coffin. *Forty-six inches,* she remembered from her first measurements of Anna. Barely more than four inches of growth for each year on earth.

"I've been lying on my bed in there wondering about you, Lib Wright."

Lib bristled. "What about me?"

"How far will you go to save this girl?"

Only when he asked it did she find she knew the answer. "I'll stop at nothing."

One eyebrow went up, sceptical.

"I'm not what you think me, Mr. Byrne."

"What do you believe I think you?"

"A stickler, a fusspot, a prudish widow. When the truth is, I'm not a widow at all." The words came out of Lib's mouth with no warning.

That made the Irishman sit up straight. "You weren't married?" His face alight with curiosity, or was it disgust?

"I was. I still am, for all I know." Lib could hardly believe she was telling her worst secret, and to a newspaperman of all people. But there was a glory in it too, that rare sensation of risking all. "Wright didn't die, he . . ." Absconded? Cut and run? Left? "He took his leave."

"Why?" The syllable erupted from Byrne.

Lib shrugged so sharply that a pain went through her

shoulder. "You assume he had cause, then." She could have told him about the baby, but she didn't want to, not now.

"No! You're taking me up wrong, you're—"

She tried to recall whether she'd ever seen this man lost for words.

He asked, "Whatever could possess a man to leave *you?*"

Now her tears brimmed. It was the note of indignation on her behalf that took her unawares.

Her parents hadn't been sympathetic. Appalled, rather, that Lib had been so unlucky as to lose a husband less than a year after catching him. (Thinking that she'd been negligent, perhaps, to some degree, though they never said that aloud.) They'd been loyal enough to help her move to London and pass herself off as a widow. This conspiracy had shocked Lib's sister so much, she'd never spoken to any of the three of them again. But the one question her mother and father hadn't asked Lib was, *How could he?*

She blinked hard, because she couldn't bear the idea that Byrne might think she was weeping for her husband, who was really not worth a single tear. She smiled a little instead.

"And Englishmen call Irishmen stupid!" he added.

That made her laugh out loud. She stifled it with her hand.

William Byrne kissed her, so fast and so hard that she almost tipped over. Not a word, only that single kiss, and then he walked out of her room.

*

Strangely enough, Lib did sleep then, despite all the clamour in her head.

When she woke, she fumbled for her watch on the table and pressed the button. It beat out the hours inside her fist: one, two, three, four. Friday morning. Only then did she remember how Byrne had kissed her. No, how the two of them had kissed.

Guilt brought her bolt upright. How could she be sure that Anna hadn't worsened in the night, hadn't taken her last ragged breath? *Ever this night be at my side, to light and guard.* She longed to be back in that small airless room. Would the O'Donnells even let her in this morning, after what she'd said at the meeting?

Lib dressed herself by feel, not even lighting her candle. She patted her way down the stairs and struggled with the front door until the bar heaved up and let her out.

Still dark; a cloud loosely bandaged the waning moon. So quiet, so lone, as if some disaster had laid waste the whole country and Lib was the last to walk its muddy paths.

There was one light in the small window of the O'Donnells' cabin that had not stopped blazing for eleven days and nights now, like some awful eye that had forgotten how to blink. Lib walked up to the burning square and peeped in at the scene.

Sister Michael sitting beside the bed, her eyes on Anna's profile. The tiny face transfigured by light. Sleeping beauty; innocence preserved; a child who looked perfect, perhaps because she wasn't moving, wasn't asking for anything, wasn't causing any trouble. An illustration out of a cheap paper: *The Final Vigil.* Or *The Little Angel's Last Rest.*

Lib must have moved or else Sister Michael had that uncanny ability to feel herself being watched, because the nun looked up and nodded a wan greeting.

Lib went to the front door and let herself in, braced for a rebuff.

Malachy O'Donnell was drinking tea by the fire. Rosaleen and Kitty were scraping something from one pot into another. The slavey kept her head down. The mistress glanced Lib's way, but only briefly, as if she'd felt a draught. So the O'Donnells weren't going to defy the committee by barring Lib from the cabin, at least not today.

In the bedroom, Anna was so deeply asleep that she looked like a waxwork.

Lib took Sister Michael's cool hand and squeezed it, which startled the nun. "Thank you for coming last night."

"But it did no good, did it?" asked Sister Michael.

"Still."

The sun came up at a quarter past six. As if summoned by the light, Anna lurched off the pillow and put her hand out towards the empty chamber pot. Lib rushed to give it to her.

What the girl retched up was sunshine yellow but transparent. How could this hollowed-out stomach make such a gaudy shade out of nothing but water? Anna shuddered, contracting her lips as if to shake the drops off.

"Are you in pain?" asked Lib. These were the last days, surely.

Anna spat, and spat again, then settled back on the pillow, head turned towards the dresser.

Lib filled in her memorandum book.

Brought up bile; half a pint?
Pulse: 128 beats per minute.
Lungs: 30 respirations per minute; moist crack-
    ling bilaterally.
Neck veins distended.
Temperature very cool.
Eyes glassy.

Anna was ageing as if time itself were speeding up. Her skin was wrinkled parchment, blemished as if messages had been inked on it then scratched out. When the child rubbed her collarbone, Lib noticed that the skin stayed ruched. Dark red strands were strewn across the upper pillow, and Lib scraped them up and tucked them into the pocket of her apron. "Is your neck stiff, child?"

"No."

"Why do you turn it that way, then?"

"The window's too bright," said Anna.

Use your influence, Byrne had said. But what new arguments could Lib muster?

"Tell me," she said, "what kind of God would take your life in exchange for your brother's soul?"

"He wants me," whispered Anna.

Kitty brought in breakfast on a tray and spoke in an uneven voice about the extraordinarily fine weather. "And how are you today, pet?"

"Very well," Anna told her cousin wheezily.

The slavey pressed her reddened hand to her own mouth. Then went back to the kitchen.

Breakfast was griddle cakes with sweet butter. Lib thought of Saint Peter standing at the gate, *waiting for a buttered cake.* She tasted ash. *Now and at the hour of our death, amen.* Sickened, she set the griddle cake back on the plate and put the tray by the door.

"Everything's stretching, Mrs. Lib," said Anna in a catarrhal murmur.

"Stretching?"

"The room. The outside fits in the inside."

Was this the start of delirium? "Are you cold?" Lib asked, sitting next to the bed.

Anna shook her head.

"Hot?" asked Lib.

"Not anything. No difference."

Those glazed eyes were reminding her of Pat O'Donnell's painted gaze in the daguerreotype. Every now and then they seemed to twitch. Troubles of vision, perhaps. "Can you see what's right in front of you?"

A hesitation. "Mostly."

"Meaning most of what's there?"

"Everything," Anna corrected her, "most of the time."

"But sometimes you can't?"

"It goes black. But I see other things," said the girl.

"What kind of things?"

"Beautiful things."

This is what comes of starvation, Lib wanted to roar. But whoever changed a child's mind by shouting at her? No, she needed to speak more eloquently than she ever had in her life.

"Another riddle, Mrs. Lib?" the child asked.

Lib was startled. But she supposed even the dying liked a little entertainment to help the time pass. "Ah, let me see.

Yes, I believe I have one more. What's — what thing is that which is more frightful the smaller it is?"

"Frightful?" repeated Anna. "A mouse?"

"But a rat scares people as much if not more, though it's several times bigger," Lib pointed out.

"All right." The girl heaved a breath. "Something that causes *more* fear if it's smaller."

"Thinner, rather," Lib corrects herself. "Narrower."

"An arrow," Anna murmured, "a knife?" Another ragged breath. "Please, a hint."

"Imagine walking on it."

"Would it hurt me?"

"Only if you stepped off."

"A bridge," cried Anna.

Lib nodded. For some reason she was remembering Byrne's kiss. Nothing could take that away from her; for the rest of her life, she'd have that kiss. It gave her courage. "Anna," she said, "you've done enough."

The child blinked at her.

"Fasted enough, prayed enough. I'm sure Pat is happy in heaven already."

A whisper: "Can't be sure."

Lib tried another tack. "All your gifts — your intelligence, your kindness, your strength — they're needed on earth. God wants you to do his work *here*."

Anna shook her head.

"I'm speaking as your friend now." Her voice shook. "You've become very dear to me, the dearest girl in the world."

A tiny smile.

"You're breaking my heart."

"I'm sorry, Mrs. Lib."

"Then eat! Please. Even a mouthful. A sip. I beg of you."

Anna's look was grave, inexorable.

"Please! For my sake. For the sake of everyone who—"

Kitty, from the doorway: "'Tis Mr. Thaddeus."

Lib leapt to her feet.

The priest looked uncomfortably hot in his layers of black. Had Lib managed to prick his conscience at the meeting last night? His mouth still turned up as he greeted Anna, but his eyes were woebegone.

Lib pushed down her dislike of the man. After all, if anyone could convince Anna of the folly in her theology, it would logically be her priest. "Anna, would you like to speak to Mr. Thaddeus alone?"

A tiny shake of the head.

The O'Donnells were hovering behind him.

The priest picked up Lib's cue. "Do you wish to make your confession, child?"

"Not now."

Rosaleen O'Donnell knotted her knobby fingers. "Sure what sins would she be after committing, lying there like a cherub?"

You're afraid of her telling him about the manna, Lib said in her head. *Monster!*

"Will we have a hymn, then?" asked Mr. Thaddeus.

"There's an idea," said Malachy O'Donnell, rubbing his chin.

"Lovely," gasped Anna.

Lib offered the glass of water, but the child shook her head.

Kitty had sidled in too. With six people in it, the room felt unbearably full.

Rosaleen O'Donnell began the verse.

From the land of my exile
I call upon thee,
Then Mary, my mother,
Look kindly on me.

Why is Ireland the land of exile? Lib wondered.

The others joined in — the husband, the slavey, the priest, even Anna from her bed.

Then Mary, in pity,
Look down upon me,
'Tis the voice of thy child
That is calling on thee.

Wrath was a spike in the back of Lib's head. *No, this is* your *child, who needs* your *help,* she told Rosaleen O'Donnell silently.

Kitty sang the next verse in a surprisingly sweet alto, all the creases of her face smoothened out.

In sorrow, in darkness,
Be still at my side,
My light and my refuge,
My guard and my guide.
Though snares should surround me,
Yet why should I fear?
I know I am weak
But my mother is here.

Lib grasped it now: This whole earth was the land of exile. Every interest, every satisfaction life could offer, was scorned as a *snare* for the soul bent on hurrying to heaven.

But the snares are in here. This cabin held together by dung and blood, hair and milk — a trap to hold and mangle a little girl.

"Bless you, my child," Mr. Thaddeus said to Anna. "I'll look in again tomorrow."

Was that it, the best he could do? A hymn and a blessing and *off went he?*

The O'Donnells and Kitty filed out after the priest.

No sign of Byrne at the spirit grocery. No answer when Lib knocked on his door. Might he be regretting the kiss?

All afternoon she lay on top of her bed, eyes as dry as paper. Sleep was a distant country.

Do your duty while the world whirls, her teacher ordered.

What was Lib's duty to Anna now? *Deliver me out of the hands of my enemies,* Anna had prayed. Was Lib her deliverer or another enemy? *I'll stop at nothing*, Lib had boasted to Byrne last night. But what could she do to save a child who refused to be rescued?

At seven she made herself go downstairs and have some dinner, as she was feeling faint. Now broiled hare lay in her stomach like lead.

The August evening was stifling. By the time Lib reached the cabin, the dark horizon was swallowing up the sun. She knocked, tight with dread. Between one shift and the next, Anna could have slid into unconsciousness.

The kitchen smelled of porridge and the fire's perpetual blaze. "How is she?" Lib demanded of Rosaleen O'Donnell.

"Much the same, the little angel."

Not an angel. A human child.

Anna was weirdly yellowish against the dull sheets.

"Good evening, child. May I look at your eyes?"

The girl opened them, blinking.

Lib pulled the skin underneath one eye down to check it. Yes, the whites were the buttery hue of a daffodil. She threw a look at Sister Michael.

"The doctor confirmed it was jaundice when he looked in this afternoon," murmured the nun as she fastened her cloak.

Lib turned to Rosaleen O'Donnell, standing in the doorway. "That's a sign that Anna's whole constitution is breaking down."

The mother didn't have a word to say to that; she received it like news of a storm or a distant war.

The chamber pot was dry. Lib tilted it.

The nun shook her head.

No urine passed at all, then. This was the point to which all the measurements were leading. Everything inside Anna was grinding to a halt.

"There's to be a votive mass tomorrow evening at half past eight," said Rosaleen O'Donnell.

"Votive?" asked Lib.

"Dedicated to a particular intention," explained Sister Michael under her breath.

"For Anna. Isn't that nice, pet?" asked her mother.

"Mr. Thaddeus is offering a special mass because of you not being well, and everyone will be there."

"Lovely." Anna breathed as if it required her whole attention.

Lib pulled out her stethoscope and waited for the other two women to leave.

She thought she heard something new in Anna's heart this evening, a gallop. Could she be imagining it? She listened hard. There: three sounds instead of the usual two.

Next she counted the breaths. Twenty-nine in a minute; speeding up. Anna's temperature seemed lower too, despite the heat of the past two days.

She sat down and took Anna's scaly hand. "Your heart's starting to jump. Have you felt it?" Something about the way the girl lay, arms and legs held so still. "You must be in pain."

"That's not the word," whispered Anna.

"Whatever you call it, then."

"Sister says 'tis the kiss of Jesus."

"What is?" Lib demanded.

"When something hurts. She says it means I've got close enough to his cross that he can lean down and kiss me."

The nun had meant it as comfort, no doubt, but it horrified Lib.

A rattling breath. "I just wish I knew how long it'll take."

Lib asked, "Dying, you mean?"

The girl nodded.

"It doesn't come naturally at your age. Children are so

very alive." This was quite the strangest conversation Lib had ever had with a patient. "Are you afraid?"

A hesitation. Then a tiny nod.

"I don't believe you truly want to die."

She saw such misery in the child's face then. Anna had never let this show before. *"Thy will be done,"* the girl whispered, crossing herself.

"This is not God's doing," Lib reminded her. "It's yours."

The limp lids fluttered and finally shut. The loud breathing softened and evened out.

Lib kept hold of the swollen hand. Sleep, a temporary mercy. She hoped it would last the night.

The Rosary began on the other side of the wall. Muted this time; the chanting low. Lib waited for it to be over, for the cabin to settle down as the O'Donnells retreated to their hole in the wall and Kitty bedded down on the settle in the kitchen. The fading of all the small sounds.

Finally Lib was the only one awake. The watcher. *Ever this night be at my side.*

It occurred to her to ask herself why she wanted Anna to live through this Friday night, and the next night, and however many nights were left. As a matter of compassion, shouldn't Lib be wishing for this to be over? After all, everything she did to make Anna more comfortable — a sip of water, another pillow — was just prolonging her suffering.

For a moment, Lib let herself imagine bringing on the end: lifting and folding a blanket, setting it down over the child's face, and bearing down on it with all her weight. It wouldn't be difficult, or take more than a couple of minutes. It would be an act of mercy, really.

A murder.

How had Lib reached the point of contemplating killing a patient?

She blamed the lack of sleep, the uncertainty. Everything a muddle and a mess. A swampy wilderness, a child lost, and Lib stumbling after her.

Never despair, she ordered herself. Wasn't that one of the unforgiveable sins? She remembered a story about a man wrestling with an angel all night and being thrown down over and over again. Never winning, but never giving up.

Think, think. She struggled to apply her trained mind. *What history has a child?* Rosaleen O'Donnell had asked that in reply to Lib's questions that first morning. But every disease had a story with a beginning, middle, and end. How to trace this one all the way back?

Her eyes roamed the room. When they fell on Anna's treasure chest, she remembered the candlestick she'd cracked, and the dark curl of hair. The brother, Pat O'Donnell, whom Lib knew only from a photograph with painted-on eyes. How had his little sister become convinced that she needed to purchase his soul with her own?

Lib laboured to take Anna's struggle on its own terms. To put herself in the position of a girl for whom these ancient narratives were literal truth. Four and a half months of fasting; how could that much sacrifice not be enough to make amends for the sins of a mere boy?

"Anna." Only a whisper. Then more loudly. "Anna!"

The child struggled to surface.

"Anna!"

Her heavy lids batted.

Lib put her mouth very close to the girl's ear. "Did Pat do something bad?"

No answer.

"Something nobody else knows about?"

Lib waited. Watched the flickering lids. *Leave her be,* she told herself, suddenly exhausted. What did any of this matter now?

"He said it was all right." Anna barely voiced the words. Eyes still shut, as if she were still in her dream.

Lib waited, breath held.

"He said it was double."

Lib puzzled over that. "Double what?"

"Love." A push of tongue for the *L,* the merest puff of breath, teeth pressed to the lower lip for the *V.*

My love is mine, and I am his; one of Anna's hymns. "What do you mean?"

Anna's eyes were open now. "He married me in the night."

Lib blinked once, twice. The room stayed still, but the world plunged dizzyingly around it.

He comes in to me as soon as I'm asleep, Anna had said, but she hadn't meant Jesus. *He wants me.*

"I was his sister and his bride too," the girl whispered. "Double."

Nausea rose through Lib. There wasn't another bedroom; the siblings must have shared this one. That folding screen she'd put outside the room on her first day had been all that had separated Pat's bed — this bed, his deathbed

— from Anna's mattress on the floor. "When was this?" Lib asked, the words scraping her throat.

A tiny shrug.

"How old was Pat, do you remember?"

"Thirteen, maybe."

"And you?"

"Nine," said Anna.

Lib's face puckered. "Did this happen just once, Anna — on a single occasion — or . . ."

"Marriage is forever."

Oh, the terrible innocence of the child. Lib made a small sound, encouraging her to go on.

"When brothers and sisters marry, it's a holy mystery. A secret between us and heaven, Pat told me. But then he died," said Anna, voice cracking like a shell, eyes fixed on Lib. "I wondered if maybe he'd been wrong."

Lib nodded.

"Maybe God took Pat because of what we'd done. 'Tisn't fair, then, Mrs. Lib, because Pat's bearing all the punishment."

Lib pressed her lips together so the child would keep talking.

"Then at the mission —" Anna let out a single hard sob. "The Belgian priest, in his sermon, he said brother and sister, 'tis a mortal sin, the second worst of the six species of lust. Poor Pat never knew!"

Oh, *poor Pat* knew well enough to spin a glittering web around the thing he was doing to his little sister night after night.

"He died so fast," the girl wailed, "he never got a chance to go to confession. Maybe he went straight to hell."

The wet eyes looked greenish in this light, and the words came out in gulps. "In hell the flames aren't for cleaning, they're for hurting, and there's no end."

"Anna." Lib had heard enough.

"I don't know if I can get him out, but I have to try. Surely God must be able to pluck someone —"

"Anna! You did nothing wrong."

"But I did."

"You didn't know," Lib insisted. "This was a wrong your brother did to you."

Anna shook her head. "I loved him double too."

Lib couldn't say a word.

"If God grants it, we can be together soon, but no bodies this time. No marrying," Anna pleaded. "Just brother and sister again."

"Anna, I can't bear this, I—" Lib was crouching on the edge of the bed now, blinded, as the room turned to water.

"Don't cry, Mrs. Lib." Those spindly arms were reaching out for her, enclosing Lib's head, pulling her down. "Dear Mrs. Lib."

She muffled her weeping in the blankets, the hard double ridge of the child's lap. The upside-downness of it: to be consoled by a child, and such a child.

"Don't fret, 'tis all right," Anna murmured.

"No, it's not!"

"All's well. All will be well."

Help her. Lib found herself praying to the God that she didn't believe in. *Help me. Help us all.*

She heard only silence.

*

306

In the middle of the night — Lib couldn't wait any longer — she felt her way through the kitchen, past the shape of the sleeping maid on the settle. The skin of Lib's cheeks was still tight and salty from weeping. When her fingers found the rough curtain that partitioned off the outshot, she whispered: "Mrs. O'Donnell."

A stir. "Is it Anna?" asked Rosaleen hoarsely.

"No, she's fast asleep. I need to speak to you."

"What is it?"

"In private," said Lib. "Please."

After long hours of brooding, she'd come to the conclusion that she had to reveal Anna's secret. But only to one other person, perversely the one Lib trusted least: Rosaleen O'Donnell. Lib's hope was that this revelation might wake Rosaleen to a sense of mercy for the tormented girl at last. This story was the family's, and the mother of Pat and Anna was entitled, if anyone was, to hear the truth about what one of them had inflicted on the other.

The hymn to Mary sang in Lib's head: *My mother, look kindly on me.*

Rosaleen O'Donnell shoved the curtain aside and climbed out of the little chamber. Her eyes were uncanny in the trace of red light from the banked-up fire.

Lib beckoned, and Rosaleen trailed her across the hard earth floor. Lib opened the front door and Rosaleen hesitated for only a moment before following her out.

With the door shut behind them, Lib spoke fast, before she could lose her nerve. "I know all about the manna," she began, to gain the upper hand.

Rosaleen looked back at her, unblinking.

"But I haven't told the committee. The world doesn't need an explanation of how Anna's lived all these months. What matters is whether she'll go on living. If you love your daughter, Mrs. O'Donnell, why don't you do everything in your power to get her to eat?"

Still not a word. Then, very low: "She's chosen."

"She's been chosen?" Lib repeated, disgusted. "You mean by God? Called to martyrdom at the age of eleven?"

Rosaleen corrected her: "She's made her choice."

The absurdity of it choked Lib. "Don't you understand how desperate Anna is, how racked with guilt? She's not *choosing* any more than she might choose to fall down a bog hole."

Not a word.

"She's not intact." Lib's circumlocution sounded absurdly prim.

Rosaleen's eyes narrowed.

"I must tell you that she's been interfered with, and by your own son." The syllables plain and brutal. "He began tampering with her when she was only nine."

"Mrs. Wright," said the woman, "I won't stand for any more scandalmongering."

Was it too inconceivable a horror for Rosaleen to take in? Did she need to believe Lib was making it up?

"That's the same filthy falsehood Anna came out with after Pat's funeral," Rosaleen went on, "and I told her not to be slandering her poor brother."

Lib had to lean on the gritty wall of the cabin. So this wasn't news to the woman at all. *A mother understands what a child doesn't say,* wasn't that how the proverb went? But Anna *had* said it. Grief for her dead Pat had given her the courage to confess the whole shameful story to her mother, back in November. Rosaleen had called her a liar and maintained that now, even as she watched her daughter pine away.

"Not another word out of you," growled Rosaleen, "and may the devil take you." She swept back inside.

Just after six, Saturday morning. Lib pushed a note under Byrne's door.

Then she left the spirit grocery and hurried away across the muddy field under a shrinking moon. This was the kingdom of hell, drifting irretrievably out of the orbit of heaven.

The hawthorn at the tiny holy well stood up before her, its disintegrating rags dancing in a breath of warm wind. Lib saw the point of such superstition now. If there was a ritual she could perform that offered a chance of saving Anna, wouldn't she try it? She'd bow down to a tree or a rock or a carved turnip for the child's sake. Lib thought of all those people walking away from this tree over the centuries, trying to believe that they'd left their aches and sorrows behind. Years on, some of them reminding themselves, *If I still feel the pain, that's only because the rag's not quite rotten yet.*

Anna wanted to leave her body, drop it *like an old coat.* To shed her creased skin, her name, her broken history; to be done with it all. Yes, Lib would have liked that for the girl, and more — for Anna to be born all over again, as people in the Far East believed was possible. To wake up tomorrow and discover that she was someone else. A little girl with no damage done to her, no debts to pay, able and allowed to eat her fill.

And then came a hurrying outline against the lightening sky, and Lib felt at once what she'd never really known until this moment: the body's claims were undeniable.

William Byrne's curls were snakish and his waistcoat was buttoned up wrong. He clutched her note.

"Did I wake you?" Lib asked foolishly.

"I wasn't sleeping," he said, grabbing her hand.

Despite everything, warmth spread through her.

"At Ryan's, last night," he said, "no one could talk of anything but Anna. Word's spread about you telling the committee that she's failing fast. I believe the whole village will attend this mass."

What collective madness had the townspeople in its grip? "If they're concerned that a child is being allowed to kill herself," Lib demanded, "why don't they storm the cabin?"

Byrne gave a great shrug. "We Irish have a gift for resignation. Or, put another way, fatalism."

He tucked her arm through his, and they walked under the trees. The sun was up, and it looked set to be another horribly lovely day.

"Yesterday I was in Athlone," he told her, "arguing with the police. This officer, a piece of apathetic pomposity with his hat and musket — he kept stroking his moustache and saying that the situation was *one of considerable delicacy*. Far be it from the constabulary, says he, to invade a *domestic sanctum* in the absence of any evidence of a crime having been committed."

Lib nodded. And, really, what could the police possibly

have done? Still, she appreciated Byrne's impulse to try something, anything.

How she wished she could tell him all that she'd learned the night before, and not just for the relief of sharing it but because he cared for Anna as she did.

No. It would be treachery to expose the secret that the child carried within her puny body to a man, any man, even one who was Anna's champion. How could Byrne ever look at this innocent girl the same way afterwards? Lib owed it to Anna to keep her mouth shut.

She couldn't tell anyone else either. If Anna's own mother had called her a liar, most likely so would the rest of the world. Lib couldn't put Anna through the violation of a medical examination; that body had endured so much probing already. Besides, even if the fact could be proved, what Lib saw as incestuous rape, others would call seduction. Wasn't it so often the girl — no matter how young — who got blamed for having incited her molester with a look?

"I've come to a dreadful conclusion," she said to Byrne. "Anna can't live in this family."

His brows contracted. "But they're all she's got. All she knows. What's a child without a family?"

The nest is enough for the wren, Rosaleen O'Donnell had boasted. But what if a baby bird of rare plumage found herself in the wrong nest, and the mother bird turned her sharp beak on the chick? "Trust me, they're no family," Lib told him. "They won't lift a finger to save her."

Byrne nodded.

But was he convinced? "I've watched a child die," she said, "and I can't do it again."

"In your line of work—"

"No. You don't understand. *My* child. My daughter."

Byrne stared. His arm tightened around hers.

"Three weeks and three days, that's how long she hung on." Bleating, coughing like a goat. There must have been something sour in Lib's milk, because the baby had turned away or spat it out, and what little she got down had made her dwindle as if it were the opposite of food, a magical shrinking potion.

Byrne didn't say, *Such things happen.* He didn't point out that Lib's loss was only a drop in the ocean of human pain. "Was that when Wright left?"

Lib nodded. "Nothing to stay for, was how he put it." Then she added, "Not that I much cared, at that point."

A growl: "He didn't deserve you."

Oh, but none of it was a matter of deserving. She hadn't *deserved* to lose her daughter; Lib knew that even on her bleakest days. She'd done nothing that she shouldn't have, for all Wright's dark hints; had left nothing undone that she should have done. Fate was faceless, life arbitrary, *a tale told by an idiot.*

Except at rare moments such as this one, when one glimpsed a way of wrestling it into a better shape.

In her head, Miss N. asked: *Can you throw your whole self into the breach?*

Lib held on to Byrne's arm like a rope. She found her mind hadn't been quite made up till this minute. She told him, "I'm going to take Anna away."

"Away where?"

"Anywhere but here." Her eyes scoured the flat horizon. "The farther the better."

Byrne turned to face her. "How would that persuade the child to eat?"

"I can't be sure, and I can't explain it, but I know she must leave this place and these people."

His tone was wry. "You're buying the damn spoons."

For a moment Lib was confused, then she remembered the hundred spoons at Scutari and almost smiled.

"Let's be clear," he said, urbane again. "You mean to kidnap the girl."

"I suppose they'd call it that," said Lib, her voice rough with fright. "But I'd never compel her."

"Would Anna go with you willingly, then?"

"I believe she just might, if I can put it to her the right way."

Byrne was tactful enough not to point out the unlikelihood of this. "How do you propose to travel? Hire a driver? You'll be caught before you get to the next county."

All at once, Lib felt her tiredness catching up with her. "Odds are I'll end up in prison, Anna will die, and none of it will have made any difference."

"Yet you mean to try."

She struggled to answer. *"Better to drown in the surf than stand idly on the shore."* Absurd to quote Miss N., who'd be appalled to hear that one of her nurses had been arrested for child abduction. But sometimes the teaching held more than the teacher knew.

What Byrne said next astonished her. "Then it must be tonight."

When Lib arrived for her shift, at one o'clock on Saturday, the bedroom door was closed. Sister Michael, Kitty, and the O'Donnells were all on their knees in the kitchen; Malachy held his cap in one hand.

Lib went to turn the door handle.

"Don't," snapped Rosaleen. "Mr. Thaddeus is in the middle of giving Anna the sacrament of penance."

Penance; that was another word for confession, wasn't it?

"Part of the last rites," murmured Sister Michael to Lib.

Was Anna dying? She swayed on her feet, and thought she might fall.

"It's not only to help a patient make a *bona mors*," the nun assured her.

"A what?"

"A good death, that is. It's also for anyone in danger. It's even been known to restore health, if God wills it."

More fairy tales.

A high bell rang in the bedroom and Mr. Thaddeus opened the door. "You may all come in for the anointing."

The group got off their knees and shuffled in after Lib.

Anna was lying with her blankets off. The dresser was spread with a white cloth on which was a thick white candle, a crucifix, golden dishes, a dried leaf of some kind, little white balls, a piece of bread, dishes of water and oil, and a white powder.

Mr. Thaddeus dipped his right thumb in the oil. *"Per istam sanctam unctionem et suam piissima misericord-iam,"* he intoned. *"Indulgeat tibi Dominus quidquid per visum, auditum, gustum, odoratum, tactum et locution-em, gressum deliquisti."* He touched Anna's eyelids, ears, lips, nose, hands, and, finally, the soles of her misshapen feet.

"Whatever's he doing?" Lib whispered to Sister Michael.

"Wiping away the stains. The sins she's committed with each part of her body," the nun said in her ear, eyes still faithfully on the priest.

Anger surged in Lib. *What about sins committed against Anna?*

Then the priest took the dish of white pellets and dabbed each spot of oil with one of them; cotton? He set down the dish, rubbed his thumb on the bread. "May this holy anointing bring consolation and ease," he said to the family. "Remember, *God shall wipe away all tears from their eyes.*"

"Bless you, Mr. Thaddeus," cried Rosaleen O'Donnell.

"Whether it be in a little time, or not for many years to come" — his voice was lullingly musical — "we will all meet again to part no more forever, in a world where sorrow and separation are at an end."

"Amen."

He washed his hands in the dish of water and dried them on the cloth.

Malachy O'Donnell went over to his daughter and bent as if to kiss her forehead. But then he stopped himself, as if Anna were too holy to touch now. "Anything you need, pet?"

"Just the blankets, please, Dadda," she told him through chattering teeth.

He drew them up and covered her to the chin.

Mr. Thaddeus stowed all his equipment in his bag, and Rosaleen showed him to the door.

"Wait, please," Lib called to him, crossing the room. "I need to speak to you."

Rosaleen O'Donnell gripped Lib's sleeve so hard that a stitch popped. "We don't detain a priest in idle conversation when he's carrying the Blessed Eucharist."

Lib pulled away from her and rushed after him.

Out in the farmyard, she called, "Mr. Thaddeus!"

"What is it?" The man stopped and kicked away a pecking hen.

She had to find out whether Anna had told him just now of her scheme to ransom Pat with her own death. "Did Anna talk to you about her brother?"

His smooth face tautened. "Mrs. Wright, only your ignorance of our faith excuses your attempt to induce me to breach the seal of the confessional."

"So you do know."

"Such calamities should be kept in the family," he said, "not bruited abroad. Anna should never have entered on such a subject with you."

"But if you reason with her, if you explain that God would never—"

The priest spoke over her. "I've been telling the poor girl for months that her sins are forgiven, and besides, we should speak nothing but good of the dead."

Lib stared at him. *The dead.* He wasn't talking about Anna's plan to trade her life for her brother's redemption. *Her sins;* Mr. Thaddeus meant what Pat had done to her. *I've been telling the poor girl for months.* That had to mean that after the mission, back in the spring, Anna had opened her heart to her parish priest, told him of all her confusion about the *secret marriage,* all her mortification.

And unlike Rosaleen O'Donnell, he'd been clear-sighted enough to believe the girl. But the only comfort he'd offered was to tell her that *her sins* were forgiven and she should never mention it again!

The priest was halfway to the lane by the time Lib recovered herself. She watched him disappear around the hedge. How many such *calamities* were there in how many other families over which Mr. Thaddeus had drawn a veil? Was that all he knew how to do with a child's pain?

Inside the smoky cabin, Kitty was throwing the contents of the little dishes on the fire: the salt, the bread, even the water, which spat fiercely.

"What are you doing?" asked Lib.

"They've the traces of the holy oil on them still," the slavey told her, "so they have to be buried or burnt."

Only in this country would anyone burn water.

Rosaleen O'Donnell was putting canisters of tea and sugar in a paper-lined cupboard in the wall.

"What about Dr. McBrearty," asked Lib, "did you think to send for him before the priest?"

"Wasn't he in this morning?" Rosaleen answered without turning around.

Kitty busied herself scraping burnt porridge into a basin.

Lib pressed on. "And what did he say about Anna?"

"That she's in God's hands now."

A tiny sound from Kitty; was that a sob?

"As are we all," muttered Rosaleen.

Rage went through Lib like an electric shock, rage at the doctor, the mother, the maid, and the committee men.

But she had a mission, she reminded herself, and she

couldn't allow anything to distract her from it. "This special mass tonight, at half past eight," she said to Kitty in as calm a voice as she could muster, "how long do these ceremonies last?"

"I couldn't say."

"Longer than on an ordinary occasion?"

"Oh, much longer," said Kitty. "Two hours, maybe, or three."

Lib nodded as if impressed. "I was thinking that I should stay late tonight so that Sister can accompany you all to the mass."

"No need," said the nun, appearing in the doorway of the bedroom.

"But Sister—" Panic in Lib's throat. Improvising, she turned to Malachy O'Donnell, who was brooding over a newspaper by the hearth. "Shouldn't Sister Michael go too, as the child is so fond of her?"

"Indeed she should."

The nun hesitated, frowning.

"Yes, you must be there with us, Sister," said Rosaleen O'Donnell, "bearing us up."

"Gladly," said the nun. Her eyes were still puzzled.

Lib hurried into the bedroom before they could change their minds. "Good day, Anna." Her voice oddly bright with relief that she'd manage to arrange to stay late, at least.

The child's face gaunt, sallow. "Good day, Mrs. Lib." Inert, as if her thick ankles fettered her to the bed, except for a shudder every now and then. Her breaths were noisy.

"A little water?"

She shook her head.

Lib called to Kitty to bring in another blanket. The slavey's face was rigid as she handed it over.

Hold on, Lib wanted to whisper in Anna's ear. *Wait just a little longer, just until tonight.* But she couldn't risk saying a word, not yet.

It was the slowest day Lib had ever known. Yet the house was in a sort of low fever. The O'Donnells and their maid hung about in the kitchen speaking in doleful murmurs, looking in on Anna every now and then. Lib went about her business, propping Anna up on pillows, wetting her lips with a cloth. Her own breaths were coming quick and shallow.

At four, Kitty brought in a bowl of some kind of vegetable hash. Lib forced herself to spoon it down.

"Would you like anything, pet?" the maid asked the child in an incongruously cheerful voice. "Your thingy?" She held up the thaumatrope.

"Show me, Kitty."

So the slavey twirled the cords and made the bird appear in the cage, then fly free.

Anna heaved a breath. "You can have it."

The young woman's face fell. But she didn't ask what Anna meant; she just set down the toy. "Would you like your treasure chest on your lap?"

Anna shook her head.

Lib helped the girl a little higher up on the pillows. "Water?"

Another shake of the head.

At the window, Kitty said, " 'Tis that picture fellow again."

Lib jumped to her feet and looked over the maid's

shoulder. REILLY & SONS, PHOTOGRAPHISTS, said the van. She hadn't heard the horse pull up. She could just imagine how artfully Reilly would pose the figures for the death-bed scene: soft light from the side, the family kneeling around Anna, the uniformed nurse at the back with her head bowed. "Tell him to make himself scarce."

Kitty looked startled but didn't argue; she left the room.

"My holy cards and books and things," Anna murmured, looking towards her chest.

"Would you like to see them?" asked Lib.

She shook her head. "They're for Mammy. After."

Lib nodded. There was a kind of poetic justice in that, paper saints standing in for a child of flesh. Hadn't Rosaleen O'Donnell been nudging Anna towards the grave all along — perhaps ever since Pat's death, last November?

Once the woman lost Anna, perhaps she'd be able to love her without strain. Unlike a live daughter, a dead one was impeccable. This was what Rosaleen O'Donnell had chosen, Lib told herself: to be the sorrowful, proud mother of two angels.

Five minutes later, Reilly's van moved slowly off. Lib, watching at the window, thought: *He'll be back*. She supposed a posthumous composition would be even easier to arrange.

An hour later, Malachy O'Donnell came in and knelt down heavily beside the bed where his daughter was dozing. He joined his hands — his knuckles making white spots on the red skin — and muttered an Our Father.

Watching his bent, greying head, Lib wavered. This man had none of his wife's malignity, and he did love

Anna in his own passive way. If he could only be roused from his stupor, to fight for his child . . . Perhaps Lib owed him one last chance?

She made herself go around the bed and lean down to his ear. "When your daughter wakes," she said, "beg her to eat, for your sake."

Malachy didn't protest; he only shook his head. "It'd choke her, sure."

"A drink of milk would choke her? But it's the same consistency as water."

"I couldn't do it."

"Why not?" demanded Lib.

"You wouldn't understand, ma'am."

"Then make me!"

Malachy let out a long, ragged breath. "I promised her."

Lib stared. "That you wouldn't ask her to eat? When was this?"

"Months back."

The clever girl; Anna had tied her fond father's hands. "But that was when you believed her able to live without food, correct?"

A bleak nod.

"She was in good health at the time. Look at her now," Lib said.

"I know," muttered Malachy O'Donnell, "I know. Still and all, I promised I'd never ask that."

Who but an idiot would have made such a commitment? But it would do no good to insult the man, Lib reminded herself. Best to focus on the present. "Your promise is killing her now. Surely that cancels it?"

He writhed. " 'Twas a secret and solemn vow, on the Bible, Mrs. Wright. I'm telling you only so you won't blame me."

"But I do," said Lib. "I blame all of you."

Malachy's head drooped as if it were too heavy for his neck. A stunned bullock.

Valiant in his own dull way; he'd risk any consequences rather than break his word to his daughter, Lib realized. Would see Anna die before he'd let her down.

A tear jerked down his unshaven cheek. "Sure I still have hope."

What hope, that Anna would suddenly call out for food?

"There was another little colleen stone-dead in her bed, eleven years old."

Was this a neighbour? Lib wondered. Or a story out of the newspaper?

"And you know what Our Lord said to the father?" said Malachy, almost smiling. *"Fear not. Fear not, only believe, and she shall be safe."*

Lib turned away in revulsion.

"Jesus said she was only sleeping, and he took her by the hand," Malachy went on, "and didn't she get up and have her dinner?"

The man was in a dream so deep that Lib couldn't wake him. He clung to his innocence, refusing to know, ask, think, question the vow he'd made to Anna, do anything. Surely being a parent meant taking action, rightly or wrongly, instead of waiting for a miracle? Like the wife he was so unlike, Lib decided, Malachy deserved to lose his daughter.

The pale sun edged lower in the sky. Would it never go down?

Eight o'clock. Anna was shaking. *"How long,"* she kept mumbling. *"Be it done. Be it* done."

Lib had Kitty warm flannels at the fire in the kitchen and then laid them over Anna, tucking them in on both sides. She caught an acrid whiff. *You,* she thought. *Every flawed, scrawny, or bloated part, every inch of the real, mortal girl, I treasure you.*

"Will you be all right if we go to the votive mass, pet?" asked Rosaleen O'Donnell, coming in and hovering over her daughter.

Anna nodded.

"Sure now?" asked the father at the door.

"Go on," the girl breathed.

Get out, get out, Lib thought.

But then, after the couple withdrew, she hurried after them. "Say good-bye." Her voice a low caw.

The O'Donnells goggled at her.

Lib whispered, "It could come at any time now."

"But—"

"There isn't always a warning."

Rosaleen's face was a torn mask. She returned to the bedside. "I think maybe we shouldn't go out tonight, pet."

Now Lib cursed herself. Her one chance, the one possible time to put her outrageous plan into action, and she'd thrown it away. Did she lack the nerve, was that it?

No; it was a matter of guilt, because of what she was about to try. All she knew was, she had to let the O'Donnells take a proper leave of their child.

"Go on, Mammy." Anna's head lifted heavily off the bed. "Go to the mass for me."

"Will we?"

"Kiss." Her swollen hands reached for her mother's head.

Rosaleen let herself be pulled down. She placed one kiss on Anna's forehead. "Good-bye now, lovey."

Lib sat turning the pages of *All the Year Round* blindly so none of them would guess how much she wanted this to be over.

Malachy leaned over his wife and child.

"Pray for me, Dadda."

"Always," he said thickly. "We'll be seeing you later."

Anna nodded, then let her head drop onto the pillow.

Lib waited for them to go into the kitchen. Their voices, Kitty's. Then the thump of the front door. Merciful silence.

Now it began.

She watched Anna's narrow chest rise and fall. Listened to the small creak of her lungs.

She hurried into the empty kitchen and found a can of milk. Sniffed it to make sure it was quite fresh, and found a clean bottle. She half filled that with milk, stopped it up with a cork, and chose a bone spoon. There was a discarded oatcake too; Lib broke off a piece. She wrapped everything in a napkin.

Back in the bedroom, Lib drew up her chair very close to Anna. Was it sheer hubris to believe that she could succeed where everyone else had failed? She wished she had more time; greater powers of persuasion. *O God, if by any chance there is a God, teach me to speak with the tongue of angels.*

"Anna," she said, "listen to me. I have a message for you."

"From who?"

Lib pointed upwards. Her eyes rose too, as if she saw visions on the ceiling.

"But you don't believe," said Anna.

"You've changed me," Lib told her, honestly enough. "Didn't you once tell me that he can pick anyone?"

"That's true."

"Here's the message: What if you could be another girl instead of yourself?"

The eyes went wide.

"If you could wake up tomorrow and find that you're somebody else, a little girl who's never done anything wrong, would you like that?"

Anna nodded like a very small child.

"Well, this is holy milk." Lib held up the bottle as solemnly as any priest in front of an altar. "A special gift from God."

The girl didn't blink.

What gave Lib's tone conviction was that it was all true: Didn't the divine sunshine soak into the divine grass, didn't the divine cow eat the divine grass, didn't she give the divine milk for the sake of her divine calf? Wasn't it all a gift? Deep in her breasts Lib remembered how her milk had run down whenever she'd heard the mewing of her daughter.

"If you drink this," she went on, "you won't be Anna

O'Donnell anymore. Anna will die tonight, and God will accept her sacrifice and welcome her and Pat into heaven."

The girl didn't move a muscle. Her face a blank.

"You'll be another little girl. A new one. The moment you take a spoonful of this holy milk — it has such power that your life will start all over again," said Lib. She was rushing so fast now that she stumbled over the words. "You're going to be a girl called Nan who's only eight years old and lives far, far away from here."

Anna's gaze was dark.

Here's where it was all going to fall apart. Of course the girl was sharp enough to see right through this fiction, if she chose. All Lib could gamble on was her instinct that Anna must be desperate for some way out, longing for a different story, inclined to try something as improbable as tying a rag on a miracle tree.

A moment went by. Another. Another. Lib didn't breathe.

Finally the muddy eyes lit like fireworks. "Yes."

"Are you ready?"

"Anna will die?" A whisper. "That's a promise?"

Lib nodded. "Anna O'Donnell dies tonight." It occurred to her that the girl — who was so rational in her own way — perhaps thought Lib was giving her poison.

"Pat and Anna, together in heaven?"

"Yes," said Lib. What had he been but an ignorant, lonely boy, after all? *Poor banished children of Eve.*

"Nan," said Anna, repeating the syllable with a grave delight. "Eight years old. Far, far away."

"Yes." Lib was well aware she was taking advantage of

a child on her deathbed. She wasn't the girl's friend at this moment; more like a strange teacher. "Trust me."

When Lib produced the milk bottle and filled the spoon, Anna shied away a little.

No reassurance now, only rigour. "This is the only way." What was it Byrne had said about emigration? "The price of a new life. Let me feed you. Open your mouth." Lib was the tempter, the polluter, the witch. Such harm this sip of milk would do to Anna, shackling her spirit to her body again. Such need, such cravings and pains, risk and regret, all the unhallowed mess of life.

"Wait." The girl held up one hand.

Lib shook with dread. *Now, the hour of our death.*

"Grace," said Anna. "I must say grace first."

The grace to take food, Lib remembered the priest praying for that. *Grant her the grace.*

Anna dipped her head. *"Bless us O Lord and these thy gifts which we are about to receive from thy bounty, amen."*

Then her ragged lips parted for the spoon, as simple as that.

Lib didn't say a word as she tipped the liquid into the girl's mouth. Watched the throat move like a wave. She was ready for choking, retching, cramps, or spasms.

Anna swallowed. Just like that, the fast was broken.

"Now a little crumb of oatcake." As much as Lib could hold between finger and thumb. She put it on the purplish tongue and waited till it had gone down.

"Dead," Anna whispered.

"Yes, Anna's dead." On an impulse, Lib brought her

palm down, covering the girl's face and closing the swollen eyelids.

She waited a long moment. Then: "Wake up, Nan. Time to begin your new life."

The child's wet eyes blinked open.

Through my fault, through my fault. It was Lib who'd bear all the blame for luring this radiant girl back into the land of exile. Weighing her spirit down again, anchoring her to the tarnished earth.

Lib would have liked to give her more food right away, to fill that shrunken body with four months of meals. But she knew the danger of overtaxing the stomach. So she put the bottle and spoon into her apron with the bit of oatcake rolled up in the napkin. Little by little; the way out of the mine was as long as the way in. Lib stroked the girl's forehead very lightly. "We must go now."

A quiver. Thinking of the family she was leaving behind? Then a nod.

Lib wrapped the girl up in the warm cloak from the dresser, put two pairs of stockings on the misshapen feet as well as the brother's boots, mittens on her hands, and three shawls, making a dark bundle of her.

She opened the door to the kitchen, then the two halves of the cabin's front door. Sun blood-red in the west. The evening was warm, and a lone hen clucked in the yard.

Lib went back to the bedroom and scooped her up. Not heavy at all. (She thought of her own baby, that minute heft in her arms, as light as a loaf of bread.) But as she carried the girl around the side of the house, Lib could feel her own legs shaking.

And then there was William Byrne holding his mare,

looming out of the dark. Even though Lib had been watching for him, she jumped. Had she lacked faith that he'd be there as he'd promised?

He said, "Good evening, little—"

"Nan," Lib interrupted before he could wreck things by saying the old name. "This is Nan." No going back now.

"Good evening, Nan," said Byrne, catching on fast. "We're going for a ride on Polly. You know Polly, I believe. You won't be scared."

Huge-eyed, the child said nothing at all, only wheezed and clung to Lib's shoulders.

"It's all right, Nan," said Lib. "We can trust Mr. Byrne." She met his eyes. "He's going to take you to a safe place and wait with you, and I'll be along in a little while."

Was that true? She meant it, if that was enough; she wanted it with all that she was.

Byrne jumped up into the saddle and leaned down for the girl.

Lib inhaled the scent of the horse. "You were seen leaving this afternoon?" she asked, delaying them for one more moment.

He nodded, patting his satchel. "While I was saddling up, I complained to Ryan about having been called back to Dublin posthaste."

Finally Lib held out her burden.

The girl clung hard before letting go.

Byrne got her settled on the saddle in front of him. "It's all right, Nan."

He gripped the reins in one hand and fixed his eyes on Lib in a curious way, as if he'd never seen her before. No,

329

she thought — as if he were seeing her for the last time and memorizing her features. If their plot went awry, they might never meet again.

She tucked the food in his satchel.

Has she eaten? he mouthed.

Lib nodded.

His grin lit up the darkening sky.

"Another spoonful in an hour," she murmured. Then she went up on her toes and kissed the only part of him she could reach, the warm back of his hand. She patted the child through the blanket. "Very soon, Nan." She turned away.

When Byrne clicked his tongue and Polly moved off across the field — heading away from the village — Lib looked back over her shoulder and saw the scene for a moment as if in a painting. Horse and riders, the trees, the fading streaks in the west. Even the bogland with its patches of water. Here at the dead centre, a sort of beauty.

She hurried back into the cabin, feeling to make sure that her memorandum book was still in her apron.

First Lib knocked over both chairs in the bedroom. Next her own bag of equipment; she kicked it towards the chairs. She took her *Notes on Nursing* and forced herself to toss it onto the pile, where it landed open like a bird's wings. Nothing could be saved if her story was to be convincing. This was the opposite of nursing: a rapid, efficient work of chaos.

Then she went into the kitchen and retrieved the whiskey bottle from the nook beside the fire. She sloshed the stuff across the pillows and dropped the bottle. She picked up the can of burning fluid and shook a quantity all over the bed, the floor, the wall, the dresser with its little chest tipped open, baring its treasures. She put the lid back on the can only very loosely.

Lib's hands stank of the burning fluid now; how would she explain that afterwards? She rubbed them hard on her apron. Afterwards didn't matter. Was everything ready?

Fear not. Only believe, and she shall be safe.

She grabbed a lace-edged card from the treasure chest — some saint she didn't know — and lit it in the chimney of the lamp. It flared up, the holy figure haloed with flame.

Cleaned by fire, only by fire.

Lib touched it to the tick, which puffed to life, the old straw hissing crisply. A burning bed, like some miracle in bright pastels. The surge of heat on her face reminded her of bonfires on Guy Fawkes Night.

But would the whole room go up in flames? This was their one slim chance of getting away with the fraud. Was the thatch dry enough after three days of sunshine? Lib glared at the low ceiling. The old beams looked too sturdy, the thick walls too strong. Nothing else to be done; the lamp swung in her hand, and she hurled it into the rafters.

Rain of glass and fire.

Lib ran through the farmyard, her apron flaming in her face, a dragon she couldn't escape. She beat it with her hands. A screech that sounded as if it were coming from some other mouth. She stumbled off the path and threw herself down into the bog's wet embrace.

It had been raining all night. The constabulary had sent two men down from Athlone, even though it was the

Sabbath; right now they were picking through the mucky remains of the O'Donnells' cabin.

Lib was waiting in the passage behind the spirit grocery, her burnt hands swaddled in bandages, reeking of ointment. Everything hinged on the rain, she thought through waves of exhaustion. On when the rain had begun last night. Would it have put the fire out before the beams could fall in? Was the narrow bedroom reduced to indecipherable cinders, or did it tell — plain as day — the story of a missing child?

Pain. But that wasn't what held Lib in its grip. Fear — for herself, of course, but also for the girl. (*Nan,* she called her in her head, trying to get used to the new name.) There was a stage of starvation from which there could be no recovery. Bodies forgot how to deal with food; the organs atrophied. Or perhaps the child's small lungs had strained too long, or her worn-out heart. *Please let her wake up this morning.* William Byrne would be there to take care of her, in the most anonymous lodging he knew in the back streets of Athlone. That was as far as he and Lib had planned. *Please, Nan, take another sip, another crumb.*

It occurred to Lib that the fortnight was up. Sunday was always meant to be the day when the nurses reported to the committee. Two weeks ago, newly arrived, she'd imagined herself impressing the locals with her meticulous account of exposing a hoax. Not looking like this: ash-streaked, crippled, trembling.

She was under no illusions about the conclusions that the committee members were likely to reach. They'd make a scapegoat of the foreigner if they could. But what exactly

would the charge be? Negligence? Arson? Murder? Or —
if the police realized there was no trace of a body in the
smouldering mud — kidnapping and fraud.

*I'll join you both in Athlone tomorrow or the next
day,* Lib had told Byrne. Had her confident manner fooled
him? She was inclined to think not. Like Lib, he'd put on
a brave face, but he knew there was a strong possibility
that she'd end up behind bars. He and the girl would board
a ship as father and child, and Lib would never breathe a
word about their destination.

She checked her notebook with its blackened cover.
Were the final details plausible?

> *Saturday, August 20, 8:32 p.m.*
> *Pulse: 139.*
> *Lungs: respirations 35; moist crackling.*
> *No urine all day.*
> *No water taken.*
> *Inanition.*
> *8:47: Delirium.*
> *8:59: Breathing very distressed, heartbeat irregular.*
> *9:07: Gone.*

"Mrs. Wright."

Lib fumbled the book shut.

The nun was at her side, dark under the eyes. "How
are your burns this morning?"

"They don't matter," said Lib.

It was Sister Michael, coming back from the votive
mass, who'd found Lib last night, who'd dragged her out
of the bog, led her back to the village, and bandaged her

hands. Lib had been in such a state, no acting had been required.

"Sister, I don't know how to thank you."

A shake of the head, gaze lowered.

One of the many things on Lib's conscience was that she was repaying the nun's care with cruelty. Sister Michael would spend the rest of her life convinced that the two of them had brought about, or at least failed to prevent, the death of Anna O'Donnell.

Well, it couldn't be helped. All that mattered was the girl.

For the first time, Lib understood the wolfishness of mothers. It occurred to her that if by some miracle she came through today's trials and got away to that room in Athlone where William Byrne was waiting, she'd become the girl's mother, or the nearest thing to it.

Take oh take me for thy child, was that how the hymn went? In times to come, when Nan-who-was-once-Anna blamed someone, it would be Lib. That was part of motherhood, she supposed, bearing responsibility for pushing the child out of warm darkness into the dreadful brightness of new life.

Mr. Thaddeus walked past just then, with O'Flaherty. The gleam had been knocked off the priest; he was showing his age. He nodded to the nurses, gloomily abstracted.

"There's no need for you to be questioned by the committee," Lib told the nun. "You know nothing." That came out too brusque. "I mean, you weren't there — you were at the chapel — at the end."

Sister Michael crossed herself. "God rest her, the creature."

They stepped aside to make room for the baronet.

"I shouldn't keep them waiting," said Lib, moving towards the back room.

But the nun put a hand on Lib's arm, above the bandage. "Best not do or say anything till you're called on. Humility, Mrs. Wright, and penitence."

Lib blinked. "Penitence?" Her voice too loud. "Isn't it they who should be penitent?"

Sister Michael shushed her. "Blessed are the meek."

"But I *told* them, three days ago—"

The nun stepped closer, her lips almost touching Lib's ear. "Be meek, Mrs. Wright, and just maybe they'll let you go."

It was sound advice; Lib shut her mouth.

John Flynn strode by, his face set in hard lines.

And what comfort could Lib offer Sister Michael in return? "Anna had — how did you put it the other day? — she made a good death."

"She went willingly? Unresisting?" There was something troubled in those big eyes, unless Lib was imagining it. Something more than misery; doubt? Suspicion, even?

Her throat tightened. "Quite willingly," she assured the nun. "She was ready to go."

Dr. McBrearty hurried down the passage, his face caved in, panting as if he'd been running. He didn't so much as glance at the nurses as he went by.

"I'm sorry, Sister," said Lib, her voice uneven, "so very sorry."

"Shush," said the nun again, softly, as if to a child. "Between you and me, Mrs. Wright, I had a vision."

"A vision?"

"A sort of waking dream. I came away from the chapel early, you see, as I was fearful for Anna."

Lib's heart started to pound.

"I was walking down the lane when I thought I saw . . . I seemed to see an angel riding away with the child."

Dumbstruck. *She knows.* Loud in Lib's head. *She has our fate in her hands.* Sister Michael was vowed to obedience; how could she not confess what she'd seen to the committee?

"Was it a true vision, would you say?" asked the nun, her gaze burning into Lib.

All she could do was nod.

A terrible silence. Then: "His ways are mysterious."

"They are," said Lib hoarsely.

"Has the child gone to a better place — can you promise me that much?"

One more nod.

"Mrs. Wright." Ryan, jerking his thumb. " 'Tis time."

Lib left the nun without a word of good-bye. She could hardly believe it. She was still steeled against the possibility of a shouted accusation, but none came. She couldn't stop herself from glancing over her shoulder. The nun had her hands joined and her head bowed. *She's setting us free.*

In the back room, there was a stool placed before the trestle tables where the committee sat, but Lib stood in front of it, to look humbler, as Sister Michael had advised her.

McBrearty tugged the door shut behind him.

"Sir Otway?" That was the publican, deferential.

The baronet made a limp gesture. "Since I'm here not as resident magistrate but only in a private capacity—"

"I'll begin, so." It was Flynn who spoke up in his bearish tone. "Nurse Wright."

"Gentlemen." Lib could hardly be heard. She didn't have to force her voice to quiver.

"What in all the blazes happened last night?"

Blazes? For a moment she feared she was going to laugh; did Flynn even hear the pun?

Lib adjusted one of her bandages where it was digging into her wrist, and a stab of pain cleared her mind. She closed her eyes and bent her head as if overcome, producing a series of racked sobs.

"Ma'am, you'll do yourself no good by giving way in such a manner." The baronet's voice was peevish.

No good legally, or did he mean only her health?

"Just tell us what happened to the little girl," said Flynn.

Lib wailed, "Anna just, she wouldn't — that evening she got weaker and weaker. My notes." She lunged at McBrearty and laid her memorandum book in front of him, open where the words and figures ran out. "I never thought she'd go so fast. She shivered, and fought for breath — until she suddenly stopped." Lib gulped the air. Let the six men think about the sound of a child's last breath. "I shouted for help but I suppose no one was within hearing distance. The neighbours must have been at the church. I tried to get some whiskey down her throat. I was distracted; I ran about like a mad thing."

If they knew anything about Nightingale-trained nurses, they'd realize the unlikelihood of this. Lib sped on. "Finally I tried to lift her, to put her in the chair so I could push her into the village in search of you, Dr. McBrearty, to see if she could be revived." She fixed her eyes on his. Then she heard what she'd just said. "I mean, she was stone-dead, but I hoped against hope."

The old man had his hand over his mouth as if he were about to vomit.

"But the lamp — my skirt must have knocked it over. I didn't know I was in flames till they reached my waist." Lib's mummified hands throbbed, and she held them up in the air as evidence. "By then one of the blankets had caught fire. I dragged her body off the bed but it was too much for me, I saw flames licking the can—"

"What can?" asked O'Flaherty.

"The burning fluid," Mr. Thaddeus told him.

"Lethal stuff," growled Flynn. "I wouldn't have it in the house."

"I'd been refilling the lamp, to keep the room bright so I could see. So I could watch her every minute." Now Lib was weeping in earnest. Odd, that it was this detail she couldn't bear to remember: the constant light on that small sleeper. "I knew the can was going to explode, so I ran. God forgive me," she threw in for good measure. Tears plummeted off her jawline; truth and lies so mixed up she couldn't tell them apart. "I raced out of the cabin. I heard it blow up behind me with an awful roar and I didn't stop to look, I just ran for my life."

The scene was so vivid in Lib's mind, she felt as if she'd truly lived it. But would these men believe her?

She covered her face and steeled herself against their response. Let the police not be prising up blackened rafters right now, or examining the timbers of the bed and dresser, or digging around in that ashy mess. Let them be lazy and resigned. Let them conclude that the tiny charred bones must be irretrievably buried in the ruins.

It was Sir Otway who spoke up. "If you hadn't been so shockingly careless, Mrs. Wright, we could have gotten to the bottom of the matter, at least."

Carelessness — was that the only charge Lib was facing? *The matter* — meaning the death of a child?

"A postmortem examination would surely have determined whether the intestines contained any partially digested food," added the baronet. "Correct, Doctor?"

So the real issue was that there was no little girl they could cut up to satisfy the general curiosity.

McBrearty just nodded, as if he couldn't speak.

"Of course there'd have been *some* food," muttered Ryan. "The talk of a miracle was all nonsense."

"On the contrary, when nothing was found in Anna's intestines," John Flynn burst out, "the O'Donnells' name would have been cleared. A pair of good Christians have lost their last child — a little martyr! — and this imbecile has destroyed all evidence of their innocence."

Lib kept her head down.

"But the nurses bear no responsibility for the child's death." That was Mr. Thaddeus, speaking up at last.

"Certainly not." Dr. McBrearty found his voice. "They were only servants of this committee, working under the authority of myself as the girl's physician."

The priest and the doctor seemed to be trying to clear Lib and the nun of blame by calling them brainless drudges. She held her tongue, because it didn't matter now.

"This one shouldn't get her whole pay, though, because of the fire," said the schoolteacher.

339

Lib almost screamed. If these men offered her even one Judas coin she'd fling it in their faces. "I deserve none, gentlemen."

THE ENGLISH & IRISH MAGNETIC
TELEGRAPH COMPANY
Received the following message the 23rd day
of August 1859
From: William Byrne
To: Editor, Irish Times
Final article follows by post have accepted
position private secretary to gentleman bound
Caucasus excuse lack of notice change good as
rest et cetera not ungratefully W.B.

Here follows this correspondent's last report on the Fasting Girl of Ireland.

At seven minutes past nine on Saturday night last, while virtually the whole Roman Catholic population of her hamlet was pressed into the little white chapel to pray for her, Anna O'Donnell expired — it is to be presumed, from simple starvation. The exact physiological cause of that death cannot be determined by postmortem because of this tale's appalling coda, which this correspondent has heard from one who attended the final meeting of the committee.

The nurse in attendance was naturally distressed on the child's sudden death and attempted extraordinary measures to rouse her, in the course of which she accidentally dislodged the lamp. A crude device borrowed from a neighbour, it had been adapted to run not on whale oil but a cheaper product known as burning fluid or camphine. (This mixture — alcohol adulterated with turpentine in a ratio of four to one, plus a little ether — is notoriously combustible, and is reported to have caused more deaths in the United States than steamboat and railway accidents combined.) The lamp smashing to the ground, the flames engulfed the bedding and corpse of the child, and although the nurse made valiant attempts to put it out — injuring herself severely in the process — it was to no avail. The entire can of burning fluid went up in an explosion, and the nurse was forced to flee the inferno.

The next day Anna O'Donnell was declared dead *in absentia,* as her remains could not be unearthed from the ruins. According to the constabulary, no charges have been or are likely to be laid.

This does not put the matter to rest. Foul play, it should be called, when a girl not suffering from any organic illness is allowed — nay, incited by popular superstition — to starve herself to death in the midst of plenty during the prosperous reign of Victoria and no one is punished or even held to account. Not the father, who abrogated his legal as well as moral responsibility. Not the mother, who broke the law of nature by — at the very least — standing by while her little one weakened. Certainly not the eccentric, septuagenarian physician under whose so-called care Anna O'Donnell wasted away. Nor her parish priest, who failed to use the powers of his office to dissuade the girl from her fatal fast. Nor any other member of that self-appointed surveillant committee who heard evidence that the girl was on her deathbed and refused to believe it.

None are so blind as those who will not see. The same could be said of the many inhabitants of the locality who, by laying floral and other tributes at the blackened remains of the cabin in recent days, seem to express a naïve conviction that what happened there was the apotheosis of a local saint rather than the unlawful killing of a child.

What none can dispute is that the watch that was set a fortnight ago wound up the clockwork of death, most likely by blocking a covert means of feeding, and contributed to the destruction of the little girl it was designed to study. The committee's last act before dissolving itself was to declare the death to have been an *act of God* proceeding from *natural causes*. But neither the Creator nor Nature should be blamed for what human hands have wrought.

Dear Matron,

You may have heard by now of the tragic conclusion to my recent employment. I must confess myself so shaken — my whole system so broken down — that I will not be returning to the hospital for the foreseeable future. I have accepted an invi-

tation to stay with my remaining connections in the north.

Yours truly,
Elizabeth Wright

ANNA MARY O'DONNELL
7 APRIL 1848–20 AUGUST 1859
GONE HOME

EPILOGUE

Sixty degrees below the equator, in the mild sunshine of late October, Mrs. Eliza Raitt spelled her name for the chaplain. She adjusted the gloves she always wore over her scarred hands.

He moved on to the next line in his log. "Wilkie Burns. Occupation?"

"Until recently, manager of a printing concern," she told him.

"Very good. Does he mean to found a press in New South Wales, put out a paper for the miners, perhaps?"

She gave a ladylike shrug. "I shouldn't be at all surprised."

"A widow and a widower," the chaplain murmured as he wrote. He glanced east, over the waves. *"To shake off the dust of sorrow in pastures new,"* he quoted sententiously.

Eliza nodded with a half smile.

"British subjects, Church of England—"

"Mr. Burns and his daughter are Roman Catholics," Eliza corrected him. "We'll go through another ceremony in that church once we land."

She'd thought the chaplain might balk at that, but he nodded benignly. She watched over the man's shoulder as he noted down the name of the vessel, the day's date, the precise latitude and longitude. (She remembered dropping her memorandum book in the waves a month ago.) What could be keeping the other two?

"And Nan Burns," asked the chaplain, "is she still troubled by stomachaches and melancholy?"

"The sea air is doing her some good already," she assured him.

"Motherless no more! Such a delightful story, the way you and the little girl happened to strike up an acquaintance in the ship's library in the easy way that custom allows at sea, and all that's followed . . ."

Eliza smiled, modestly silent.

Here they came down the deck now, the bearded Irishman with close-cropped red hair hand in hand with the little girl. Nan was clutching a set of glass rosary beads and a bouquet of paper flowers she must have made herself, the paint still wet.

Eliza thought she might weep. *No tears,* she told herself, *not today.*

The chaplain raised his voice. "Let me be the first to congratulate you, Miss Nan."

Shy, the child pressed her face against Eliza's dress.

Eliza held her tight and knew she'd give Nan the skin off her body if she had to, the bones out of her legs.

"Are you amusing yourself well enough on this great clipper?" the chaplain asked the child. He pointed over their heads. "Eleven thousand yards of sail, fancy that! And two hundred and fifty souls aboard."

Nan nodded.

"Perhaps you're looking forward to your future home, though. What appeals to you most about Australia?"

Eliza murmured in the small ear, "Can you tell him?"

"The new stars," said Nan.

That pleased the chaplain.

Wilkie took Eliza's free hand in his warm grip. So eager, but not more than she was. Hungry for the future.

"I was saying to your bride, Mr. Burns, it has real charm, your little family's shipboard romance. You might even think of working it up for the press!"

The groom shook his head with a grin.

"On the whole," said Eliza, "we'd rather our days be unwritten."

And Wilkie, looking down to meet the child's eyes, then back at Eliza, asked, "Shall we begin?"

AUTHOR'S NOTE

The Wonder is an invented story. However, it was inspired by almost fifty cases of so-called Fasting Girls—hailed for surviving without food for long periods—in the British Isles, Western Europe, and North America between the sixteenth and the twentieth centuries. These girls and women varied widely in age and background. Some of them (whether Protestant or Catholic) claimed a religious motive, but many didn't. There were male cases, too, though far fewer. Some of the fasters were put under surveillance for weeks on end; some started eating again, voluntarily or after being coerced, imprisoned, hospitalized, or force-fed; some died; others lived for decades, still claiming not to need food.

Thanks for crucial suggestions go to my agents Kathleen Anderson and Caroline Davidson and my editors Iris Tupholme at HarperCollins Canada, Judy Clain at Little, Brown, and Paul Baggaley at Picador. Tana Wollen and Cormac Kinsella kindly helped me keep my Hiberno- and British Englishes straight, and Tracy Roe's copyediting was as ever, and in both senses, priceless. Dr. Lisa Godson at National College of Art and Design in Dublin shared her knowledge of nineteenth-century Catholic devotional objects. My friends Sinéad McBrearty and Katherine O'Donnell lent some of my characters their family names, and another is named for the generous Maggie Ryan as a fund-raiser for the Kaleidoscope Trust.

If you enjoyed *The Wonder*, discover Emma Donoghue's latest novel, *Haven* . . .

Three men vow to leave the world behind them and start anew . . .

In seventh-century Ireland, a scholar and priest called Artt has a dream telling him to leave the sinful world behind. Taking two monks – young Trian and old Cormac – he travels down the river Shannon in search of an isolated spot on which to found a monastery. Drifting out into the Atlantic, the three men find an impossibly steep, bare island inhabited by tens of thousands of birds, and claim it for God. But in such a place, far from all other humanity, what will survival mean?

Haunting, moving and vividly told, *Haven* displays Emma Donoghue's trademark world-building and psychological intensity – but this tale of the island now known as Skellig Michael is like nothing she has ever written before.

Discover more from
Sunday Times bestselling author
Emma Donoghue

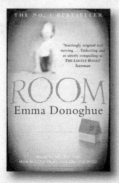

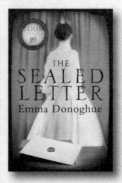